Cross Check

A Bayard Hockey Novel

Kelly Jamieson

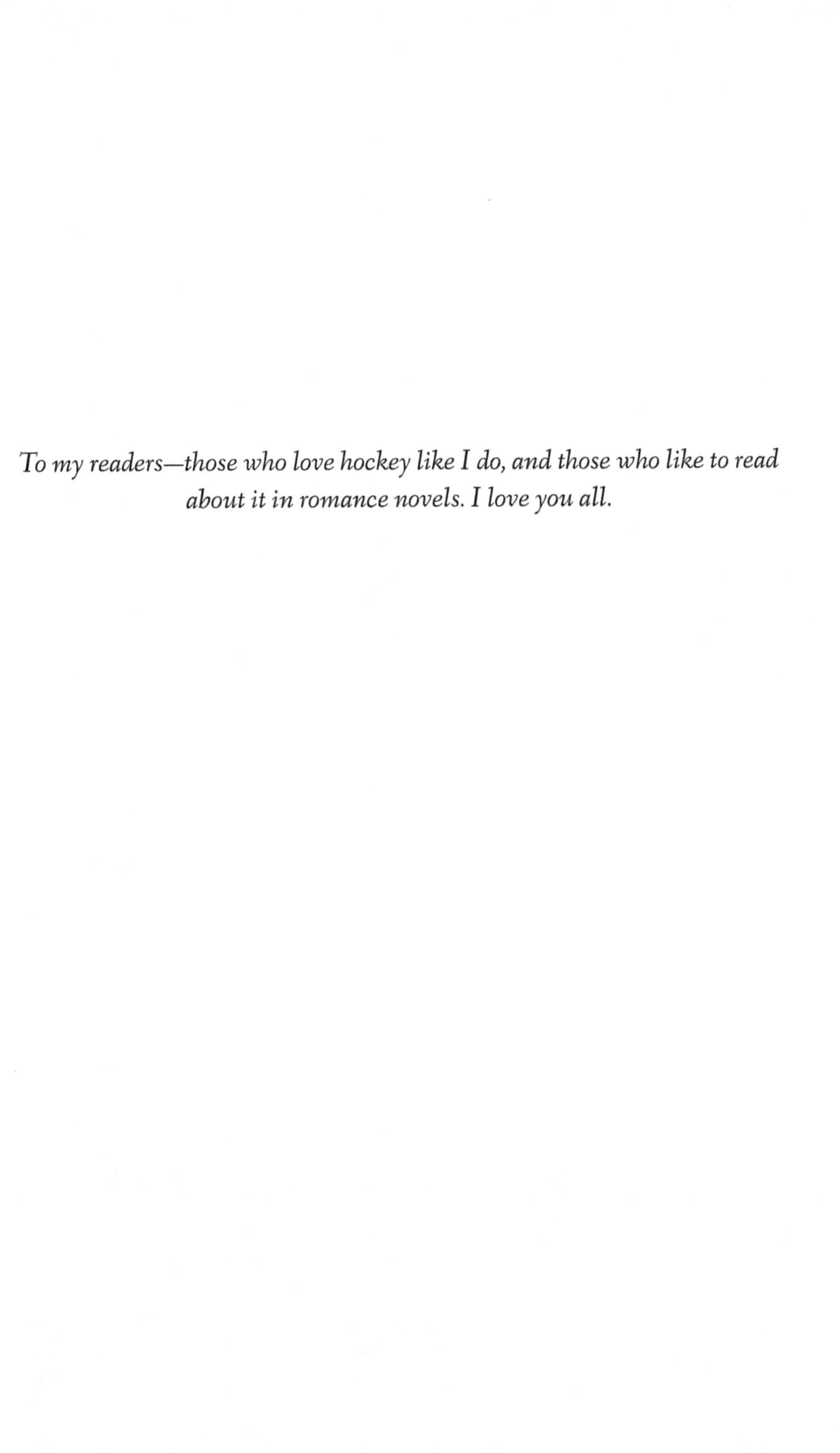

To my readers—those who love hockey like I do, and those who like to read about it in romance novels. I love you all.

Chapter 1

Ella

Academic probation.

I bite my lip as I reread the letter in my hand, my stomach knotting.

At the end of each semester, the Academic Achievement Committee reviews the records of all students and takes appropriate action, including issuing warnings, placing students on probation, granting leaves of absence, advising students to withdraw, or suspending or expelling students.

Sitting on my bed in my room in the house I share with three friends, I drop my chin to my chest and squeeze my eyes shut.

I've already read the letter, but I tried to forget about it over the winter break. Now I'm back at college. Classes start tomorrow and shit just got real. I have to meet with my academic adviser next week and figure out how I'm going to pull my grades up.

This has never happened to me before. I may not have been a straight-A student in high school, but I never got below a B. Of course, I had my parents always on my back about getting my homework done, helping me with projects, and looking at every test and paper I brought home.

A knock on my bedroom door has me jerking my head up. I shove the letter under a pillow and call, "Come in!"

The door opens and Skylar bursts in. "Hey, you're awake."

"I am." I make myself smile at her. I've been faking smiling through the whole winter break so my family wouldn't guess how messed up I am. Although yesterday, my brother Gareth had a "big brother talk" with me about my behavior last term, so he suspects. Ugh.

Our housemates, Brooklyn and Natalie, appear in the door too.

"Hi!" My smile widens. "You're back!"

"Just got here." Natalie moves into the room with a big smile that slips as she studies me. "Your aura is looking a little brown. Is everything okay?"

I blink. "Brown? Is that bad?" What am I saying? A brown aura *has* to be bad.

She perches on the side of my bed. "It can mean confusion or discouragement." She eyes me.

I'm a little skeptical of Natalie's ability to read auras, but right now she's nailed it. Hell yeah, I'm confused and discouraged.

"You usually have such a bright aura," Natalie continues. "Beautiful bright orange."

She's told me that means I am an outgoing social person who likes to party. Which is what got me into this confused and discouraged state. I summon all my energy to try to create a bright orange aura, imagining flames outlining my body. However, it appears I can't really fake that the way I faked being happy and carefree at home with my family. I need to deflect Natalie's attention from me. "How's *your* aura, Brook?" I joke.

Brooklyn grins, leaning against the door. "Very bright," she assures me. "Break was good."

"And we all know Skylar is beaming because she and Jacob are back together," I add.

Skylar laughs. Yeah, she's happy. It's so nice to see. "We're going ice-skating this afternoon," she says. "I came to invite you to go with us."

"Skating? Seriously?"

"Yeah. There's a pond in Seneca Park that they turn into a skating rink. Jacob thinks it would be fun to go there and skate just for fun."

Jacob is Skylar's new boyfriend. They were pretty much inseparable before Christmas, but were apart for a few weeks over the break, so their reunion yesterday was mega-steamy. Now they want to go skating? I'd think they'd want to stay holed up in a bedroom until classes start tomorrow. But Jacob's a hockey player for the college team, so I guess he likes skating.

"I don't have skates," I say.

"Neither do I, but we can rent them there."

"Who's going?"

"I don't know. A bunch of us."

"I'm not going." Brooklyn pushes away from the door. "I don't do cold."

I look at Natalie. She shrugs. "I might go."

I debate the invitation. I'm inclined to blow Skylar off. But to do what? I don't have homework, my mom did all my laundry while I was home for the break, and on a Sunday afternoon I'm probably not going to find a party to distract me from all the shit I want to be distracted from.

A lot of stuff went down last year, and things between Skylar and me were messed up. We've been best friends since middle school, but last term we had a falling out and for a while we weren't even speaking to each other. I know it was mostly my fault, and when I finally figured that out, I knew I had to work at repairing my friendship with her. That's one of my goals for this term, along with bringing up my marks before I get kicked out of school, or my parents find out about my academic probation and drag my ass home.

So because fixing things between Skylar and me is important, I find myself agreeing to go skating.

It turns out Natalie doesn't come either, so when Jacob picks us up, it's just Skylar and me. He drives us to the pretty park off the campus of Bayard College. It snowed recently and everything is pristine white, the black tree branches layered with white and the branches of dark evergreens holding big clumps of snow. The sky is clear blue, the sun bright, and it's hard to feel glum surrounded by so much light and freshness.

We enter a small but tall building with lots of windows. Inside there's a big stone fireplace and a bunch of picnic tables and benches. Jacob leads us over to a window where we can rent skates. I ask for size eights, hoping there's room for the thick socks I've donned. When I turn around to find a place to sit, I see Jacob's friend Ben waving at us.

Ugh.

I detest Ben Buckingham.

He's a pompous, pretentious ass who thinks he's all that, with his designer clothes and perfect hair and all the adulation that goes with being a star hockey player on campus. But even more than that, I despise him because he judges me.

I know he does. I've seen him at parties, watching me flirt with other guys, leave with other guys, and I can feel the waves of disdain coming from him. He thinks I'm a slutty tramp.

But that's *his* problem, because I'm not going to be ashamed of owning my sexuality.

I should have known he'd be coming along with Jacob, since they live together and play hockey together. I look around for Jacob's other friends, but Ben appears to be alone. Reluctantly, I cross the room toward him.

"Hi." I take a seat on the bench, not close to him. "Where's everyone?" Hopefully already out there skating.

"Nobody else wanted to come." He leans forward, elbows on his knees, already wearing his hockey skates.

Shit. When Skylar said a bunch of people were going skating, I figured I could handle it. Now this is just weird, with two couples, one of them being Ben and me, and we are definitely *not* a couple.

"How was your winter break?" I ask stiffly, pulling off my boots.

"Okay." He shrugs. "I went home to Buffalo for a few days."

"That's nice."

"Not really. But whatever."

His response makes me pause and flash him a curious look.

"And we had that tournament in Florida," he adds.

"I heard the Bears were runner-up."

"Yeah." He makes a face that clearly tells me he's not satisfied with being runner-up.

I guess when you're competitive, you don't like losing. Ever. "Well, win some, lose some."

His eyes flash with annoyance. Which makes me want to annoy him even more.

I take in his perfectly tousled brown hair, dark designer jeans, black pea jacket, and the scarf he wears looped perfectly around his neck, looking like he's here for a fashion photo shoot.

"Do you have a suit and tie under there? Who dresses like that to go skating?" I ask him, waving a hand up and down. In contrast, Jacob is wearing a knit cap and a plaid scarf tucked inside a big thick hoodie over loose, faded jeans.

Ben looks down at himself, then gives me a once-over. "I do," he says easily. "And I don't know if you're one to talk, party girl. Better zip that jacket up or your hooters are going to freeze."

I glance down at my chest and my cheeks flush hot. My long-sleeved top *is* low cut, but it's not like I have a lot of cleavage to worry about, and I brought a scarf too. I bend to wrestle the skates on, a little ashamed of how bad-mannered I am around Ben.

That's not me.

But I've been doing a lot of things lately that aren't me.

I try to ignore him, mostly out of embarrassment, as I fight with the skate laces to get them tight enough. Skylar and Jacob join us on the bench and start putting on their own skates and I glance up and freeze. Ben is looking down my shirt.

He looks away quickly and I don't know if he even realized I caught that. I swallow and blink at the laces in my hands. Well, I guess I gave him a bit of a show, bending forward in my low-cut top, but like I said, there's not much to see so he was probably pretty disappointed.

I sigh and resume my struggles with the skate laces.

"Here."

To my shock, Ben moves into a crouch in front of me, picks up one of my feet, rests the boot of the skate on his knees and starts working on the laces. "You do know how to skate, don't you?"

"Of course I know how to skate." Well, sort of. I've never taken lessons or anything, but I skated as a kid. Although that *was* a few years ago.

"Okay, good. 'Cause I'm not going to hold you up the whole time."

I roll my eyes. "That won't be necessary, Mr. Hotshot Hockey Player."

He expertly ties the laces on my second skate and stands. I set my blades on the rubber floor mat and push my jeans down over the tops of the figure skates. I glance over at Skylar and Jacob, also finishing lacing their skates.

"Ready?" Skylar asks brightly.

"Ready." I zip up my jacket to my throat and loop my scarf around my neck, annoyed again about Ben's comment about my top. As if I planned to ice-skate with my boobs hanging out.

We all stand and follow Ben out the door. Walking in skates across the rubber mat is a little ungainly, but I'm feeling pretty good as I reach the door. Outside, more rubber mats lead down to the pond. I pull on my mitts as we tramp along the path.

We reach the pond and there's a bunch of loose snow at the edge. I set my foot into it as carefully as I can. The first step is okay but my second step has the blade sliding out from under me. I flail and grab at the railing. Luckily, I keep myself from going down.

"Whoa!" Skylar and Ben both grab for me.

"I'm good!" I laugh to cover my embarrassment. Hell. Why am I doing this? Making a fool of myself with a bunch of friends is one thing, but making a fool of myself in front of Ben Buckingham, star hockey player lusted after by every girl on campus? That's just painful.

I find my balance on the skinny blade edges and slide my feet along the ice. Skylar follows me, a little more gracefully. Ben and Jacob push off with enviable ease and skill. They skate ahead of us, then Jacob loops back to skate closer to Skylar.

"How are you doing, babe?"

"Good!" She beams a smile at him as we slowly cross the pond.

"You *are* doing good," I tell her.

"I went skating at Christmas a couple of times with my sister."

"Ah."

My shins start burning with the unfamiliar movements, but I keep going, wobbling a little as I try to push off. After one round of the pond, I'm in pain. Jesus.

I'm a dancer . . . for years I took ballet, hip-hop, and jazz classes, and competed at a pretty high level. I should be good at this, and it annoys me that I'm not.

Ben skates up beside me. "Keep your knees bent," he says.

I shoot him a sideways glance. "I don't need your advice."

But I do bend my knees. God, I hate him.

I pause next to a snow bank and turn my face to the weak sun, pulling in a deep breath of fresh, cold air.

A sharp scrape of ice and shower of snow make me jump, and I nearly fall over. Ben has skated up to me and stopped abruptly. He grins and grabs my arms to steady me. "Sorry."

"No you're not. You did that on purpose. Show-off."

He laughs. "Come on. Why are you standing here?"

"Just enjoying the nice day."

He shrugs and takes off again, flying across the ice with smooth moves that irritate me.

He rounds one end of the oblong pond with easy swings of his legs, his blades scratching into the ice, and I can't help but watch him. It's like watching dancing . . . graceful and beautiful. And I hate it that he's so good at something.

I mean, I already knew that. I've been to games with Skylar, and I've seen him play hockey. It just seems different now, with me on the ice so ungainly and slow, him dressed in street clothes and yet so expert.

I look around for Jacob and Skylar and see Jacob skating backward facing her, the two of them smiling into each other's eyes. Jacob is skilled like that too, his backward glide effortless.

I turn and push away again. I can't just stand there all day. As I make another loop on the pond, I feel a little steadier. There are quite a few other people out enjoying the nice day too, kids who skate way better than I do along with kids using little walker-type things, adults who are wobbling more than me, and others almost as good as Jacob and Ben. I watch Ben and Jacob skate together for a minute, laughing about something, and I notice the attention they're getting from pretty much everyone on the ice, male and female. They're both big and handsome and great skaters.

I catch up to Skylar and we skate together. "This is so fun," she says.

"Yeah." I'm probably not having as much fun as she is, but I'm not going to ruin the day. "It's a great day for it. Not too cold."

"I'm going to try skating backward." Skylar does a little twirl, wobbles, laughs, and then makes some tentative pushes outward with her feet.

I grin at her. "Good work."

Jacob skates up behind her, slows, and grabs her waist, startling her. She glances over her shoulder and laughs. "You scared me!"

He skates backward too, still holding her, pulling her with him.

"Slow down!" she cries, and he does, though he's smiling.

Ben joins us too then. "Hanging in there, Franklin?"

"Franklin?"

"Franklin the Turtle."

I roll my eyes. "Thanks a lot."

"It's okay. Better to take it slow at first."

Ugh. Annoyance buzzes in my veins. I try to skate a little faster, but the first push off I take makes me wobble. I wave my arms and catch my balance without falling, then skate on, focusing on my feet and not on Ben. Which is pretty easy, because he ditches me yet again for another fast loop around the ice.

A girl falls just as he gets close to her and he immediately stops to help her up. I watch her flutter her eyelashes at him and smile prettily. They stand talking for a few minutes. As I near I can hear them talking about Bayard, so she must be a student there too. I ignore them as I chug slowly past, concentrating on my strides so I don't fall as well. She might be happy to have Ben Buckingham, star forward for the Bayard Bears, help her up, but I definitely don't want that.

As I'm focusing, gliding along and feeling more confident, a little kid comes barreling toward me, skates flying, but not very steady. I watch in horror as he falls right in front of me. I've finally gotten a bit of speed up but I don't know how to stop! A little screech leaves my lips and my arms start windmilling as I head right toward the boy on the ice. I'm going to hit him and go down on top of him!

Strong arms grab me and lift me off my feet, swinging me up over the boy. It's Ben, and he's actually carrying me, gliding steady and sure on his blades. Then he lowers me to the ice and we slow to a stop.

His arms are strong, his body big and solid against mine, and I can even breathe in his scent—a woodsy clean smell that makes me want to lean in closer and breathe deeper.

He looks down into my face. "You okay?"

I'm shaking. "Yeah."

"You don't know how to stop, do you?"

I grit my teeth. "No."

"Come on. I'll show you."

"That's okay. I'm good."

"No, really. It's easy."

"Usually I just crash into the boards," I mutter, since most times I've skated have been indoors. "But there aren't any here."

"Yeah. Okay." He faces me and takes my mittened hands in his. "Push out with your right leg. Like this." He demonstrates with his left leg.

I don't want to do this, but I grit my teeth and make an attempt. The outside edge of my blade scrapes out and I wobble, but Ben's holding me steady.

"Good. Again. And again."

We stand there doing that until he's satisfied.

"Now your other leg. One side . . . then the other."

I'm just standing there pushing each leg out to the side. Ben nods. "Okay, you got it. Now put your right leg out in front of you, turn it in, and push into that edge the same way." He lets go of my hands and glides backward away from me, then toward me to demonstrate.

He makes it look so damn easy.

I try to copy his action, barely moving, my skate pushing out.

"Take a bit more weight on your back leg," he says.

I do that, and it feels more comfortable.

"Again."

He makes me do it over and over, getting a little faster each time, and a little more secure. I can't help the smile that pulls at my lips as I glide along the ice, slide my foot out in front and push into the edge, coming to a neat stop.

"Perfect!" Ben skates up to me with a grin. "There you go."

This all annoys me of course, but it also makes me admire him all the more. It's not that easy and yet he makes it look effortless, and knowing how hard it is to stop makes his halting instantly in a shower of snow even more impressive. But I'm not about to tell him that.

"Thanks," I say grudgingly.

He's also a good teacher, dammit.

I keep skating this time, to make another loop of the pond. Skylar and Jacob are skating hand in hand now. I take a shortcut across the pond to meet up with them. "My legs are getting tired," I say. "I'm going in for some hot chocolate."

"I'll come with you," Skylar replies, and says to Jacob, "You guys can do a few laps as fast as you want now."

Jacob grins and releases Skylar's hand, and yeah, he's gone in a flash of blades, soaring across the ice toward Ben. Skylar and I skate more slowly toward the warm-up building, then grab for the railings as we step off the ice and onto the rubber mat.

Inside, I pay for two hot chocolates and we find an empty picnic table. The heat from the fireplace is delicious. It feels good to sit, our legs with the heavy skates stretched out in front of us. We both pull our hats off our heads.

"Whoa, major static," Skylar says, patting her wild hair down.

"Mine too." My hair is practically standing on end. I try to smooth it.

"Feels so good to get some fresh air and exercise."

I sip my chocolate. "Those guys put us to shame."

She laughs. "I know, right? But it doesn't matter. It's just for fun. Someday they'll be earning their living from skating, but not me."

"Me either, that's for sure." I pause. "So you've really changed your mind about being a doctor?"

Last term, Skylar made a huge decision and changed her major. She'd been trying to follow in her older sister's steps and go to medical school, but she'd been struggling.

"Yeah." She meets my eyes. "It wasn't the right thing for me. It was the right thing for my sister. But not me."

"So teaching, huh?"

"Yeah!" Her eyes sparkle. "I'm excited about it."

I drop my gaze to my skates, and my stomach clenches. "Um, I haven't told you, but . . . I'm on probation."

"What?" I glance at her and she's frowning. "Probation?"

"Academic probation. My grades kind of, uh, slipped last semester. Well, and the one before that too. I found out just before Christmas."

"Ella." Her forehead creases with concern. "No, you didn't tell me that. I thought you were doing fine in your courses."

I shake my head slowly. "Not so much."

"So what happens? You have to meet with your faculty adviser?"

"Yeah. Tuesday. I don't know how that will go, but I think we have to come up with a plan for how I'm going to pull my grades up."

"Less partying, more studying?" Skylar's voice is neutral, but still my head snaps around.

I can't deny that I partied a lot last year. That was one of the sources of tension between Skylar and me—she kept bugging me about it and it felt like my parents and big brothers all over again, trying to keep me in line and control my life.

I'm the baby girl in the family. My two older brothers and my parents have always looked after me. I mean, they love me, but it gets . . . stifling. When I was in high school, it drove me crazy that they were controlling everything I did, still making decisions for me and meddling in my life.

My parents checked all my homework and wanted to help with projects and papers. They wanted to know every mark I got on every test. They enrolled me in a bajillion dance classes and pushed me to enter competitions. I was so happy to go away to college and be on my own and make my own decisions about what I wanted to do. But I may not have done so well at that.

Now, I know Skylar was just worried about me. Still, I grimace. "Yeah, I guess so."

She nods. "I went through that last year."

Last spring when Skylar failed two courses, I was shocked. She works so hard at school. It surprised me that she'd flunked when I hadn't. We both went through a rough time that semester, losing our other best friend, Brendan, to suicide. Of course, now I understand why Skylar struggled so much with school that semester. Obviously, losing a friend was tragic, but now that I know more about what happened, I get it.

Only now Skylar seems to be doing just fine, whereas I am still an epic mess.

I pull a long breath into my lungs and let it out. "I know. And apparently it worked?"

"Yeah. It also helped to know that I wasn't going to have to struggle anymore through courses I hate. That was a big relief. You're still okay with your major?"

"Oh yeah! Communications is really what I want to do." I sigh. "For a while there, I just didn't care. It didn't seem like anything was important."

"I know." She reaches out and squeezes my hand. "I felt like that too, after Brendan died."

"Then I just felt pissed. At everything. At the world." I pause. "At you."

Skylar pressed her lips together. "Even before you found out what happened with me and Brendan?"

I swallow. This is hard to admit out loud. "Yeah. Because you seemed to be coping so much better."

"I really wasn't." She rubs her forehead. "I wish we had talked about this stuff back when it all happened. It would have helped us both. I know that was my fault."

"No, it wasn't. It was on both of us."

She shakes her head. "No. It was me."

I suck in a deep breath, because this is hard to say too, but it has to be done. "Okay, yeah. You did shut down." Again I hesitate. "I felt like I'd been abandoned by both Brendan *and* you."

"Oh, Ella." She leans her head into mine, and I shift toward her too. "I'm sorry."

"I know. And I'm so sorry for what you went through."

I'm coming to know that Skylar was going through a whole lot of shit, even more than I was at that time, and that's why she closed off. And then when she was ready to open up, I was too busy getting drunk and having hookups to talk to her about it.

"We're going to get there," Skylar whispers.

My eyes sting, and I nod. I want my best friend back so much. "I know."

This is a start. Talking is a good start.

Chapter 2

Ben

It feels good to get back to a routine.

After winter break and the tournament in Florida, I'm eager to get back on a schedule. Christmas was kind of depressing. I spent a few days back in Buffalo with my mom, which was great, I love my mom, but she lives with this snooty rich family whom I hate, and she was mostly working because she's their housekeeper and it was Christmas and they were constantly entertaining. Someday I'm going to get her out of there. Someday I'll have enough money to buy her a place of her own in a nice neighborhood. I'm going to make it in the NHL and leave that shit life behind forever.

So I came back to Bayard right after our Florida trip because I'd rather be alone here than sitting in Mom's "maid quarters," trying to avoid the Winthrops. And, call me boring, but I like structure in my life. I'm happy here at Bayard, happier than I ever was back in Buffalo. Life was out of control there at times, messed up and scary, outside of my hockey. And here people don't look down on me; they admire me.

Sure, life is crazy busy, with classes, practices, study groups, workouts, team meetings, and games. But I love it.

I have two classes Monday—Business Analysis and Valuation Using

Financial Statements, and Big Data and Critical Thinking—both part of the business degree I'm working on. Bayard College is known even more for their business school and MBA program than they are for their hockey team, and I feel honored to belong to both. I hope I can finish my degree even if I do get drafted, but if I don't, I figure these kinds of courses will be good. I'm specializing in finance, and already I've learned enough about managing my money to have made some pretty sweet cash in the stock market. I also have money socked away in more secure investments. I didn't start out with much, but I've been careful and made the best of it.

After my first class, I meet up with the boys for lunch, and everyone else is slow and grumbling about being back at school. We load up with carbs and protein, then I head to my next class. After that, it's off to the DeWitt Athletic Center, Bayard's state-of-the art athletic facility. Not only is there the ice for the men's and women's hockey, but the strength and conditioning facility is full of world-class free weights and selectorized, plyometric, and cardiovascular equipment; plus, the staff there is first-rate. There are offices and locker rooms for the head and assistant coaches, a study lounge for athletes, a high-tech video room, and bikes and skating treadmill rooms. Bayard takes their athletics seriously.

I am so fucking lucky to be in a place like this. I know I come across as kind of cool and maybe a little arrogant. I may not show it, but every day, deep inside, I'm grateful for this opportunity, and I plan to make the most of it.

Now we're into spring semester and the home stretch to make the playoffs. This is also a critical time for those of us hoping to be drafted into the NHL. Scouts will be at every game, watching us, talking to the coaching staff, compiling lists. My housemates Flash (Jacob Flass) and Rocket (Grady Rockwell) and I have already made the NHL's Central Scouting list of "Players to Watch," compiled from all the major leagues around North America. This is the year it has to happen.

Okay, you *can* make it into the NHL without being drafted, but right now I've attracted enough attention that the draft looks pretty good for me. I can't let that make me complacent, though. This is when I have to play my best, not to mention stay out of trouble, because those scouts interviewing the coaching staff want to know what kind of character players have *off* the ice as well as on it.

This has been my goal for as long as I can remember—to get to the NHL. To make something of myself and leave behind the crap life I grew up with. I'd like to earn some decent money, because I want to help my mom and I don't ever want to go back to the kind of life where options are so limited, crime is the only answer. But that's not the main reason. I just love playing hockey.

Since it's Monday, we do low weights but high repetitions. This is so we can recover from the games we usually play on the weekend. Tuesdays we do high intensity but low volume work, and Wednesdays are for plyometric exercises.

As usual, Flash and I team up in the weight room. Music blasts through the stereo system—Drowning Pool's "Bodies," then Godsmack's "Cryin' Like a Bitch," and "Back for More" by Five Finger Death Punch. Along with the clanging weights, grunts, and trash talk, the music adds to the adrenaline pumping through my veins.

The four guys I live with all love playing hockey too. But even though Rocket and Soupy (Hunter Campbell) are good players, that's not their entire goal in life. Like I said, Rocket has a shot at making the NHL, but he seems kind of surprised by that. Flash, on the other hand, is as driven as I am. Maybe that's why we sort of bro bonded when he moved in with us in September.

I didn't like Flash at first, because he was some hotshot player from Canada. Nobody could figure out why he'd all of a sudden decided to play American college hockey. I have to admit to a little cringe of shame remembering how shitty we were to him. We'd been strictly forbidden to haze him, and anyway hazing at Bayard is seriously prohibited after an ugly incident a couple of years ago involving the football team, but we didn't exactly welcome him.

Jaegar, our strength and conditioning coach, meets with me to go over some new things he wants me to focus on.

"You need to work more on your core for dynamic strength," he tells me. "Not just abs, but your back too. This'll improve your slap shot."

I lift my eyebrows at him.

"You need enough movement in your core to generate torque, which is relayed to the extremities to create power, which is released from your stick to the puck to create velocity." He demonstrates the movement slowly with an imaginary stick. "You need strength and stabilization in your back and shoulders."

I've put on about twenty pounds of lean muscle since I started at Bayard as a freshman, which puts me at just over two hundred pounds on my six-foot-two frame. I'm happy about that because I was kind of a late bloomer, small for my age until I was eighteen and then I was kind of scrawny. That was why I didn't enter the draft last year; Coach thought if I waited a year and tried to bulk up more, I'd go higher. I wouldn't mind a few more pounds, so I'm working on it.

After my workout, we head to the locker room to get ready for our first practice after the break.

We played well in Florida, and I hope we can keep up that level of compete into the next stretch of our season. Sure, I'm focused on the scouts who'll be here in advance of the NHL draft, which will happen in June, but there's also the playoffs to be concerned about. The Frozen Four. My goal is to be drafted in the spring, but the competitor in me can't ignore the need to fucking *win*.

Coach Klausen is a great coach, the best I've ever played for. He's been really supportive of me and my goal of making the NHL, and I know he's also talking me up to the scouts who've been hanging around and will be even more later this semester. I would walk across a mile of burning broken glass for him.

Coach starts us off with a drill that gets our feet and hands warmed up and has us giving and receiving passes, and also warms up the goalies. Rocket is on the blue line and I'm skating backward exchanging one-touch passes with him. "Stay low!" Coach yells at me. When I reach the hash mark, I stop and then rush forward, getting my feet active, still passing. At the blue line I pivot and fan out across the ice, taking a long pass from Rocket. With the puck, I stay wide and take a shot at Freddy in the net, and he makes the save. I grin, but he's already squaring himself for the next player's shot in the drill.

Coach makes us work hard, shoving us back into the thick of things. I don't mind. I *want* to work hard. My body needs it and my mind kind of needs it too.

After that leisurely skate yesterday on the pond at Seneca Park, I want to go hard, skate full out. I want that puck on my tape. I love the speed, the puck handling, shooting it at the net.

Skating yesterday was okay. It might have been more fun if some others had joined us. Instead I had to hang around with Ella the party girl. Christ, she annoys me. It's great that Flash has a girlfriend, and Skylar's awesome. I'd be jealous, except the last thing I need right now is a girlfriend. I'm happy for them, but why does Skylar's best friend have to be such a bitch?

Okay, she's not always a bitch. I've seen her with her friends, and they all love each other. Guys like her too; they're all over her at parties. Ugh. It's just *me* she's like that with, and it's not hard to figure out why it bugs me. I spent my teenage years living with a family of girls around my age; they treated me like a servant because my mom worked for them . . . and made fun of me and looked down on me because of that. I get the feeling Ella looks down on me like that too.

It was kind of cute how Ella didn't really know how to skate, yet she was so determined to do it. No idea why. If I were her, I would've stayed home. I *should* have stayed home. But Flash convinced me to go, and then when nobody else wanted to, I kind of felt obligated to show up.

Yeah, it was okay, a fun outdoor skate on a nice winter day. I haven't played hockey outdoors for years. And showing Ella how to skate was a little ego-stroking.

I stay after the practice to shoot some pucks, assistant coach Art Backes remaining on the ice to work with me. The individual attention I've gotten from the coaching staff here has really improved my play. Some days I shoot a handful, some days fifty or a hundred, and I like it when Art passes to me, because his passes aren't as good as my teammates'. No offense to Art, he's a great coach, but it makes me move my feet more and get off shots that are more of a challenge, like in a real game.

Most of the guys are gone by the time I hit the showers, but Coach Klausen is still there and he calls me into his office when I'm dressed. I'm pretty sure I'm not in trouble, so I'm mostly curious as I saunter in and take a seat.

"You don't have a family adviser," he says to me.

"No." I suck briefly on my top lip. I know some guys do—Butch has one, but he's already been drafted.

"You need one."

I nod slowly. My gut tightens. This means there are scouts who are seriously interested in me. "Okay." Fuck. I have no idea how to go about this.

"Your family's not involved much in your hockey, are they?"

"No sir. My dad's deceased, as you know. And my mom . . . well, she doesn't know much about hockey." My mom struggles to support herself, never mind worry about me. It sucks, but it's been that way for a long time. My uncle Dave has been great, but he doesn't know anything about hockey either. I'm on my own in this.

Coach nods and pushes a paper across the desk to me. "Here. Some names. These guys are expecting a call from you. Call all of them. And here are some questions you should ask them. Don't just go with the first one you talk to. They know the NCAA rules and I trust all of them." He pauses. "Do you know the rules?"

I take the paper and stare at it. Holy shit. I suck air into my lungs and look up at Coach. "Um, yeah. I think. I can't take any money from him."

"Right. No gifts either. He can't market you to NHL teams, and you can't enter into any agreement to have him represent you as an agent in the future."

"Got it."

"You do have to compensate him for his services, though."

"Oh." I swallow. I have some money, hopefully enough.

"Let me know if that's a problem," Coach says, eyeing me shrewdly.

"Okay. Thank you."

"Also let me know what you decide. Or if you have questions, come see me. Got it?"

"Yes, sir."

I rise and leave his office, clutching the piece of paper.

Holy shit. This is really going to happen.

The paper tucked carefully into my messenger bag, my heart is thudding as I leave the facility and walk to my car. It's older, but it's cool, a black 2000 Ford Mustang. I got a good deal on it years ago because it needed work. I spent summers working in a body shop, so I was able to fix it up pretty cheap, and now it looks sweet. In the driver's seat, I start the car and pull my phone out to check for messages while I give the engine a minute to warm up in the cold evening air. There's a text message from Rocket, telling me the guys are at the Taste of Heaven Diner getting dinner. I send a reply that I'll be right there.

Rocket, Soupy, Flash, and Freddy are all crammed in a booth in the diner, and I grab a chair and sit at the end of it. Some waitresses wouldn't be cool with me doing that, but luckily, Skylar's working tonight and she lets us get away with it. She comes right over.

"We already ordered," Flash says.

Without looking at the menu, I order the pulled pork and slaw sandwich and a chocolate-banana milk shake, and Skylar flashes me a smile before sauntering away in her tight little pink uniform.

I look around at the guys. "Coach says I need an adviser."

They all stare at me.

Flash says, "Yeah, me too." XX

I meet his eyes and we both break out in huge grins. I reach over to bump fists.

"Christ." I shake my head. "How the fuck do we do this, Flash?"

"I called my folks. They're going to help me figure it out."

"Did he give you names?"

"Yeah. And they're all guys I've looked into."

"I haven't. Jesus. I have no fucking clue."

Flash's eyes shadow a little. "Look, we'll figure this out together. Okay?"

"Yeah." I know what he's saying. He knows I don't have family to help like he does. I don't talk much about my background to people, but one night Flash and I got trashed on tequila and started sharing our deep, dark secrets. Who knew we both had such messed-up shit in our lives? Anyway, along with our love of hockey and our determination to make it into the NHL, that kind of bonded us too. "Thanks, man."

"You guys," Rocket says. "I'm already on this. I mean, my parents are already on this." He shakes his head. "They got Laurie Landon to be my adviser. I never thought I'd need one, but apparently I'm on some lists, which is freaking me the fuck out."

"Future NHL superstars!" Soupy crows and claps a hand on Rocket's shoulder, shaking him. "Fuck yeah!"

We're all in a pretty jubilant mood, and there's more backslapping and laughter as Skylar brings my milk shake. Flash fills her in and she gives me a warm smile. "That's fantastic, Ben."

"What's going on, guys?" We turn to the other female voice that speaks. It's Skylar's housemate Brooklyn.

And she's there with Natalie and Ella. Great.

Skylar relates our news to the girls, who smile but don't seem quite as impressed. I don't think they really get what's happening here, but that's okay. They take the booth next to us, and Natalie kneels on the seat to look over the divider and talk to us about how our first day of classes went.

Classes? Oh yeah. I chuckle to myself. I can't let this go to my head. I still have to pass my fucking courses.

Sitting where I am, I can see Ella on the other side of the next booth. She's smiling at her friend, and for once her smile looks soft and genuine. She's actually really pretty. Her face is small with delicate features—small nose, thinnish lips, with a little mole above the left corner of her mouth, and her eyes are big and dark. Her long brown hair is parted in the middle, kind of wavy, like a lot of girls wear it these days, and it's really shiny. She's a little on the thin side—I guess you'd say she's small-boned—but not short, probably about five foot five. But even though she's thin, she has a pretty fine ass. She doesn't have much for boobage, unfortunately. I like boobs.

Wait, why is that unfortunate? I want nothing to do with Ella's boobs. Or lack of.

She glances my way and totally busts me checking her out. Fuck. I give her a tight-lipped smile, and she gives me the same kind of smile in return. For some reason, my skin heats. I turn away from her to listen to what the others are saying.

Now I'm hyperaware of her. Christ. This is stupid. I want to look at her again, but I know I can't because if she catches me again . . . Well, I don't even know what she'd think. Probably that I'm planning to punch her or something. But the more I tell myself not to look at her, the harder it is to do that.

Fuck, I should've just gone home and made myself a sandwich.

Skylar arrives with food for the other guys. "Your sandwich will be right up," she assures me.

"Thanks, Sky."

She moves to the next table to look after her friends. And yeah, my eyes follow her and I glance at Ella and hear her order a pulled pork and slaw sandwich and a chocolate-banana milk shake.

I frown. Shut the fuck up. Did she hear me order that? No, she wasn't even here then.

We ordered the exact same meal. That is fucked-up.

Now she catches me gaping at her yet again. Shit. My face heats up as I shake my head and I rub my face.

"I say start at the top," Flash says, talking about the agents who aren't really going to be our agents, but in fact probably will. We have to follow the rules, but I know how it works. "Nuncio represents Gabriel Manson." He names last year's number one draft pick. "That has to mean he's good."

"Yeah, but he might not be good for *you*," Rocket says. "It's important to have a guy who gets you and knows what you want to do with your career.

I want to play in the NHL. But I nod. "Coach did specifically say to talk to all of them."

"Yeah," Rocket says. "One of the guys my parents talked to insisted I'd be playing the first season after the draft. Realistically, that's probably not gonna happen. You want someone who's not going to blow smoke up your ass, trying to make you think you're the next Great One."

"Butch has an adviser," Flash adds. "We should see what he thinks."

"Yeah. We can talk to him tomorrow."

Hockey players are superstitious, and I'm no exception. I have my things, as do a lot of the guys—little routines or things we have to do the same every game day. And I'm terrified that if I let myself think about being drafted, I'll totally jinx it. I can't even imagine what getting drafted would feel like, and much as I want to let my imagination conjure up images, I can't go there.

Jesus Christ. I can't look at Ella. I can't think about the draft. What the hell. I need to get drunk. Or get fucked.

Yeah. Fucking would be good.

Chapter 3

Ella

THE MEETING with my faculty adviser goes okay. Honestly, I'm embarrassed. "It's been a year since my friend died of suicide," I tell Professor Daneck. "I had a hard time dealing with it."

Her eyes shadow with sympathy. "That would be hard for anyone. Did you get some support?"

"No." I bend my head. "But I'm going to. My best friend—she was friends with Brendan too—saw a counselor."

I told Skylar before Christmas I was going to see someone. I haven't actually done anything about that yet. In fairness, it *was* winter break.

"That would be a good idea. We do need to have a plan for how you're going to get things back on track."

"I may have developed some, uh, unhealthy coping mechanisms." I swallow and meet her eyes. "I plan to spend a lot more time in the library this semester."

She nods slowly. I can tell she's genuinely concerned about me, which in a way is nice, but in another way makes me feel uncomfortable. Like I don't deserve her concern, because I know I'm the one who effed up here. We talk a bit more and she offers a few other suggestions. I don't think it's really that complicated. It's not that I don't understand the course material. I just haven't been putting in the effort.

I leave there and emerge from York Hall onto the Quad. It's late afternoon, blue-ish dusk at this time of year, snowflakes floating in the air, so light they're not really falling, just drifting around. The streetlights are on and people are rushing in all different directions.

I let out a long breath. At least that's done. But the hard work is yet to come. The weight of that burden makes my steps heavy. It would be easy to let my imagination run free, imagining all kinds of scenarios in the future, stirring up a whole bunch of anxiety, but I can only focus on right now, this day . . . this evening . . . which means I'm headed to the library to do some reading. It's early in the semester and it's tempting to believe I have lots of time, but I can't think that way.

Much as I love Nat and Brooklyn, I know if I go home I'll get sucked into all of us giving each other pedicures, or watching *The Bachelor*. Or both. I climb the big stone steps of the library and enter the spacious study hall. The hushed surroundings make my skin itch. I pause and search for an empty carrel—then, head down, I make a beeline for it.

I crash into a big, hard body just as I arrive at the carrel. "Whoa!"

Shit, that came out way too loud. People are looking at us. At me and . . . Ben.

Oh, for fuck's sake.

He grabs my arm to steady me. "Jesus, watch where you're going!"

"Shh!" I glance around. "This is a library."

"I fucking know that."

I bug my eyes out at him because he's still talking too loud. "*You* weren't watching where you were going either."

He's still holding my arms, and once again, I'm close enough to smell him, that crisp woodsy fresh scent that right now smells like he's just stepped out of the shower. And judging by his damp hair, maybe he has. "You stalking me, party girl?"

My mouth drops open. "As if!" Then I close my eyes, because my voice had gotten loud again. Yep, when I open them, people are glaring at us.

His lips quirk and he releases me.

I step away from him, clutching my bag to me.

"Never mind," I whisper, my cheeks burning. "It's all yours." I sweep a hand out and turn.

He grabs my arm again, and I give him a cool look over my shoulder.

"You take it," he whispers harshly. "I'll find somewhere else."

"There aren't a lot of places." This kind of boggles my mind. Who knew so many people wanted to study at this time of day?

"I can go to the study table at the Academic Center." But he doesn't look pleased with the idea.

"Dude." A guy behind me pops up. "I'm outta here. Take this one. Please." He's holding his jacket and books.

"Thanks, man."

So Ben slides into the carrel next to me and I move to sit. I take a deep breath. We've created quite the disturbance in the library, and I just want to sink down into oblivion. Well, and my Public Relations reading.

I'm acutely aware of Ben next to me, getting out his laptop and plugging it in, then shrugging out of his Bayard Bears jacket and draping it over the back of his chair.

What's a jock like him doing here, anyway? I have no idea what courses he's taking, and I'm suddenly painfully curious about that. Oh hell. I don't want to know anything about him. He's a pompous ass. Not to mention conceited. "Stalking him," I mutter under my breath as I open my textbook. "As if."

I hear a soft snort from the carrel beside me.

I push back my chair to glare at him.

He turns his head and lifts one eyebrow, the corners of his mouth tilted up.

He has a great mouth.

No, fuck that. He's an ass.

"What are you even studying?" I hiss at him. "You're a jock."

He gives me a look. "What are *you* studying, party girl?"

I swallow. Yeah, I was a party girl. But he's the last person to whom I want to admit that I got myself in a little trouble. "I asked you first."

"What are we, twelve?" He rolls his eyes. "Managing International Trade and Investment."

I blink. "What?"

"That's what I'm studying. My major's Business. What's yours? Oh wait, let me guess . . . a double major in partying and drinking?"

I narrow my eyes at him. "You f—"

I hear a throat clear loudly behind me and turn to see a couple of people glaring at us again.

"Never mind." I push back into the desk and focus on my textbook. Luckily, this topic is interesting to me, and I manage to immerse myself in it for some time. Public relations . . . managing the spread of information between an individual or an organization and the public . . . to inform them and ultimately persuade them to maintain a certain view about the individual or organization . . . This is good stuff, and I nod as I read more, highlighting text as I go.

I pull out my laptop, open it, and boot it up. As it starts, I read another paragraph.

Music blasts from my laptop

"Jesus!" I scrabble at the computer just as DNCE calls "Oh no!" the opening line of "Cake by the Ocean." Frantically, I find the volume button and punch at it until it goes quiet.

The silence in the library pulses around me as I slump into my chair. I feel eyes on me, probably belonging to every person there, including Ben. Chin on my chest, I set my fingertips to my forehead to cover my burning face.

"Oops," he whispers. "Great song, though."

I let out a big sigh.

"Ella."

Now I look the other way and see Skylar, dropping to a crouch beside my chair. "I didn't know you were here."

"I guess everybody knows I am now."

She grins.

"You better go away," I whisper. "I'm becoming hated."

"Phhht. Oh, hi, Ben." Skylar looks past me at Ben.

He lifts a hand.

"How much longer are you staying?" Skylar whispers.

"I don't know. I just got here."

"Jacob and I are going to get something to eat in about an hour. I'll come get you."

"Oh. Okay." I'm hesitant. I should stay here longer than that, but I am getting hungry. Probably should have gotten some food before I came here.

She pats my knee, then hurries back to wherever she came from. I hadn't noticed her and Jacob there.

Okay, so I'll really focus and get this reading done and then I can go eat.

I try not to be aware of Ben next to me, his big body sprawled in his chair, staring at his laptop, his left hand moving on the keyboard and track pad, his other hand resting on one very muscular, denim-covered thigh.

Hockey players have amazing thighs and asses.

I shake my head. *Come on, Ella.*

I like boys. Men. Whatever. I also like sex. But I *don't* like Ben Buckingham, and I need to stop thinking about his nice eyes and his perfect mouth and his amazing ass.

Homework. That's what I need to focus on.

I manage to succeed at this endeavor and am actually surprised when Skylar comes up and touches my shoulder. She's standing between Ben and me, and whispers to both of us, "You guys ready to go?"

Oh, hell no. I should have realized they'd include him in the invitation. I open my mouth to tell Skylar I changed my mind, but my stomach gives an audible rumble.

Shit.

"Yeah, you need food," she whispers cheerfully. "Meet you out front."

I slowly gather my things, while Ben does the same next to me. We stand at the same time. Our eyes meet.

Yep, he's as unhappy as I am about this.

However, not only am I hungry, Skylar invited me and I want to say yes, because I want her friendship back. If that means hanging out for a while with a big jerk hockey player, I can do it.

I toss my hair back and walk past him, make my way out of the library, and find Skylar and Jacob all cozy on the front steps, Jacob leaning against the stone balustrade with his arms wrapped around Skylar as they smile into each other's eyes. Snow is falling harder now, the air thick with fluffy white flakes dropping from the dark sky.

"Where are we going?" I ask.

"Mort's."

It's not walking distance. I tuck my hair behind my ear and bite my lip.

"I'll drive," Ben says. "My car's in Lot A."

"Good," Jacob says. "Because my truck's at home."

So we walk to the lot and Ben leads us to a sweet black Mustang. Of course Skylar and Jacob move to get into the backseat—well, Jacob kind of folds himself up to get in there.

"Jesus, man," he says to Ben. "Move your seat forward. I got no legroom whatsoever back here. My knees are up in my face."

"You sit up front," I quickly offer.

"Nah, it's okay, I'll slide over." Jacob moves so he's behind the passenger seat, which is farther forward than the driver's. Skylar slides in the other side, and I swallow a sigh as I take the front passenger seat. I fumble around for the handle to move the seat even more forward. I'm not tall, so I can give Jacob more room. But I can't find it.

Ben reaches over and, with a long arm, between my legs, finds the lever, and pushes on it. "Slide forward," he orders. I dig my heels in and the seat moves, although heat fills me at having Ben so close once more, with his hand between my legs.

God.

"Thanks," Jacob says behind me. "Better."

"You're probably still cramped back there." I turn to look at him.

He grins good-naturedly. "I'm fine."

It's not far to Mort's, thankfully. Ben fills the car with music, Drake and Rihanna.

We get seated in a booth, like the world is conspiring to make Ben and me feel like a couple, because of course Sky and Jacob sit on one side. I try to shrink into the corner, the windowsill jabbing my shoulder, and study the menu. I want to order everything, I'm so starving, but this place is known for its huge portions.

"Let's get some wings to share," Skylar says.

"Sure," Ben and Jacob both say.

"How hot do you like it?" Skylar asks, her gaze on the choices on the menu.

"Oh, baby." Jacob nudges her. "You know I like it hot."

She rolls her eyes. I can't help but smile at Jacob's cheesy humor.

"Ella likes it hot too," Skylar says.

Ben doesn't look at me, but I sense the waves of disapproval flowing off him.

"Can't take the heat?" I ask him. "It's okay. Men who don't like spicy foods tend to have lower levels of testosterone."

Skylar chokes on a laugh.

"Oh, we were talking about food?" Ben slaps his menu closed and slides me a sideways glance. "So, does eating the hot stuff cause an increase in testosterone? Or the abundance of testosterone makes you like spicy food?"

"Um, I don't know if researchers have actually determined that."

"Where'd you learn that useful factoid, anyway?" Ben smirks at me. "*Cosmo* magazine?"

I'm trying not to smile. "As a matter of fact, pretty boy, I think it was. I might still have that issue. I'll loan it to you. There's a side piece called 'Five Easy Ways to Increase Your Testosterone.'"

"Ha. Funny."

"Hey, low testosterone can cause a lot of problems. Including in the bedroom. I think there's another issue that has a guide to erectile dysfunction. Maybe you want to borrow that one, too."

Ben's eyes flicker and his jaw tightens. "Erectile dysfunction."

"Don't be embarrassed." I shrug. "You men are so sensitive about your sexual prowess."

"You don't know anything about my sexual prowess."

"That is true. And hopefully I never will."

I'm being a bitch. I know it. But he's been winding me up, calling me party girl. And truthfully . . . along with the nudge of guilt is a shiver of excitement that I'm getting to him.

"Okay, five-alarm hot wings!" Skylar says brightly. "With jalapeños, why not?"

"Why not?" I murmur. "Okay, I've decided." I close my menu. If we're having wings, I'll just order the sliders instead of a big meal. Maybe with some fries.

The server approaches, and it's a girl I recognize from school. "Hi, Ben!" she says with a wide, white smile and eyes only for him. "How are you?"

Ben shifts on the bench seat next to me. I can feel his unease. Huh. "Hey, Mandy. I'm good. You?"

"Awesome. Getting ready for your next game? Yale, right?"

"Right."

From all the tension emanating off of Ben, it's pretty easy to figure out that he must have hooked up with this girl. She looks completely infatuated with him. On the other hand, he clearly wants nothing to do with her.

Mandy's gaze flicks to me and she blinks. Her smile fades.

She thinks we're a couple.

Obviously, it would be awkward to say that we're not. I repress a sigh and stop myself from banging my forehead on the table.

"Are you ready to order?" Mandy asks.

"Yeah, I think so." Ben glances around the table. We all nod.

Mandy looks at him expectantly. "We're going to share some five-alarm wings to start," Ben says. "With jalapeños." He shoots me a sidelong smirk. "And I'll have the sliders. With cheese. And an order of fries."

My mouth drops open. "Seriously?"

He frowns. "Uh, yeah. Problem?"

Oh my God. I grab the menu and flip it open again. I can't order the same thing he has. No freakin' way. My gaze bounces blindly around over the menu. "Uh, you guys order, I need a minute."

"I thought you said you knew what you want?" Ben demands.

I press my lips together while Jacob and Skylar order.

"Chicken fingers," I say, and hand over the menu.

Ben gives me a weird look.

I look out the window and drum my fingers on the table.

"How did your meeting with your faculty adviser go this afternoon?" Skylar asks me.

I freeze. Then I bug my eyes out at her. I don't want to discuss my academic probation in front of other people, especially Ben. Has Skylar told Jacob about that? Damn. Then he could have told Ben already . . . I give Skylar a sharp look and say, "It went fine."

She blinks and then sucks on her bottom lip. "Oh. Right. Good. So, hey. You'll come to the game Friday night with me, right?"

Yeah, she's trying to change the topic to help me out, but she's only making things worse. I don't want to go to the effing hockey game.

Well, that's not totally true. Skylar made me go to a few games with her last semester when she started seeing Jacob, and they're actually a lot of fun. Those hockey fans are crazy, and even though I don't know much about the sport I have to admit it's a fast-paced, exciting game to watch.

And again . . . I want my friendship with Skylar back. So how can I say no?

Chapter 4

Ben

I SPEND the rest of the week in a blur of practices, workouts, classes, and playing phone tag with the agents Coach gave me the names of. On Thursday night, Flash and I Skype with his parents to talk about all this. They're pretty cool, really down to earth and sensible about things. I think I'm pretty independent and mature for my age—Flash and I are both twenty—and I can handle a lot, but fuck, this is big, and if I'm totally honest, I'm a little scared. Okay, I'm fucking terrified.

I wouldn't admit that out loud to anyone, not even Flash, but then again, with him I don't *have* to because I know he feels the same without either of us even saying anything about it. We get each other. This is huge for us, so goddamn important that not making it would wreck us.

I'm envious of Flash for having such great parents behind him, but thankful for our friendship.

I do manage to finally have conversations with the agents. I scribble some notes and, like Mr. and Mrs. Flass made me promise, I tell all of them I'll get back to them. They all want to come to Ridgedale to meet with me, which freaks me out.

This weekend Flash and I are going to compare notes. Neither of us is really sure what the hell we're doing. Coach said he'll help us too, and his input will be good because he knows both of us and how we play, what our strengths and weaknesses are, and what the scouts are saying about us.

Finally, it's Friday night, and we get to play. Practices are intense, and workouts are strenuous, but I live for the game. I love to play hockey.

Like I said, I'm a bit superstitious. I think most hockey players are, and it's part of our Bears Bro Code that you never interfere with a teammate's game day routine. That's a level-five infraction, which is bad. Punishment for that might be running around the Quad naked. No, wait, some of the guys would do that anyway. Well, it would be bad.

Things I do before a game that are always the same—I chug a bottle of lemon-lime Gatorade (and it *has* to be lemon-lime); I do my stretches in the same order every time; I take my time taping my sticks, to get them precisely how I like them.

First I tape the blade. Every player does this differently, and I have my set way of taping. I always go from toe to heel, and there's a reason for it, because that way the ridges are away from the puck as it moves from heel to toe, and it won't stick on them. I start the black tape about an inch from the end of the blade, overlapping the strips precisely. It has to be perfectly smooth. I tear it off at the top, then run the roll of tape over both sides of the blade to smooth down all the edges.

Then I tape my knob.

Yeah, yeah, we've all made jokes about our knobs. Some guys like a really big knob. Some don't, and tape lower down the shaft. Yep, there are all kinds of dirty jokes to be made. So I'm smiling as I wrap white tape around the stick. I like white tape for the knob because it doesn't mark my gloves up as much as black. I like a small knob and a bit of a grip. After wrapping the tape once around the top, I let the roll dangle with about a foot of tape, then spin it. When it's like a rope, I spiral it around the shaft, carefully making sure each wrap is the same distance apart. Yeah, I'm anal that way.

More dirty joke material. It amuses me.

I wrap the flat tape back up the shaft nice and tight. Heh.

At the top, I rip the tape off. Then I carefully pull at the tape on the roll to split it in half, making a narrower strip, and wind that around the top of the stick. I finish off with more wide tape to make it nice and smooth.

The DeWitt Center is buzzing tonight because there's a huge traditional rivalry between Bayard and Yale. The arena will be packed with fans. This should be a fun night.

There are more rituals as we head onto the ice for the game—the secret handshakes, the order in which we all go on—always, *always* our goalie Freddy is the first one on the ice, and big D-man Trent Abraham is last.

I stand on the blue line, listening to the Bayard Pep Band play the national anthem, shifting my weight from one foot to the other as I visualize winning the opening face-off. Then I skate to center ice to actually do it.

I'm facing off against Matt Brigham. I grip my stick, one hand low on the shaft, the other about a quarter of the way down, and crouch with my body and head low, my body alive and alert, stick on the ice. The puck drops and I snap it over to Flash and we're off.

Yale has a good team this year, and we have to battle hard for puck possession. But we're doing it. Controlling the neutral zone. They can't get any kind of momentum going. We're outshooting them. But fuck, their goalie is standing on his head to make the saves, and by the end of the first period the score is tied at zip.

As we file off the ice, I look up and see Skylar and Ella sitting in the stands. Skylar is watching Flash, behind me, but Ella seems to be looking right at me. I pause for a fraction of a second, then keep going without acknowledging her.

We tramp into the dressing room. I pull off my helmet then my jersey and shoulder pads, and collapse onto the bench in front of my cubby. Sweat is running down my face, soaking my long-sleeved T-shirt, the tech fabric wicking moisture away from my skin. Thank fuck. I grab a towel and rub my face.

"What the fuck," Flash says. "I swore that shot was going in."

"I know." I shake my head. "Jesus. I don't know how the hell Ranta stopped that."

"He's hot tonight," Soupy agrees.

"Just keep it up!" Coach calls to us. "We controlled that first period. Keep getting the puck to the net. Eventually, it'll go in."

Ranta is from Finland, and he's another one apparently on the scouts' lists of possible draft picks. I can see why.

When we start the second period, I find myself aware that Ella is in the crowd watching me. I mean, watching the team. She wasn't really looking at me as I was leaving the ice.

Fuck, I shouldn't be thinking about her. I should be thinking about the NHL scouts who hold my future in their hands. I focus mentally. Not only do you need physical strength to be a pro athlete, you need mental strength. You need to be able to focus, no matter what. That's what a professional does, and I need to show everyone I can be a professional hockey player.

My next shift, I do that. I focus. I skate hard. I hit hard. I take out one of the Bulldogs' top scorers with a hard check in the corner. My teeth rattle too, but it's worth it as I gain control of the puck and spin around to shoot at the net. Goddamn Ranta blocks it, but the rebound pops out and Flash catches it on his blade and releases it so fast it's a fucking miracle. I follow the puck with my eyes, right past Ranta and into the net. *Yeah!* The red light goes on, the horn blasts, and the crowd cheers.

Flash's arms go up in the air and his smile beams. I skate at him and hug it out as the rest of the team converges on us, patting Flash's helmet, slapping my back. We all skate by the bench to bump gloves with the rest of the team.

The pep band is playing the Bayard Fight Song and the crowd is still going crazy. The announcer calls out, "Baaaayard Bears goooooal, his eleventh of the season, scored by nuuuuuumberrrrr eight . . ." And he pauses as the crowd screams, *"Jacob Flass!"*

"Assisted by . . . number fifteen . . ." And they scream, *"Ben Buckingham!"*

I grin as I settle onto the bench. Coach slaps my shoulder and Franco gives my helmet a tap as we watch Jimmy take the face-off at center ice.

Fuck, I love this game.

The crowd now takes up the chant where the people at the home end of the arena stand up, point at Freddy, and yell, *"Goalie!"* and then the people at the other end of the arena do the same, yelling at Yale's goaltender, *"Sieve!"* This goes back and forth for a while as the play continues.

"People don't do that in Canada," Flash says beside me, grinning. "That is so not cool."

"It's cool as fuck," I argue.

He just laughs.

We know one of Ranta's weaknesses is his rebound control. That's exactly how we got that last goal, and this is playing through my head for the rest of the period. So I'm parked in front of him when Franco has the puck and shoots. And I'm ready when that puck bounces out, pouncing on it and flicking it into the net over Ranta's shoulder.

Fuck yeah!

It's my turn to pump my hands in the air and be swarmed by my teammates. But weirdly, as that happens, my gaze goes up into the stands where Ella is sitting with Skylar, and I see them on their feet, cheering.

We're up two–nothing, but we can't slack off and sit on the lead. We have to keep on the offense. I want to stay in front of the net again, but after that last goal, the Bulldogs are on to me and are doing everything they can to get me out of there, pushing, shoving, fucking cross-checking . . .

The sharp blast of a whistle stops the play, and I grin as O'Connor from the Bulldogs heads off for two minutes for cross-checking. Flash comes by, gives me a pat, and says "Attaboy, Buck" for drawing the penalty. I ignore the pain across my shoulder blades from the hit.

O'Connor protests loudly to the ref, following him to the timekeeper's bench. "That's fuckin' bullshit!" he yells.

I roll my eyes.

Okay, we've been working on our special teams and now have a power play. I win the face-off against Ciceron, drawing the puck back to Soupy. I take a second to give Ciceron a shove before we set ourselves up. Soupy hangs on to it, gliding back to the blue line then passing across to Danny. He passes to Flash, beside the net. I'm out front again with two Bulldogs trying to fuck me up. We play with it a bit, cycling the puck around until fucking finally I have an opening. I bang my stick on the ice and Danny passes it to me and I snap it in again over Ranta's shoulder.

The horn blasts, the arena goes nuts, and guys all leap on me to celebrate. I'm grinning like a fool as I head to the bench.

The second period ends with us up three–nothing. The mood in the dressing room is definitely upbeat, with lots of trash-talking of the Bulldogs. Coach reminds us we still have twenty minutes to play, though.

Remember that superstitious thing? The one thing nobody mentions in the dressing room is a hat trick. I don't even want to *think* about it, never mind say it. I can't let that affect how I play.

So when Flash and I have a two-on-one, I have to think fast. I've got the puck and I could shoot, but it's straight on the net. Ranta could kick out a rebound, which Flash *might* be able to grab. Nah. I meet Flash's eyes and drop the puck. I continue left as he circles behind me to pick up the puck, come around, and shoot at the wide opening Ranta has left because he's watching me.

Another goal.

"You two are on fucking fire tonight!" Franco yells as we celebrate again.

So, I don't get my hat trick, but we still win four–nothing, and that's the most important thing.

I get some rare words of praise from Coach after the game. Flash and I have to talk to some media people—a college blogger and a guy from the local newspaper. Then we shower and dress and head out to meet up with the rest of the guys at Curly's to celebrate the win.

"Skylar coming too?" I ask Flash.

"Yeah. She's meeting us there."

We walk into the bar, known for being a hockey hangout. The place is packed and music pounds from the speakers. In the dark, we find our teammates at some high-top tables pushed together. Skylar's blond hair glows in the dim light, and Flash heads straight to her. She throws her arms around him in a hug. I see Ella next to her. Whatever.

The other guys who are there all greet us with fist bumps and bro hugs and some "fuck yeahs." It's hard not to be pumped about how we all played tonight against our archrival.

I order my usual beer. Even though we're underage, Curly's serves hockey players and everyone just kinds of turns a blind eye to it. Flash is driving tonight, so I can have more than one.

"Congratulations, pretty boy," Ella says to me after the commotion has died down.

"Thanks." I want to roll my eyes at her nickname for me.

"Why didn't you shoot the puck?"

"What?"

"That last goal. You had the puck. Why didn't you shoot it?"

I shrug. "I didn't have the best shot. Figured we could do better."

"You could have had a hat trick."

I eye her. "I didn't know you were that into hockey."

She wrinkles her nose, and it's kind of cute. "It's hard not to get into it when the arena is full of four thousand screaming fans."

I laugh. "Yeah, I guess."

"So you let Flash get the goal."

"It's a team sport. We don't score for ourselves. We score for the team." She's looking at me as if I just told her I eat pucks for breakfast. "What?"

She shakes her head.

"You look surprised," I persist. "Because I'm not the asshole you think I am?"

"I don't think you're an asshole."

"Yes, you do."

"Well, you think I'm a slut."

Guilt smacks me upside the back of the head, and I almost wince.

The truth is, I did once call her a slut. Not to her face; it was a stupid comment I made to some of the other guys, and Flash called me on it immediately. My gut cramps up a little, remembering that. "No, I don't."

"Party girl?" She lifts one eyebrow.

Fuck.

The waitress arrives with beers for Flash and me. I reach for mine and guzzle down about half of it in one go.

Why do I feel like apologizing to her? The truth is, she does like to party and sleep around. And honestly, I don't have a problem with that. Lots of *guys* do it—hell, *I* do it—and everybody looks *up* to them for it. Why shouldn't a girl be able to do whatever she wants?

But when *she* does it . . .

"Never mind," she mutters, and starts to turn away.

I stop her with a hand on her forearm. I don't know why. I don't even like her, but the vulnerable droop of her lips and shadows in her eyes get to me. "You're not a slut. And there's nothing wrong with partying. If that's what you want to do."

She stares at me. The air crackles around us, the noise and other bodies fading away. For some reason all I can see is her face, a perfect, pale oval with big dark eyes and the tiny mole above her mouth that draws my attention to her lips. The moment stretches out. Then she says, "Thanks," and moves away to disappear into the crowd.

Chapter 5

Ella

WHILE SKYLAR GOES to work at the Taste of Heaven diner on Saturday, I go to my job, which isn't really a job because I don't get paid. Saturday mornings I help teach ballet to five-year-olds. It's a volunteer thing, but I love dance and I love little kids, so I enjoy it.

I haven't had to get a part-time job since I started college, because my mom and dad pay for everything. I do have a job in the summer and save up, but my parents are so protective of me, they don't want me to have to work and take classes at the same time, in case my grades suffer.

If they only knew.

I've always felt lucky that I didn't have to get a job, but now I realize that having my parents there to support me no matter what is a little . . . immature. If I had to pay for some things myself, maybe I wouldn't have made the bad choices I have lately.

This realization makes me feel pretty shitty.

Dammit, not only do I have to bring my grades up, and make things better with Skylar, now I also need to take responsibility for my own life.

I almost laugh out loud at myself because, wow, am I ever spoiled if taking responsibility for my own life annoys me. This shit is hard.

But I can do it.

I spend an hour positioning tiny feet and hands, redirecting distracted little princesses and demonstrating first position and pliés. They're so cute in their little pink leotards and tights, some of them still with round bellies, their hair pulled up into buns. I especially like little Cleo, whose hair is too short for a bun so she has about five hundred bobby pins holding it back.

Then I head to the library to get some homework done.

I settle in with my laptop, carefully making sure the sound is off. I shake my head and smile, remembering my last study session here, with Ben next to me, no doubt enjoying my humiliation.

Then I remember last night at Curly's, talking to him, and that weird moment when we were insulting each other and . . . it didn't feel right. He kinda looked ashamed, and honestly I felt guilty about thinking he was a pompous asshole, after watching him play and seeing his unselfish moves on the ice, and then later seeing how much his teammates like and respect him.

I almost want to go to tonight's game. But Skylar's not going because she's working this afternoon and she needs to get some homework done. I admire her self-discipline. And I will emulate it and stay home with her. After the game, Jacob's taking her to a party, though, and she invited me to go with them. I'm torn.

Maybe this is how an addict feels. Like if you get a taste of the thing you're addicted to and you're too weak to resist wanting more . . . what if I go to this party and end up getting drunk and making out with some guy? I don't want to do that anymore. But staying home alone on a Saturday night doesn't appeal either.

I'm not addicted to partying. And I'm not an alcoholic. I had one drink last night at Curly's and that's the first drink I've had since New Year's. But I'm an extrovert and I need be around people. I can do this.

By about four o'clock, I'm done. I'm antsy and starving for human interaction. I got a lot done, though. There's a four-thirty Zumba class at Carol Carson Hall that I often go to. That's what I need. Fun music and dancing with a bunch of girls. Even though my parents made me take all those ballet, jazz, and hip-hop classes, I really do love to dance.

I change into a pair of cropped yoga pants and a tank top and lace up my Nikes, then walk into the Zumba room with the big wall of mirrors on the far side. There are a few girls I know there, and we chat until class starts. The instructor starts off with "El Taxi." which has a sexy Latin feel. I love Pitbull's voice. I love dancing too, and I put my whole body into the moves, swiveling my hips, pumping my arms. Maybe I can dance at the party tonight, too.

Soon I'm sweating but it feels good. This. *This* is a good way to deal with my feelings.

My mind wanders as I dance. The hockey game starts at seven. What's Ben doing right now? Is he at the arena, getting ready? Is he already sweaty too?

Gah! Why am I thinking about him? I give my head a shake and follow the instructor's footsteps.

After Zumba class, Skylar and I arrive home around the same time.

"Hey, how was work?" I ask, dropping my bags onto a chair in the living room.

"Busy. But I made lots of tips, so that's good. How was the library?"

"Quiet." I make a face. "You know I don't do well with silence."

She laughs. "No blasting of music accidentally?"

"Not today, thank God. I got lots done. Then I went to Zumba class. Hence the sweatiness. I need to shower."

"Oh, me too."

"You go first. I'll make us something to eat and I can shower after."

"Okay, thanks."

I put on some music while I move around the kitchen. There aren't a lot of groceries to choose from, but I put together a pasta dish with some bottled sauce that I jazz up with hot pepper flakes, black olives, and a jar of roasted red peppers I find at the back of the cupboard.

Natalie and Brooklyn are both out, and Skylar and I sit at the little kitchen table to eat.

"So are you coming to the party tonight?" Sky asks.

"Yeah, I guess I will."

"You don't sound enthusiastic." She gives me a curious look.

"No, no, I'm sure it'll be fun."

"You love to party."

"That's what got me into this mess, remember?"

"But you don't have to become a hermit."

"I'm not!" *I'm going to the damn party, dammit.*

"No, I know, I know. You came out last night. Thank you, by the way. I hate going to a hockey game alone."

"It was fun."

"And it'll be fine if you come to the party tonight."

I give her a wry smile. "Last semester *you* were the one who refused to go out, like you were afraid to. You spent all your time studying until you started seeing Jacob. You know I have to get my grades up. Now you're encouraging me to go out?"

"I'm encouraging you to not feel guilty about having some fun once in a while."

I blink at her.

"You can set goals for yourself and that's great, but you can't do homework twenty-four/seven. I'm just saying, you can still have fun. You act like coming to this party is going to be as much fun as a gynecologist appointment."

I have to laugh at that. "Shit."

She smiles. "That's not like you. You're so outgoing and bubbly . . . you love going to parties and meeting new people."

I bite my lip, because I immediately think that "meeting new people" means meeting guys to hook up with. Okay, I'm oversensitive about this. And anyway, what's wrong with hooking up if you meet someone you're attracted to?

Yeah, there's nothing wrong with it. Except . . . I'm having another one of those painful moments of honesty with myself. Half those hookups I barely remember because I was so drunk or, in a few cases, stoned. And many of them weren't that great. Some were fun, yes, but after a while, meaningless sex starts to make you feel kind of . . . lonely.

I blow out a long breath. "When I was home at Christmas, my older brother Gareth had a little talk with me."

Skylar blinks. "About what?"

"Well, even though he graduated from Bayard a couple of years ago, he still knows people here, and apparently they alerted him to the fact that I was drinking and partying and sleeping around a lot. He basically threatened to tell Mom and Dad if I don't get my shit together."

Skylar's forehead furrows. "Oh no."

"Yeah." I grimace.

I've never been one to care what people think. My family just shook their heads when I had mismatched socks as a kid. They indulged me when I wore my Little Mermaid costume to school on picture day and shrugged when I put blue streaks in my hair.

"I don't care if people are talking about me," I continue. "But even though I don't like being smothered by my family, I really hate the thought of causing them grief. So I have to clean up my act. That's why I'm not all thrilled about going to the party. But I'll come. I just won't drink. And I probably won't stay late."

Skylar nods. "Sure."

I move on to other important topics. "What are you wearing?"

We discuss wardrobe options for a while. Then Skylar says, "Have you contacted SAPAP yet about going for some counseling?"

That's the Sexual Assault Prevention and Awareness Program we have at Bayard. Skylar volunteers there after she got counseling through them last year.

I focus on my plate of half-eaten pasta. "Not yet."

"But you will. Right?"

"Yes." I feel my defenses going up and the urge to snap back at Skylar, and I fight with it. "I'm doing fine, okay?" I try to keep my tone gentle so it doesn't come across wrong.

"Okay." After a pause, Skylar says, "I'll do the dishes, since you cooked."

"I'll help."

We get things tidied up and then go up to our rooms. Skylar needs to put in a few hours of homework. Jacob's going to pick us up after the game, which will be about ten, so I have time to shower, do more home-work, and figure out what to wear.

I like clothes and fashion, putting together new outfits and trying new makeup. Maybe it's superficial, but it's fun, and everyone needs some kind of creative outlet, right? In my early teens I used to write angsty poetry. Maybe I should take that up again to express my emotions. Or interpretive dance. Ha! That idea makes me smile.

I have to finish this assignment for Research Methods in Communication Studies, but first I open my closet and study the contents. The right clothes can totally give you confidence, and tonight I need confidence, since I won't be numbing all my feelings with alcohol. I pull out a black dress. It's the perfect combination of sexy and classy. I don't want to look like I'm going to my grandmother's funeral, but I don't want to be broadcasting "on the prowl" either. I grab a pair of heels and plug in my curling wand to touch up my waves.

Then I bury myself in Research Methods.

Around nine-thirty, Skylar knocks on my door and pops her head in. "Hey. Can you help? I don't know which outfit to wear."

I smile and push away from my desk. Helping Skylar figure out what to wear is familiar territory. In her room, we decide on leggings and a long sparkly top.

"Thank you!" Dressed, she inspects her reflection in the mirror. "You always know what's right."

I wish. But I smile.

The doorbell rings.

"He's here!" Skylar whirls around and rushes out to let Jacob in, and I follow.

The party's off campus. We've been to this house before. On the way there, Skylar says to Jacob, "This is where we met."

It makes me sad that I don't even know that. I guess I was busy with other things that night.

The Bears lost tonight. Apparently, Yale regrouped after their beating last night and came out strong: Final score, two–one. "They scored the winning goal with forty seconds left in the game," Jacob grumbles. "We had no chance to come back, dammit."

Skylar pats his shoulder. I want to say something stupid like "You can't win them all," but Jacob already knows that, and it's not going to make him feel any better, so I say nothing.

The party isn't too crazy, but I'm sure that will change when it gets later and more people arrive. Music blasts as we make our way through the crowd. Jacob finds his hockey buddies in the kitchen, including Ben. He's changed out of his game day suit into a pair of narrow tan pants and a pink-and-brown plaid shirt that's fitted perfectly to his muscled body, as usual stylish and perfectly groomed, his hair tousled on top, sideburns neatly trimmed.

I've seen him play hockey before, but last night was weird, because suddenly I was comparing him on and off the ice. Off the ice, he's all polished and sophisticated and cool, with perfect beard stubble and designer clothes. *On* the ice . . . he was sweaty, with dripping hair and a red face, his eyes intense, his jaw set. Tough. Raw.

Here he's back to his usual urbane self, even though he's sipping beer from a red Solo cup like almost everyone else there.

Skylar hands me a cup too, and I hesitate and lift my eyebrows at her. She just smiles and I take a tiny sip. Sparkling water. I smile back at her gratefully. She's a true friend.

The guys are in the middle of a conversation.

"I like a really sticky shaft," Grady says.

My eyebrows rise as I meet Skylar's wide eyes.

"Stiffness is important too," Ben says. "I like a stiff shaft."

I blink. "That's what she said."

The guys all look at me and then burst out laughing. But they continue their conversation. "Franco's is super stiff too," Ben goes on. "His shaft is probably the only one harder than mine."

I'm shaking my head, trying not to collapse into giggles.

"What?" Ben looks at me. "Sticks are important to hockey players."

I suck on my bottom lip, laughter still bubbling up inside me. "I'm sure they are."

"Length matters too," Jacob says. "The shortest player on our team has the longest stick."

Now I can't stop myself and I fall against the counter, laughing. "Length does matter," I manage to choke out.

"Because he spends a lot of time on the penalty kill," Hunter adds. "He needs a longer stick to poke check. And a lighter stick too, so that he can wave it faster back and forth."

My eyes widen as I picture this image and I laugh even harder.

"His blade is really curved too," Jacob puts in.

Skylar and I are now both dying.

"There are so many differences," Ben says, his lips twitching. "Curve, texture, feeling, thickness of the shaft, stiffness, roundness . . ."

I'm crying, tears running down my face.

"We can spend hours fiddling with our sticks," he ends, grinning.

I can't even speak, and Skylar is likewise laughing so hard she's crying.

"And we won't even talk about our knobs," Jacob adds with a huge smile.

"Stop, please," Skylar begs. "My abs hurt."

"Mine too." I press a hand there and wheeze for air.

My eyes meet Ben's, and for once his hold a teasing glint, his lips curving into a smile. He totally knew what that conversation sounded like. I shake my head, and I'm holding Ben's gaze and we're relaxed and smiling at each other . . .

Heat pulses around us, something intangible curling around me and drawing me to him . . . the pounding music and loud voices surrounding us dulls and all I can hear is my heartbeat in my ears. My gaze moves over Ben's face . . . he really has a very attractive mouth . . . and his face is put together so nicely . . . oblong, lean cheeks, a strong jaw. I meet his eyes again, a brown a little lighter than his hair—caramel-colored.

A sizzle runs down my spine, and when his gaze drops to my mouth, I pull in a quick breath. I start to touch my tongue to my bottom lip, but then realize how that's going to look, so I quickly draw my top teeth over my lip and try to relax. I watch as his eyes darken.

Holy hell, Ben Buckingham and I are eye fucking.

I can tell when a guy's attracted to me, and he is, even if he does hate me. And at that moment, with my skin tingling everywhere, my mouth longing to kiss him, I have to admit the truth . . . I'm attracted to him too.

God. I swallow and break eye contact, turning away. My fingers tighten on my plastic cup to keep them from trembling.

Maybe it was all that dirty talk about hockey sticks. I don't want to be one of those girls who sees a hockey player on the ice and gets all silly. Surely that's not what this is. But I'm feeling a little hot and bothered.

Ice. For my drink.

I turn my head and find a cooler across the room, then dive toward it. Why do we always end up in the kitchen at parties? I need to go dance.

I find some ice, drop it into my cup, and press it against my burning cheek. When I turn back around, Ben is watching me. One corner of his sexy mouth lifts.

Of course that makes my cheeks even hotter.

I head back toward Skylar and grab her hand. "Let's go dance." I love to dance.

She gives Jacob big blinky eyes, and he laughs and comes with us. I don't realize until we're trying to fit ourselves in between bodies in the crowded living room that Ben came too.

It's so crowded, everyone's dancing with everyone, bodies bumping. I try to ignore Ben and move my body to the beat of "Burnin'" by Calvin Harris, my arms up, my hair flying. Like in the class earlier, I dig my hips into the music and let it fill me up. Skylar moves with Jacob and Ben stays close to me, and I can't ignore him. I'm impressed with the hockey dude's dancing. He's got rhythm, nothing flashy, but he looks at ease, not like some guys on the dance floor who're stiff and awkward.

Our eyes meet again, the music throbbing around us, and I find my body moving in time with his. More heat swells inside me, warming my skin. The music is fast and hot, almost . . . erotic. We're not touching, but there's barely a breath between our bodies, our gazes fastened on each other in a way that's making my core melt. When the music shifts into another tune, a Don Diablo mix, I give Ben my back . . . and then I move my ass into him.

His hands come to my hips and we're grinding, moving to the music together, my body undulating against his. I think I hear him mutter, "Jesus" near my ear. My hands go to my hair, my head tossing, and his fingers tighten on me.

I hate him. He's stuck-up and superior, judgy and full of himself. But he's a great dancer, and I don't want to stop. A mist of perspiration dampens my bare arms and my chest in the round neckline of my dress.

The music changes again, the beat slowing, melding into another song . . . a slow song by Avicii, still sultry . . . Ben's hands turn me to face him, but he keeps hold of me and now our bodies are touching, hip to hip, thigh to thigh. I look into his eyes and he meets my gaze steadily, hotly. Heat smolders between us, and I'm breathless and on edge. My nipples tingle and my thighs quiver.

Ben's watching my mouth and it's the sexiest thing ever. My lips part with hunger.

"Not here," he murmurs, easing me between writhing bodies, across the room toward the French doors. We're still dancing; when we get clear of the crowd he takes my hand and spins me. Delight courses through my veins as I let myself twirl back to him, this time right up against his big body.

Damn, he's hard everywhere, all thick muscles . . . ripped as fuck. I'm dying to know what he looks like with his clothes off. My pussy is aching and molten heat pools low down inside me.

He doesn't hold that position long, though, leading me out of the room and down a hall. The music fades but I can still feel it pulsing in my body. He spins me again, this time into a room . . . possibly a bedroom? I see nothing, because it's dark and also because I'm crashed up against him and he's kissing me.

Chapter 6

Ben

My mouth can't get enough of hers. Christ. I'm all over Ella, and she's right there with me, arms around my neck, hands in my hair. My dick is huge and throbbing, my balls aching relentlessly as I eat at her mouth. Heat burns over my skin, from my face all the way down to my groin.

I slide my tongue into her mouth and she meets it with hers and a groan rumbles up from my chest. I grip her ass with both hands, and fuck, she's got a nice ass, firm and round. Her tits are pressed into my chest and when she rubs a little against me there, electric jolts shoot right to my nuts.

I slide a hand up her back and twist it into her long hair, pulling her head away so I can glide my mouth over her cheek. I kiss her jaw, catch her earlobe between my lips, then drag my tongue down the side of her neck. She shivers and gives the hottest little moan.

"Christ," I mutter. "You pushed this tight little ass up against me out there. You made me so fucking hard."

She rocks her pelvis into me, against that hardness, and more heat and pressure builds inside me.

"Feel that?" I mumble, seeking her mouth. "Feel how hard I am for you?"

"Yesssss. Oh God, yes."

I capture her mouth with mine again, opening wide, licking inside. We're practically fused together, rubbing against each other, and I bump my hips harder, giving some friction to my aching dick against her mound.

She gasps. "Oh my God. Ben . . . more . . ."

"I'll give you more, baby." And I pull her even tighter to me, hands on her ass, our hips rocking together, dry humping each other as our mouths slide and suck at each other, our gasps and whimpers and groans filling the dark silence.

I spin Ella and shove her against the wall, which is vibrating with the deep bass of the music. Grabbing her butt, I hoist her up and she wraps her legs around my waist. She grips my shoulders and her head falls to one side as I lick and suck at her neck and her shoulder. I find one breast and cover it with my palm, giving it a firm squeeze. She sucks in a sharp breath again, lifting her hips into me in a needy rhythm. And I know just what she needs, because I need it too—*Christ, do I.* My heart is pounding, my blood pumping hot through my veins.

I could shove her short dress up and have my fly down and be inside her in seconds. My dick jumps with joy at this thought. Her skirt's already ridden up on her smooth, warm thighs, and I start to work it higher, higher. I find the edge of her panties and I curl my fingers around what is basically a string on her hip.

"Ben," she whispers, and I kiss her again, deep and thorough. Tingles race up my spine.

The door bursts open, light stabs my eyes, and people fall into the room. All I can hear is a girl sobbing. I freeze.

"He's such an asshole!" the girl cries.

"I know, I know," another female voice consoles her.

"Oh . . ." They see us, practically fucking against the wall, and now they go motionless. "Uh, sorry . . ."

The girl takes a long, ragged breath in, then sobs again.

I lower Ella's legs, and she finds the floor with her high heels, both of us tugging her dress down. "It's okay," I say, turning and hiding Ella from view so she can make whatever adjustments she needs to. I hope the two girls won't drop their gaze below my waist, because there's no hiding my raging hard-on. "We're leaving." I wave a hand to the room.

The first girl stumbles to the bed and collapses onto it, covering her face in her hands and weeping loudly. I glance at Ella over my shoulder, then let her precede me out of the bedroom. I shut the door behind me, and we pause in the hall, the music louder here.

We're both still vibrating with lust, but the interruption has knocked some sense into my head, if not my dick, which still pulses with urgent need. What the hell am I doing? This is Ella. I don't even like her.

I may have slept around my share, but I've never slept with a girl I don't like. I'm not that desperate, although the guy downstairs might beg to differ.

"Well, party girl, looks like we were just saved from making a horrible mistake."

Her face changes, from soft and dreamy to completely blank. She lifts a hand to her throat and rubs. "Right." She shakes her hair back and lifts her chin. "Lucky us."

I'm not feeling real lucky right now, but I go with it. "Yeah. Let's get back to the party."

"I'm going to find a bathroom." She gives me a tight smile and pivots on one spiky heel, and I watch her ass swing in the body-hugging dress as she walks down the hallway. She disappears through another door, closing it behind her with a crack that's just short of a slam.

I run a hand through my hair and suck in air, then let it out with a burst. Fuck. We may have been saved from an even worse mistake, but clearly we already fucked up.

I'm cursing myself as I return to the kitchen to search out another beer. Maybe two. Or ten.

There are even more people here now, and more arriving all the time. The music seems louder. I find Soupy and Rocket talking to a couple of girls, so I slide into their conversation. Tiffany gives me a flirty smile as she plays with the straw in her drink. I wink at her. I haven't slept with her, but I think nearly every other player on the team has.

"I just don't understand guys," the other girl says. I think her name's Brandi. She's hot, but the slight whiny tone in her voice puts me off. "I thought everything was going fine and then he ghosted. What do guys really want in a relationship?"

"Sex," Rocket offers helpfully.

Both girls laugh. "No, really," Tiffany says. "Besides that."

"Space," Soupy says. "It's nice when you pay attention to us and send us cute text messages, but sometimes you have to back off. If you were texting him ten times a day, maybe that scared him. Guys need time with their buddies or time to study or whatever."

"Especially hockey players," Rocket adds. "Man, our schedules are full."

Tiffany and Brandi nod, Brandi shooting me a look from under her eyelashes.

"If he doesn't text you right back, it doesn't mean he doesn't care," Soupy adds. "It might just mean he's busy."

Flash joins us then, along with Brooklyn and Natalie, all looking damp and out of breath from dancing. "Who else needs a beer?" he asks.

I lift my nearly empty bottle that I've sucked back in record time and Flash disappears.

"Hi, Nat, Brooklyn." I lift my beer at them, and they grin, raising their red cups to tap my bottle in a toast. "You just get here?"

"A few minutes ago."

Jacob returns and hands me a nice cold, full beer.

"Hey, Jacob." Tiffany smiles at him. "How are you?"

"Great."

She's apparently noticed that Skylar isn't with him and moves closer. So close she can touch him. And she does, laying a hand on his biceps. "I like your shirt."

Oh yeah—pretty sure Flash is the one other guy on the team Tiffany hasn't slept with, though not from lack of trying on her part.

"Uh . . . thanks." Flash glances down at his blue plaid shirt.

"Great game tonight."

"We lost." He edges away, but in the crowded room it's not that easy, and she sticks to him like a tick on a dog. I see Brooklyn and Natalie exchange frowns.

"I know, but you played well. You always play well. You're amazing."

I close my eyes so they don't roll back in my head. Jesus.

She's stroking his arm when Ella appears, back from her trip to the bathroom. Her eyes meet mine briefly and there's a flash of awareness between us that changes the air in the room from flat to electric. Then her gaze moves to Tiffany's hand on Flash and the way she's pressing her tits against his upper arm. Ella's eyes widen then narrow, and before I can even blink, she inserts herself between Tiffany and Flash.

"Back off, Barbie," she says. "He's got a girlfriend, and you don't want to get her or me angry."

Tiffany's mouth tightens as she takes a forced step back. "Skylar? That victim feminist? Right."

Oh, fuck me sideways. She did not just say that.

It's like everyone standing there goes on alert . . . Flash, Soupy, Rocket, Natalie, and Brooklyn . . . even me. And especially Ella.

"What did you just say?" Ella demands in a low tone, her eyes flashing.

"Jesus," Flash says, looking at Tiffany in horror.

"You don't even know how truly disgusting what you just said is." Ella takes a step toward Tiffany. Flash grabs her arm and I'm glad because I'm a little worried she's going to slap Tiffany and there's going to be an actual catfight.

"You can talk, slut," Tiffany says, backing away.

Ella's eyes go wide, and the air in the room nearly catches on fire. I make a noise in my throat, and all the other guys make it too, a low "uh-oh" of disgust.

I wish I had some kind of smart answer or put-down, but I got nothin'.

Then Natalie steps forward and goes nose to nose with Tiffany. "What did you just call her?"

"Uh . . ."

Brooklyn slides over and has Natalie's back. She points at Tiffany. "Girl, get with the times! Slut shaming is so *over*. Women are sexual. We are free to express our sexuality all over the damn place. Owning our sexuality is empowering, not a reflection of whether we're good or bad."

"It's *okay* for women to enjoy sex," Natalie adds. She gives Tiffany a fake smile. "So stop being such a jealous hypocrite."

Tiffany's eyes widen as she gapes at Natalie. Then she whirls around and stalks away.

Brooklyn and Natalie immediately turn to Ella. Her face is tight and pale, her mouth a straight line. Her friends put their arms around her. "She's a bitch," Natalie whispers. Ella closes her eyes briefly, and I actually feel a pain in my chest. She stepped up to help her friend out and ended up being called that in front of a bunch of people.

But wow . . . I'm all kinds of impressed with her friends and how they backed her up.

"Hey!" Skylar approaches and slides under Flash's arm with a bright smile. Then she looks around at us, all silent, all wearing various looks of shock and horror on our faces, Natalie and Brooklyn still with an arm around Ella. Her forehead creases. "What's going on?"

"Nothing." Ella smiles at Skylar. "You need another drink?"

"Yeah, come on, let's go get one." She and Ella head off arm in arm, followed by Brooklyn and Natalie.

We all gaze after the girls.

"Wow, that was weird," Rocket says.

"No shit." I shake my head. "Good riddance to Tiffany." I chug more beer.

I watch the girls across the room, smiling and laughing as they get drinks. I can tell even from here that Ella is faking her smile. And I'm filled with awe because of what I just witnessed—the obvious love Ella has for Skylar. And the equally obvious love Ella's other friends have for her.

Hearing someone call Ella a slut and seeing the flash of hurt on her face made my insides burn and made me want to punch that bitch. This confuses me.

Skylar comes back, but the others don't, joining in a conversation with a group of three guys. One of them greets Ella with a smile, throws an arm around her neck, and pulls her in for a kiss on her forehead.

Yeah, that makes me want to punch someone, too.

I watch her smile up at the dude as she sips from her red cup. I watch her toss her hair back and laugh at something, then reach out and tap one of the guys on the arm in a flirtatious gesture. And I watch him grin at her, obviously liking what he sees.

She *feels* good too, dammit; I know that now and also know how her mouth tastes. How the hell am I going to forget that?

"And then I fucked her up the ass."

I blink and turn my gaze to Rocket. "Whaaaat?"

He laughs and punches my arm. "That got your attention. Jesus, I asked you three times what you're doing tomorrow."

I shake my head at him. "Asshole. What am I doing tomorrow? Studying, that's what."

"Me too," Flash says. "Skylar's working—right, babe?"

"Yeah." She grimaces.

"Beer me," I say, handing my empty to Rocket.

"Fuck you, get your own."

"It was worth a shot." I push my way through the crowd, trying to ignore Ella flirting with those guys in the corner. This time I take two beers because I'm knocking them back pretty fast. Maybe too fast. I don't give a shit.

The rest of the party passes in a blur of alcohol, loud music, and several rounds of flip cup. By the time Skylar and Jacob are ready to go, I'm shitfaced.

"You're supposed to be our designated driver tonight," Flash reminds me with a frown.

"Oh yeah . . . shit."

"Yeah, no kidding. I can't drive. Neither can Skylar."

Ella appears next to Flash and plucks his keys from his hand. "I'll drive."

We all gape at her. Then Skylar smiles. "Sure, El?"

"Sure." They exchange a look.

"Party girl," I mumble. "You don't wanna drive drunk."

"I'm not drunk." She gives me a sharp look. "You, on the other hand, appear to be wasted."

"Nah." I wave a hand and wobble a little. "I'm good. Just a little drink. Drunk."

She purses her lips like she's trying not to laugh.

"Serioushly, Ella. How many drinks have you had?" I demand. I'm not so drunk that I don't know what's going on.

"None."

I squint at her. "I saw you drinking."

"Club soda, dude."

"Oh." I pause. "Okay, then."

We all stagger out the front door and across the lawn of the frat house. Flash's truck is parked down the street. I point at the moon, a full moon with a cloud partially obscuring it, bare black tree branches in front. "Look at the moon! That's so creepy!"

"It is," Skylar agrees. "Like a horror movie."

I howl like a coyote. Everyone laughs except Ella.

"Don't do that," Skylar says. "You're scaring me."

"Oh my God," Ella mutters as she unlocks all the doors.

Jacob and Skylar get in the small backseat, even though it's his truck, so I'm in the front seat, my head leaning into the headrest.

"Seat belt," Ella reminds me.

"Oh right." I pull the belt across me but can't get it fastened. "I can't get it in."

"I've heard you have that problem," Flash says from behind me. Skylar giggles and Ella's lips twitch.

"Ha-ha. Very funny. I have no trouble getting it in. I just can't find the hole . . . you know. The vagina for the seat-belt penis." I laugh at my own joke.

"That was terrible." Ella reaches over, grabs the buckle, and clicks it into place. "There you go."

"Thank you. Wake me up when we get home."

"You staying at my place?" Flash asks Sky.

"I don't know . . ."

"You can take my truck, Ella," Flash says.

"It'd be easier if you come back to our place," Sky replies.

"Right." A pause, then Flash leans forward between the seats. "You gonna be okay, man?"

"Hell yeah."

"Turn this song up." Skylar requests.

I reach for the radio. "Great song."

Panic! at the Disco blasts around us.

Ella winces and turns it down. I shrug.

She's not impressed with me, I can tell. I don't give a shit.

She soon pulls up in front of our house. I roll out of the car, nearly onto the ground, but I keep my balance. "Okay! 'Night, everyone. Thanks for driving, party girl."

I peer into the backseat and see Flash and Skylar making out.

"Oh, man, come on, enough swapping spit."

A hear what sounds like a choked laugh from the driver's side.

I think I do a pretty good job of walking to the front door. It takes a couple of tries to get the key in the lock, but I accomplish that and wave the others away.

Then I manage to get my sorry ass upstairs, get my clothes off, and pass out naked.

The next afternoon Flash and I are at home watching *How It's Made,* our laptops in front of us, educating ourselves on how to make gin as we compare notes on the various agents we've talked to over the last few days.

"Ugh. Gin." I don't even want to think about booze.

"Juniper berries." Flash shoves another Dorito in his mouth. "Who knew."

"I hate gin."

"Yeah, not my fav either."

"You need to lay off the junk food, man. This is a critical time of year to be in shape."

One of Flash's eyebrows flies up. "Says the guy who consumed a dozen beers last night. What the fuck?"

I shrug and reach for a Dorito myself. Yeah, I'm feeling a tad under the weather today. Okay, I feel like I was eaten by a wolf and puked up over a cliff, and my mouth tastes like the bottom of a birdcage. I should definitely not be judging Flash for eating junk food. I'm also embarrassed, thinking about Ella's reaction to me being hammered. Christ. I slouch down deeper into the couch. She has a low enough opinion of me already. "Might have overdone it a bit."

I usually pride myself on being in control. Last night, I wasn't.

"Yeah, I'd say so. You know you committed an infraction."

I wince. "Yeah." Promising to be designated driver and then getting drunk is definitely an infraction of the Bears Bro Code.

"Oh yeah." Flash grins, and it's kind of evil. "I've been waiting for a chance to inflict my own punishment. I think that's at least a level-two infraction."

"Lay it on me. I deserve it."

"I need to think about it. Who would have thought that Ella would be the sober one who could drive us home, eh?"

"Eh?" He's Canadian and we like to ride his ass when he says that. He lifts his middle finger at me, and I laugh. "Yeah, who woulda thought."

Because at a party, Ella was usually (a) too drunk to drive and (b) off fucking some guy somewhere.

Christ. My gut cramps and I rub my face. I'd wanted to be the guy she was off fucking somewhere. She's hotter than a firecracker lit at both ends. That girl is sex on wheels. Even if she is annoying as hell.

She'd given me a look . . . and instead of pissed or judgmental like I would have expected, she'd looked amused. As if she knew I drank my face off because I was so horned up I felt like a three-peckered goat in a field of nannies.

"Okay, here's your punishment," Flash says. "You have to help me with this program I'm working on."

I narrow my eyes at him. "The sex program?"

He closes his eyes and shakes his head. "It's not a sex program."

"Oh right, it's an *anti*-sex program."

"No, it's not!"

"I thought the point of it was to tell guys to keep their dick in their pants."

Flash sighs. "No, that's not the point. The point is to educate athletes about sexual assault, sexual harassment, and to raise awareness of rape culture. And to teach them about bystander intervention so we all know how to step in when we need to."

I'm really just yanking his chain; I know what the point is.

Flash came up with this idea just before Christmas. Because of some trouble he'd gotten into up in Canada, where he played hockey last year—as in, he'd been accused of gang-raping a girl he'd never touched—he had to go through this new program Bayard was making all freshman take—the Sexual Assault Prevention and Awareness Program. And I guess it kind of opened his eyes or something, especially after one night at Curly's, when one of our teammates who's kind of an asshole got overly aggressive with Ella. Flash stepped in and stopped it, but Black Jack was pissed about it. He didn't even get what was wrong with what he was doing. And Flash came up with the idea that all the hockey players should go through that training. Actually, he proposed all the *athletes* at Bayard go through the program.

This won't be an easy sell to all the testosterone-fueled, entitled, macho athletes at Bayard, including assholes like our teammate Black Jack. "Really? You want me to help?"

The truth is, that's not much of a punishment, because Flash is my buddy and I'd help him even if he didn't force me. But I'm not going to say that, because I might end up with some other punishment, like washing the car of every Bayard Bear player for the rest of the year, or having my eyebrows shaved off.

"Yeah. I mean, assuming this goes through. We're making another presentation to the president and the executive officers of the college on Wednesday."

"Another one?"

"Yeah. They're interested, but Victoria says they want to hear more details. So Skylar's coming too, to talk about how the training will be structured."

"Ah.

"Victoria wants us to do most of the talking. Fuck." He scrunches his face up.

"You're a good talker, Flash." He is. He's one of the guys who'll be a media favorite when he makes it into the NHL, because he's smart and well-spoken and he has personality. And I say *when* he makes it into the NHL because I'm convinced he will. He should have already been drafted, but because of the shitty situation that happened to him last year, he had to take himself out. But this year . . . he's got it.

"Thanks. Anyway, if they approve this, we have a lot of work to do to make it happen."

I emit a heavy sigh. "Okay, fine. I'm in."

"Oh hey, this is better." Flash points at the TV. "Garage door openers."

We watch and learn how garage door openers are made while I try not to think about kissing Ella.

Chapter 7

Ella

I've finally gotten the guts to make an appointment with a counselor. My stomach is tight as I sit in the waiting room, scrolling through Instagram on my phone. I see the selfie that Skylar posted of her and me at the party the other night, with our big smiles, then a picture of Jacob and Ben, all handsome. Aw. What a cute brodak moment.

Ben.

Look at him with his perfectly styled hair, his stubble, his chiseled jaw, his perfect teeth. How does he have such perfect teeth, anyway? Hockey players are known for having their teeth knocked out.

Why does he have to be so perfect? It pisses me off.

I wasn't even drunk, so I can't explain how the hell that little incident in the bedroom happened. All I know is . . . it was so good.

I close my eyes, but when I reopen them the picture of Ben is still on my phone. Damn him, he's even a good dancer, and an amazing kisser. I get that flippy feeling low in my belly all over again, remembering his lips on mine, his tongue in my mouth, his hard body against mine . . .

"Ella Verran?"

I jump, and quickly darken the screen of my phone. I fumble for my purse and my backpack and stand. "Yes."

"I'm Frances. Come in."

I enter the room and it's not really the office I'd expected, but more like a sitting room with a love seat, a couple of armchairs, a coffee table with a box of Kleenex on it, and lamps providing soft light. There's even a big potted palm in the corner and some nice art on the walls.

I take one of the armchairs, setting my things on the other, and Frances sits on the love seat, across the coffee table from me.

"Before we start, I need you to fill out this form and sign it for me." She passes over a clipboard. I take it and the pen and quickly do that then hand it back.

"Thank you. Now tell me what's happening with you and why you're here." Her voice is gentle and warm.

I take a breath. "You actually already know some of this, because my friend has been to see you. Skylar Lynwood."

She nods, smiling faintly. "Yes, I know Skylar. But tell me the story anyway."

I tell her about Brendan—about how I started to care for him as more than a friend, about his not realizing it, about his suicide, and about how devastated I was. "I didn't handle it very well. I started going out a lot. Drinking a lot. And having sex with a lot of guys."

I'm not going to feel ashamed about this. That bitch Tiffany humiliated me by calling me a slut the other night at the party. I was so tempted to just act the way everyone expected—get drunk, leave with a guy, and have sweaty, meaningless sex. With that ache in my chest and the tightness in the pit of my belly, it had been so hard not to do those things that would make me feel better, like they have in the past. But I didn't.

I know Tiffany's not the only one who thinks that of me, and, geez, she sleeps around even more than I have, so where does she get off with the slut shaming? But it's just a word, and I'm not going to let anyone make me feel ashamed. Why does that word even exist? And why do girls think it's an insult?

I keep my chin up as I talk, telling Frances about the things I've done to try to cope with the pain.

"So, this gets even more complicated," I continue. "Because I found out some things that I didn't know. Skylar and I were best friends, but we weren't talking much. I felt so alone. So I started partying a lot, and then I felt like she was judging me for what I was doing. Then Brendan's parents gave me his cellphone when I was home one weekend. It was dead, but they thought I could charge it and see if there was something on it that would be a clue about why he committed suicide. It took me three tries to figure out Brendan's password. And I did find some things. Some very disturbing things."

I rub my face. This part is actually harder than talking about my feelings for Brendan. "I found out that Skylar and Brendan had slept together a few days before he died. At least, that's what I assumed had happened, from the texts I read. He said he loved her and he wanted to talk to her, and she wasn't answering."

"How did that make you feel?" Frances asks quietly.

I hate admitting to such an ugly, petty emotion, but I know I have to be honest here. "Betrayed. Jealous. I was jealous of Skylar. I was jealous because Brendan loved her and not me. I hated her. Sort of. Actually, I don't know if I really hated her. I was confused."

I realize I'm talking all garbled.

"That's understandable."

"That didn't help things between Skylar and me. She had a new boyfriend, she was spending all her time studying and doing her important volunteer work, and that made me feel like I was . . . nothing."

I suck in another breath. "It gets worse. I didn't want to talk to her about it at first, but eventually we did. And she told me that she and Brendan hadn't slept together—he'd raped her."

I almost forgot that Frances already knows this. She doesn't react, just keeps her expression warm and sympathetic.

"Then I was even more confused."

"Tell me about that. What was confusing?"

"I couldn't believe Brendan would do that. I just couldn't. He was our friend. I thought maybe Skylar was lying about it. But I knew she wasn't. And then I felt so angry at Brendan. How could he do that to Skylar? To anyone? I still don't understand it." I swipe at a tear that has appeared in my eye, then grab a tissue. "I knew I was going to need these, dammit."

Frances smiles. "Help yourself."

"Brendan struggled with depression. We knew that. He had a lot of ups and downs, but he was a great guy. I read an email he sent to his psychiatrist, and it sounded like Brendan had been caught cheating on a test, and he was worried about what was going to happen. He also said something else had happened and he needed to talk about it." I swallow. "I think he was referring to what happened with Skylar. He sounded super-anxious about it. He was supposed to see the psychiatrist Monday . . . but he never got there."

Frances nods. "There's a lot to unpack there."

"Oh God, I know." I wipe my eyes.

"So there's your reaction to Brendan's death. Which alone is a hard thing to deal with. Losing a friend, especially to suicide, is certainly a difficult thing."

I nod quickly.

"There's also your relationship with Skylar. How is that?"

"Getting better. It's been rough. But she's my best friend."

"And then there's dealing with knowing things about your friend Brendan that change how you see him."

"Yes." I drag air into my lungs.

"Well, we'll talk about that. We won't get to all of it today, but if you're willing to come back a few times, my goals would be to help you understand the mourning process and explore some areas that may be preventing you from moving on. Also, help resolve some areas of conflict that you're still experiencing both internally and with Skylar, and help you adjust to a new sense of self." She pauses. "Ideally, this would have happened sooner after Brendan's death, but it's not too late. Are you willing to work through those things?"

Yes. *Yes*, they're what I need help with. But damn, this shit is *hard*. I straighten my shoulders and meet her eyes. "Yes."

"Let's start first with your feelings after Brendan died. A bereavement period is a confusing time involving a lot of very powerful emotions, but grief after suicide can be particularly complex. Family and friends left behind by a person who dies from suicide often experience a multitude of emotions. Many people feel angry at themselves, or guilty. They blame themselves and wonder if they could have done something to help."

"Yes." *Yes.*

"It's totally understandable for us to ask ourselves why. But we may never have answers. It's also okay to be angry. When someone takes another life, we have somewhere to direct our anger. But when someone takes their *own* life, the person who did it and the victim are the same. So we ask ourselves, *How could he do that to us?* That's perfectly natural. And it's also natural to blame ourselves. We want to think that we could have prevented it. We imagine all kinds of 'what if' scenarios. But that often only makes us feel worse. Guilt is normal, but ultimately Brendan's choice to end his life was his own."

"Yes," I whisper. "I did have those thoughts. I loved him and I had no idea things were so bad for him. God. I kept thinking over and over how he must have been feeling, how alone and hopeless he must have felt to . . . to take that step. I felt like I'd failed him. I should have been there for him. But . . ." I bite my lip.

"Did you feel angry at Brendan?" Frances asks softly.

"Yes." I swallow. "Is that terrible? Why didn't he tell us how he was feeling? How could he have done that?"

"It's not terrible. Your feelings are your feelings, whatever they are, and those are very common thoughts. Tell me what your life was like after he died."

I frown, not sure what she means. "Like, how I felt?" Because I thought I just did tell her that.

"More than that. Tell me how you acted. Did you skip classes? Did you stop taking care of yourself?"

"I, uh . . . well, I already told you I was drinking a lot." I think back. "Honestly, a lot of that time is kind of a blur. Not just because of the drinking. I mean, I wasn't drinking *that* much. But I remember thinking that I didn't really care about anything. I went to classes, but I didn't care.

I . . . I lost some weight. I started hanging out with different people, and . . . I felt angry. At almost everyone. Sometimes I maybe snapped at Skylar when she tried to talk to me about what I was doing."

"What about drugs?"

I make a face. "I may have smoked a joint or two, but that's it. I don't do any other kind of drugs."

She doesn't comment on that, which is kind of a relief, because I don't want to feel she's judging me about any of this. If she was all disapproving about a couple of joints, how was I going to be honest about all the random hookups?

"It's also common to feel numbness, or that sense that nothing matters," she says.

I tell her how sad and lonely I felt, how I'd go over and over the days before Brendan died, trying to figure out why he did it and what I could have done.

"Our time is up for today," Frances eventually says. "I want you to know that even though you may never stop missing Brendan, you *can* get to the point where you find happiness again and a new purpose for your life. You can honor the impact he had on your life, without letting his absence obscure your own future."

And that's where she nearly loses me. Because I'm so damn pissed at Brendan for what he did to Skylar, I am *not* worried about honoring the impact he had on my life.

Only, thinking that makes me feel horrible. Because he's dead. So yeah, I guess there *is* more work to do.

I gather my things and head out.

As I walk across campus in the frosty afternoon air, I shake my head. Talking about those things sure pushed away my confusion about Ben and what happened Saturday night. For a moment, I feel overwhelmed. All these feelings, trying to make sense of them . . . Wow, I've got enough issues to keep Frances employed for the next year.

The cold air stings my cheeks and my lungs as I breathe it in. I tuck my nose into the big scarf wrapped around my neck. Talking about that stuff resurrected all those feelings, but I also have a sense of accomplishment.

I pull out my phone and text Skylar. We'd talked about meeting up for coffee after my appointment, and after her and Jacob's big presentation to the president and the executive officers of the college.

We arrange to meet at Carol's Café, in Carol Carson Hall, and I start toward there. I hope it's just Skylar and not Skylar and Jacob. I like Jacob, but right now I want girl time. Because I am going to shock the hell out of her.

I run up the steps of the old stone building with ivy growing all over the front of it and push inside. The café is on the right, and it's nice and bright and warm in there, with the rich, dark scent of coffee floating on the air along with the chatter of voices and the hiss of the espresso machine.

I spot Skylar at a small table for two and head her way, unwrapping my scarf.

"Hi!" She smiles.

"Hey." I dump my stuff and drape my jacket over the back of my chair. "I'll get coffees. What do you want?"

When we have our lattes, I curve my cold hands around the cup and lean forward. "So? How'd it go?"

She hunches her shoulders up and wrinkles her nose. "I think it went great. Jacob did most of the presentation. We did some research, gave them some stats and some real-life examples . . . ugh . . . which we *don't* want to happen here at Bayard. I think they were impressed. Then I added in some thoughts about the teaching strategy, how we'd start with the coaches, and then roll it out to players, but we'd condense the materials, and make it really interactive, to hold their attention, and also deliver the course around the athletes' schedules, since they're all busy training and practicing and traveling. I suggested that we train some athletes as leaders, so there's better buy-in."

"Did they commit to doing it?"

"No." She makes a face. "They want to discuss it more, but they said they'd have a decision for us by the end of the month. Jesus! Why does it take so long? It's a no-brainer. We need to get moving."

"You think you can do it this year?"

Her shoulders slump. "Probably not. Victoria says it would be more realistic to set a target date of September."

"You want to do it now."

"I do. And Jacob does." Her eyes go dreamy. "He was so good, El. They really listened to him."

I smile at her. "That's great. It sounds positive, so hopefully they'll make the right decision. What can I do to help?"

Her face softens. "You'd help?"

"Of course."

"Thank you. Once we get going, I'll definitely include you. How did your session with Frances go?"

"Well." I let out a breath. "I think it went well. We didn't get very far. Man, I have more baggage than American Airlines."

She huffs out a sad laugh. "You and me both."

"But I have another appointment next week. So I'm working on it."

"Good. She's nice, isn't she?"

"Yeah, she seems nice." I take a sip of my coffee. "So. Just to show that over the last year one thing I've learned is that I should have talked to you more . . . I have to tell you about something."

She nods, wide-eyed, and flicks her long blond-and-pink hair behind her shoulder. "What?"

"On Saturday night, at the party . . . I kissed Ben."

She blinks. "What? Ben? Ben Buckingham?"

"Yes."

"You kissed him?" Her eyes pop open even more.

"Well, we kissed each other. It was pretty . . . intense."

"When did that happen?" She leans closer. "When he was drunk? Oh my God, he was so funny that night. I've never seen him like that."

"No, not when he was drunk." I shake my head, remembering him howling at the moon. Hey—maybe he's not so perfect. I have to admit I kind of enjoyed seeing him a little messed up. "Just after we were dancing."

"Oh. Oh yeah." She smiles. "You two were hot."

I hold up a hand. "No. This isn't what you think. I haven't said anything because he's Jacob's friend, but I do *not* like him. He's annoying as fuck."

Her smile fades. "You still don't like him?"

"No. Like I said, he annoys me."

"Oh, come on. The sparks between you two could cause a forest fire."

I frown. "Sparks?"

"Oh, hell yeah."

"You don't have some kind of matchmaking ideas, do you? Because forget it. I'm not telling you this because I have some crazy crush on the guy. I hate him."

"That's harsh," she says slowly. "He's a good guy."

"Phhht. He's obsessed with his appearance. Designer clothes. Styled hair. Mr. Perfect."

Skylar tips her head and regards me thoughtfully. "Mmm."

I frown. "What does that mean?"

"Nothing."

"Yes it does. What?"

She shakes her head.

"You don't believe me?"

"Of course I believe you. Now I feel bad that you've had to hang out with us when you dislike him that much." But she's smirking.

"You *don't* believe me!" My mouth drops open. "I'm telling you, he's an egotistical, pompous asshole. How can one person be that perfect? Right?"

She purses her lips. "I see your point."

Okay, even *I* know I'm protesting too much. I need to shut the fuck up.

"So why did you tell me that you two kissed?"

"Because I'm confused about it. It was hot as hell. Damn, he's even good at kissing! How could it be that good when I hate him?"

She taps her chin with her index finger. "I don't know, Ella. Why do you think it could be that good?"

"Jesus. You sound like Frances."

She laughs. "Well, I'm not trying to tell you how you feel, but I'll just say that sometimes really intense feelings can get . . . mixed up. You know what they say: there's a thin line between love and hate."

I narrow my eyes at her. "That's bullshit. There's a Grand Canyon between love and hate."

She laughs.

"You can't tell me you hated Jacob when you first met."

"Ha. You know what? I kind of did. Okay, not the *first* time we met. The first time we met, we ended up making out. At that same house we were at the other night. Hmm. Maybe it's something to do with the house . . . no, that's crazy. Anyway, I actually asked him to have sex with me and he turned me down."

My eyelashes flutter up and down a few times at this astonishing news. "He turned you down?"

"Yeah. Um, you know what happened with him."

Ugh. Do I. I was the one who dropped that knowledge on Skylar. Just one more piece of baggage I have to unpack. "Yes."

"He didn't want to get in trouble, or even in a position where he could be falsely accused again, so he was trying to stay away from girls."

"Ah."

"Needless to say, I was humiliated when he rejected me. So, damn right I kind of hated him. But I kind of liked him too." One corner of her mouth lifts in a wry smile.

"Okay. But I *don't* kind of like Ben." As I say the words, I almost feel as if I'm lying. Because there have been things about him lately that I do like . . . his hockey talent, his self-discipline, his dedication and loyalty to his team, the way they respect him.

"Okay. It was just some kind of hormonal thing, then. You were pressing yourselves up against each other on the dance floor and that caused hormone goggles."

"Goggles?"

"Yeah. When you're attracted to someone you normally wouldn't be." Her forehead creases. "Although it's not as if Ben is ugly."

"It was just physical, though." I nod quickly. "Okay, *that* I get. Hormones. It won't happen again. No more dirty dancing."

"Sure," she says lightly. "I'm so glad we got this straightened out."

"Me too."

Chapter 8

Ben

A BUNCH of us are over at Skylar's place to order pizza. Of course Ella is there too, along with Natalie and Brooklyn.

I haven't been able to get that kiss out of my head, and it's making me crazy. Now every time I look at Ella, I stare at her mouth and I remember the feel of her soft body against mine and the way she tasted and . . . *fuck*.

We all settle into their living room to eat, The Weeknd singing "Starboy" in the background.

"Whose *Cosmo*?" Soupy picks up the magazine from the coffee table.

No one answers.

I pick up my piece of pizza. "I think it's Ella's," I say, not looking at her. "Apparently, she gets a lot of useful information from *Cosmo*."

When she doesn't respond right away, I risk looking at her. Our eyes meet with a burst of heat and sparks.

She tosses her hair behind her shoulder. "Fine, it's mine."

"Nothing to be ashamed of," I assure her.

"Then why are you smirking?"

I totally am.

Soupy is flipping the pages. "Oh hey. Sex advice from guys."

"Yeah, let's hear this." I take a big bite of pizza.

"Oh my God," Ella mutters.

Everyone else is waiting expectantly.

"Wear a wet T-shirt to bed?" Soupy lifts bewildered eyes.

"Wet T-shirts are hot," Rocket says.

"Not in bed! Sure, they're hot to look at, but fuck, that's gonna make for some uncomfortable sleeping."

I grin. "I agree."

"Okay, the next one is to 'accidentally' splash yourself with water when doing the dishes, so your nipples show."

Flash's head whips around to stare at Skylar. "You read that in *Cosmo*?"

Her face flames scarlet. "Shush."

The guys all burst out laughing and Ella leans over to pat Skylar's knee. "So proud of you, hon."

Of course Ella's proud of her. She's known for sleeping her way across campus. She probably wears wet T-shirts to bed and does crazy sex acts like . . . Oh fuck it, I can't think about that.

"Graze his nipples with your teeth while you play with his package," Soupy reads on.

My eyebrows fly up.

"Really?" Brooklyn taps her chin. "Do guys really like their nipples played with? I tried that with a guy once and he freaked out."

I meet Soupy's eyes, then Rocket's. None of us say anything.

"Jacob likes it," Skylar says.

"Fuck," Flash mutters.

"That's payback for telling them about the wet T-shirt trick." She elbows him in the ribs and he chuckles.

"Okay, okay, I kinda like it," Flash says.

"Let's take a poll!" Ella looks around at all the guys. "Nipple play . . . yay or nay?"

Soupy shrugs and rubs his chest. "It doesn't do anything for me. But I don't think my nipples are very sensitive."

Rocket and I look at each other and one corner of my lips tugs up. "What the fuck are we even talking about?"

"Come on, inquiring minds want to know," Ella eggs me on with a little smirk on her mouth that's retaliation for laughing at her magazine choice.

"My nipples are supersensitive," Rocket admits. "So it's okay, but you gotta be careful."

"I'd say having my nipples played with is almost as good as a blow job," Flash owns up. "Feel it right in my balls."

"Oh my God." Skylar slides down into the couch. "Can we not talk about this?"

"We haven't heard from Ben yet," Ella says, that little smile still playing on her lips.

I narrow my eyes at her. What is she doing?

"So one is a nay, one is a qualified yay, one is an enthusiastic yay," Brooklyn recaps, and smiles at me.

Jesus. "Fine. I kinda like it." I lift my chin at Soupy. "What other gems of information do you have there?"

"'Play the "Dirty Dice" game,'" Soupy reads. "'For example, when she rolls a six, she has to touch herself.'"

"Another one?" Jacob says to Skylar. "Wow. You really got into that *Cosmo* article, didn't you?"

"Oh my God! You're embarrassing me!" She swats at his chest, but she's laughing along with everyone else. Even Ella has a huge smile, and holy fuck, when she laughs like that, all relaxed and happy, she's fucking gorgeous.

Rocket laughs so hard he falls off the couch, nearly losing his pizza. "Sky, honey, you should see your face," he chuckles. "Come on. You gave us advice about shaving our balls. We have no secrets between us."

She's adorably red. We all love Skylar. Well, I'll admit there was a time I wondered about her. She dumped Jacob without even hearing his side of an ugly story, and that pissed me off. But they talked it out and made up and things are good with them. Jacob sort of hinted that there was more to it than just not trusting him, which made me wonder if something had happened to Skylar in the past. I hate to think she might have been assaulted, but that would explain why she reacted the way she did.

We all flirt with Skylar, but it's only to yank Flash's chain and express our affection for her in a twisted kind of way. And she's a great hockey girlfriend because she can totally take our dirty obnoxious jokes and sexy teasing in stride.

"Put that magazine away," Skylar directs Soupy.

"No way, this is too much fun. Let's see what else we got here . . . Oh ho. Now we have advice for the men."

"This should be good." I stand to get another piece of pizza.

" 'Pay attention to your partner,' " Soupy reads. " 'Try out different things and pay attention to how she responds to find out what she likes.' "

"Huh." I slide a piece onto my plate and head back to the living room. "That's crap advice."

"So you prefer to *not* pay attention to your partner?" Ella asks.

I give her another slitty-eyed look. "I meant that's crap advice because it's a no-brainer. Every guy does that."

"Uh, no." Brooklyn raises a finger. "Every guy does *not* do that. I speak from experience. I was seeing this guy and his moves in bed were exactly the same every time. *Every* time. And not in a good way. I tried to get him to change things up, and he went along with it, but he had no idea what was good for me."

I'm really beginning to wish we weren't talking about sex, because this conversation is starting to turn me on. After kissing Ella and constantly thinking about it and thinking about what I wanted that kiss to lead to, my dick was half hard to start with. The last thing I want to do is embarrass myself by sporting a stiffy in front of her just because of a little sex talk. "Okay, so that *is* good advice, then." I take my seat again.

"Like the guys who don't know where the clit is!" Natalie says.

Oh Jesus. I close my eyes briefly.

"Or they don't know how to touch it," Brooklyn adds. "Too rough, too fast, not quite the right spot . . ."

Skylar pats Jacob's chest as if to reassure him he's got that down.

Enough. I need to go home and watch some Internet porn and spank the monkey. Consult Dr. Jerkoff. Er, get a grip on things.

The next week is crazy busy. We have a trip to New Hampshire on the weekend, and the rest of the time we're practicing, working out, and studying. I've been playing phone tag with agents again, trying to set up meetings. I can't believe these guys are really going to come all the way to Ridgedale just to meet with me. Well, there's one guy Jacob and I both are talking to, so he could kill two birds with one stone. Plus, there's some sports reporter dude from a big hockey blog going to be on campus next week, and he wants to interview me, Flash, and Rocket for an article he's writing about the difference between the Canadian hockey system and college hockey. I can see why they'd want to interview Flash, as he's one of the rare players who has played in both systems, but whatever, Coach says this is good exposure for us with the draft coming up and also good practice dealing with the media.

First we have two games to win against Dartmouth. And we do it, winning Friday three–one, and a shutout Saturday night, two–nothing. After the game, we're all buying drinks for Freddy, our goalie.

I enjoy road trips with the guys. We're like a family, more family than I had growing up. Sure, we play some juvenile pranks and talk a lot of trash, but it's all good. Luckily, no one surprises me with a fake goddamn snake. I shudder, remembering that prank. The guys know I'm terrified of snakes, and when we were in Florida, Rocket went and bought a rubber snake and put it in the cooler. When I went to grab a Gatorade, I damn near died when I saw a huge fucking snake in there. They told me I screamed like a girl, and they laughed and laughed about that. Fuckers.

Jacob is Snapchatting with Skylar while we're at the bar. I'd give him a hard time, but he's not the only one. Some of the other guys have girlfriends, and they're messaging them too.

There are a bunch of girls hanging around us, and they're all hot. I should take one of them up to the room, like I did when we were in Florida for the tournament, which made poor Flash almost blow up because he was so horny being away from Skylar.

"Hi." A cute blonde smiles at me. "Kiss me if I'm wrong, but isn't your name Matthew?"

I stare at her. "My name's not . . . oh."

She laughs. "Sometimes I really like being wrong."

I can't help but smile, because it is kind of funny. But I'm not going to kiss her. "I'm Ben."

"Tawny. My friends said you guys are hockey players."

"Yeah."

"Hockey's a crazy sport. I don't know much about it, but it seems very violent."

Actually, the fact that this chick admits she doesn't know hockey is kind of refreshing, unlike the bunnies who pretend to love hockey because they want to fuck a hockey player. "It's fast," I say. "We play hard."

"On sharp blades. With sticks. And what about the fighting?"

"Yeah, sometimes we fight."

"Do *you* fight?" She moves closer and gazes up at me, wide-eyed.

Yeah, here we go. "It's not allowed in college hockey."

Her hand closes over my biceps and gives a squeeze. "Oh yeah. You're strong."

I flex my muscle.

"Oooh." She squeezes again. "That's impressive. You must work out a lot."

"Yeah. Our strength and conditioning coach develops a whole individualized program for each of us. They hold us to a pretty high standard of fitness."

"So do you work out, like, every day?"

"Yeah, but we work on different things, and we usually have one day a week off. There are optional exercises we can do those days."

"You lift weights?"

"Yep. Other stuff too. Cardiovascular exercises. Agility and footwork training, riding a stationary bike, using slide boards, and Sleds."

"What are Sleds?"

"They're an off-ice training device. You hook your stick into it and skate. It helps develop a proper skating stride and increase power, explosion, and speed."

"Wow." Her eyelashes flutter. "This sounds way more high-tech than I would've expected."

"We're lucky we have state-of-the-art training facilities and equipment." I could go on and on about this, but that would probably change her look from impressed to tuned-out. "Hey, Tawny . . . do you need another drink?"

"I do!"

We make our way over to the bar. Flash is leaning there with Freddy. I introduce them to Tawny, and Flash gives me a smirk. "Remember, we're roommates and I need my sleep," he mutters to me.

I roll my eyes. Yeah, I thought about taking her up to the room, but for some reason I'm not really feeling it tonight.

Don't ask me why the fuck, but I keep thinking about Ella.

About how *she* wouldn't be standing there fluttering her eyelashes at me and pretending to be all impressed with my muscles. I doubt there's *anything* about me that impresses Ella; in fact, she's distinctly *un*impressed, which annoys me. Not that my ego is that fragile. Okay, maybe it is. Hell, I only *pretend* to have an ego. Inside, I'm that fatherless kid from a family of criminals, who was actually homeless for a while, then was humiliated by the family we lived with.

Maybe Tawny's not just pretending to be impressed. Maybe she really is.

Whatever. I'm not into it. I should just leave.

I force myself to hang around for one more drink, and I talk to Tawny along with the other guys, but then I say good night and head out. Flash comes with me.

He slaps a hand on my back. "So about that low testosterone issue . . ."

"Fuck off, asshole."

He laughs.

"I'm just being a considerate roommate," I tell him.

"Bullshit. You know if you want to get laid I'll go hang out with the other guys."

Then I don't know what to say because I've run out of bullshit and there's no way I'm telling him the truth . . . which is that I keep thinking about Ella.

The guy from the *Hockey World* blog meets with the three of us separately the next week, but before that, Coach meets with all three of us together.

"Okay, you guys," he begins. "This isn't rocket science, but you'd be amazed how many guys fuck it up. Dealing with the media is common sense, but then shit happens, you play a crappy game, they ask you tough questions and criticize you, and you gotta respond. Drunk Tweeting is a definite no. If you've had more than one beer, put your goddamn phone away. Same for photos. Don't take naked pics, no matter how hot she is, and for the love of all that's holy, don't take dick pics of yourself and send them out into the world."

I bite my lip and shoot Flash a glance. We all nod.

"You're going to be talking to the media a fuck of a lot over the next ten years. Yeah, that's my prediction and I'm sticking to it. I've worked with a lot of talented athletes, and you three are right up there."

Holy shit.

"You'll probably say something you regret at some point. We all do it. That's life. But I'm gonna try to help you not do that. Okay. Rule number one: Make eye contact. Look the reporters in the eye when you talk to them. Call them by name. Say hi when you see them wandering around the arena, even if they're not interviewing you. Make friends with these people. They can be a great ally or your worst fucking enemy. Think about what you want to say. You guys thought about how you're gonna answer this reporter's questions today?"

We all nod again. Not sure about the other guys, but I went online and did a bit of research.

"Good. Also be professional and respectful. Yeah, it's hard when you just played a shitty game, but it's their job to report what happened even if we don't like it. Don't take it personally." He pauses. "Humor is good, but for God's sake, keep it clean and appropriate. Don't fucking be like that NFL player who called one of his teammates the N-word. Don't make jokes on Twitter like that other NFL dude who said he'd scream if he found a gay man in his bathtub. He thought he was being funny. It wasn't funny."

Coach's thick eyebrows are pulled together over his intense blue eyes.

"Got it," I murmur. "No racial, homophobic, or sexist comments."

"Yeah." He draws a breath. "If you want to use humor, a little self-deprecation goes a long way." He tips his head. "I don't have to explain that word to you, do I?"

I bark out a laugh. "No, Coach."

He grins. "Good. Okay. Don't ramble on and on. Get to the point when you answer a question, but be thoughtful. Now this . . . you guys already know it, but what happens in the dressing room stays in the dressing room, right? We don't throw our teammates under the bus. Ever. But don't lie. That's even worse. There are times it's appropriate to say 'no comment.' As for 'off the record,' there's no such thing. Some reporter is buying you drinks and you think you're having a friendly off-the-record conversation—you're not. Ever. It will come out. And lastly, act like you're having fun. Which you will be. Got it?"

"Got it, Coach," we all say.

I meet with the reporter, Cam Carder, in a meeting room at the DeWitt Center. I try to remember Coach's advice, making eye contact, thinking about Carder's questions, and trying to answer the best I can.

"We get a lot of access to the ice here," I tell him. "We practice a lot, but we can be on the ice other times as well, and I try to take advantage of that whenever I can, if there's a break between classes or days off. Then I can work on individual skills." I tell him about the work I do with Coach Backes, shooting pucks, and how I've worked hard on my shot and my skating.

"So that's allowed you to become one of Bayard's top prospects," Carder says.

That makes me pause. I've never thought of myself that way. Butch got drafted by the San Jose Sharks last year, and I've always felt he's kind of the star of the team. "Uh, I guess, yeah."

"Last year you scored six goals and had a total of eighteen points as a freshman. You've really upped your game this year."

"Yeah. The speed of college hockey opened my eyes last year. I really wanted to improve my game, so I've taken advantage of all the supports we have here, the coaching, fitness and conditioning, and equipment. I've had every opportunity to improve, not just my skating but every aspect of my game."

"You play fewer games than major junior teams," Carder says. "Do you think the added time spent on conditioning makes up for that?"

I have to think about that. "I love to play, and I'd love to play more games. And that kind of schedule does prepare you for the NHL, because it's so similar . . . but yeah, having that extra time to work on strength and conditioning is a benefit. College does a really good job with the time you spend practicing. It's development time, instead of constantly being on the road or getting ready for a game that night. We work one-on-one with full-time strength coaches. I've put on twenty pounds of muscle since I started at Bayard last year, doing scheduled lifts during the season and the off-season, and I think that helped increase my on-ice speed and power."

"I'm going to be interviewing your coach as well," Carder says. "You three young men are attracting a lot of attention in the hockey world these days. Thanks for sitting down with me today, I appreciate your time."

Again, I feel like shaking my head, but I smile politely and stand to shake Cam Carder's hand. "My pleasure."

I kind of wish I already had a family adviser on board. In my research I've learned more about agents, and some of them work for big sports management companies who will do a lot more for me than just negotiate my NHL contract, if that happens. They'll help me with preparation for the draft, and yeah, negotiate contracts, but also help with banking services, budgeting, accounting, insurance, and taxes. Holy fuck. They also help with ongoing training and fitness, which is important, because once I'm out of college, it will be on me to stay in shape. Then there's shit like endorsement opportunities, and marketing myself, which also freaks me the fuck out.

I'm waging a war inside me on my desire to keep a low profile, as I did in Buffalo because of my family's history, and making it big when lying low will not be an option.

Then there are the things they can help me with that I really think I need right now—media exposure and publicity. Coach's advice was great, but I kind of feel like I'm in over my head.

So much pressure. Not only do I have to play well, I have scouts talking to Coach and others at the college about my character on and off the ice, and I also have to talk to these people and not screw up by saying the wrong thing. All the layers of becoming a professional hockey player are piling on and weighing me down. But dealing with pressure is part of it, and if I can't handle *this* pressure, I'll never handle being interviewed by NHL GMs, and then sitting in that fucking arena waiting for my name to be called in June. Jesus Christ. I swipe the sweat that breaks out on my brow as I head to the dressing room to get ready for practice.

After practice, though, Coach tells me that Cam Carder was impressed with how confident and well-spoken I was, so I guess I faked it pretty good.

Fake it till you make it. It's been my motto for a long time. Arriving here at Bayard where nobody knew me gave me a new start on life, a chance to be the kind of person I always wanted to be, to leave my past behind and make something of myself. And goddammit, I'm going to do that, no matter how much pressure I feel.

Chapter 9

Ella

On my way home from my ballet class on Saturday, I spot a little dog wandering down our street. I look around for his people but see nobody. Is he lost?

I approach him and show him the back of my hand to sniff. "Hey, buddy. Are you lost?" His tail wags and he gives me a sniff. Gently I reach out to stroke his back and he lets me. "We need to find your people, little guy." I pick him up, and he calmly allows me to carry him into the house.

I love dogs. I miss Gracie, our family's cockapoo, so much. Does it make me a terrible person that I miss her more than my human family members? I wish I could have a dog at college, but I know that's ridiculous. It would be nice to have all the love and affection that Gracie bestows on me. Dogs don't have any expectations beyond some Milk-Bones and a few belly rubs. They don't care what mistakes you've made or how many courses you've failed. They love you no matter what.

I've never seen this dog in the neighborhood before. He's so cute! I think he's a beagle, with big brown eyes, floppy ears, and a white snout and legs. I find the tag on his collar and peer at it. Oh good—it's a tag from a veterinarian clinic. They should be able to identify him. I manage to make out an ID number and the phone number of the clinic and jot them down on a notepad. Then I call the clinic.

They check their records, and they do know who Buddy is—only his real name is Elvis (oh my God!). I thought they could just give me his address and I'd take him home, but they can't give out personal information, so they say they'll call the owners and give them my phone number.

I'm sitting on the floor cuddling Elvis when Jacob and Ben show up at our house. Jacob and Skylar disappear upstairs, leaving me alone with Ben and Elvis, hopefully not for long, but with those two you never know.

"Cute dog," Ben says, a notch between his eyebrows. "It's not yours, is it?"

"No." I stroke my hand down Elvis's back. "I found him outside. He's lost."

"Oh." Ben crouches down and extends the back of his hand for the dog to sniff. "What are you going to do?"

"He has a tag on his collar. I already called the vet clinic. They're contacting the owners."

"Oh, that's good."

I cuddle the little guy, and he swipes my chin with his tongue. "You're so cute," I coo at him, then wince and glance at Ben.

He's watching me with a funny expression on his face. Then his gaze drops to take in what I'm wearing . . . my ballet leotard and tights, with a pair of sweatpants over them, the waistband rolled down on my hips.

"So you recovered from the party two weeks ago?" I ask him, smirking a little as I remember how drunk he was. It's the first time we've been alone together since then.

I expect him to be embarrassed, and he does look a little sheepish, but he shrugs and shocks the hell out of me when he says, "Sorry about that. I was supposed to drive that night, so thank you for stepping up."

I blink. "No problem."

"Why weren't you drinking?"

I set Elvis on his feet on the floor and stand. I move to the sink to wash my hands. "Just didn't feel like it."

Elvis starts jumping at Ben's legs, and he bends and picks up the dog and scratches his ears. "Huh. Well, I guess I drank enough for both of us."

I open the fridge to pull out some things I need to make myself a sandwich. "You were pretty entertaining."

"Great. I don't usually overdo it like that."

I don't ask *why* he did, because I suspect it had something to do with us making out in that bedroom and he was probably trying to erase the memory with copious amounts of alcohol. "Well, you know what that means."

He frowns. "What?"

"You can no longer bug me for being a party girl, when I was the sober one who bailed your drunken ass out."

A slow grin spreads across his face. "Huh. You have a point."

Another moment stretches between us, and my skin starts that hot tingle. I swallow and change the subject. "Big game tonight?" I set my ingredients on the counter and reach for a loaf of bread.

"Yeah." He lowers Elvis to the floor, and the little dog runs over to me, his nose twitching at the smell of the food on the counter. He sits and stares at me hopefully. "They're all big games at this time of year. Making the playoffs. Plus, scouts are watching."

I frown as I lay slices of deli turkey over bread, and drop a little piece of meat into Elvis's mouth. "Scouts?"

Ben grins at Elvis, then looks back at me. "Yeah. From the NHL. They're looking for players they might want to draft."

"Hmm. You might need to explain that to me."

"You might need to make me one of those sandwiches."

I meet his eyes, surprise making me go still. "Really? You're hungry?"

"Starving. And that looks really good."

I look down at the tomatoes and lettuce and mayo I've piled between slices of bread. It seems pretty basic to me, but damn, if the poor guy's hungry, I better feed him. "I can make you a sandwich, I guess."

As I get out more bread, slather mayo over a slice, then layer on the other ingredients, Ben explains the NHL draft and scouting process to me.

"So are there scouts at every game?"

"Yeah. There are thirty NHL teams and they all have scouts."

"How does that impact your play? Does it make you nervous?"

"Nervous as fuck." He gives a short laugh and his hands grip the edge of the counter.

I focus on his white knuckles for a few seconds instead of the sandwich I'm building. "This is serious stuff."

"It's my fucking life." Then he laughs, as if to make light of it, but I can tell he's super stressed.

I add some salt and pepper, top the sandwich with bread, then place my hand on it to hold it while I slice it in half. I push the plate toward him.

"Thanks." He picks up a half and takes a big bite with those perfect white teeth. When he swallows, he says, "Goddamn, this is good."

I smile, but I feel it's crooked because I'm surprised. "It's just a turkey sandwich."

"But it's *good*." He devours one half before I've taken even two bites of mine, both of us standing at the counter.

I slide a bag of potato chips toward him. "Here. Have some chips."

"Thanks." He chews and looks around. "Your kitchen's really clean."

I also do a quick survey. I don't think it's super clean—none of the four of us are really good at cleaning. I'm probably the one who cares the most, which means I'm the one who cleans the most, but even I'm not that anal. "It's not so clean."

"You should see our place."

I *have* been to his place, once, just before Christmas, and I don't remember the kitchen being a disaster. But with four guys living there, I guess I can understand if it is. "You're so meticulous about your appearance . . . you're not that meticulous about your kitchen?"

He grins. "Nope. I am pretty good at doing laundry, though."

I tip my head. "Well, that's important to know. And I guess it makes sense, since you dress so well."

He arches an eyebrow as he chews another bite and then swallows. "You think I dress well?"

"Don't get excited. It's all you have going for you."

That is such an egregious lie it's all I can do not to wince. I wait for him to be pissed, but he laughs. He *laughs*.

And I have to purse my lips to stop from laughing too. His eyes meet mine. A shiver works over my skin and my insides tighten. He licks his thumb and my gaze goes there, heat expanding through my body.

His smile is almost challenging.

Brooklyn wanders in at that moment, and I don't know whether to be annoyed or relieved.

"Hey," she says, opening a cupboard to grab a mug. "Whassup?"

Elvis bounds up to her and gives a little bark. She shrieks and nearly drops her mug. She grabs onto the counter with both hands and stares at Elvis. "What the hell? Where'd a dog come from?"

"He was lost." I move and scoop him up into my arms. "I'm just waiting to hear from his owners. Hopefully they'll come pick him up soon."

But I feel a little sad about that. Elvis is so cute. It would be nice to have a dog.

"Oh. Okay." She relaxes and stretches, and she's wearing only a tank top and a pair of boxer shorts. I look at Ben, expecting him to be taking in the sight of Brooklyn, with her arms above her head and her perfectly flat abs revealed in the gap between her tank top and low-rise shorts, but he's still watching me hold Elvis.

I swallow.

"So we're having some people over here tonight," Brooklyn says to me. "You okay with that?"

It's not like I have a lot of choice. My plans include studying, reading, and more studying. Skylar hasn't asked me to go to the game with her, so I don't know what she's doing. "Sure, no problem."

Brooklyn smiles at Ben as she pours herself a cup of cold coffee. "You guys should come after the game."

He shrugs. "Yeah, maybe."

Brooklyn sets her mug in the microwave and, with a few quick beeps, has it heating. "Invite the rest of the hockey team. Some football players are coming."

"Okay." Ben wipes his fingers on a paper napkin he snags from the holder on the counter.

"Want something to drink?" I ask Ben, moving to the fridge. "Water? Coke? Kool-Aid?"

"Kool-Aid?" He lifts a brow.

"It's Skylar's favorite drink."

"Right, right. That's why Flash keeps making jugs of the stuff."

I set Elvis back on the floor, hoping he won't bark at Brooklyn again. She seems a little nervous about him. But Elvis is more interested in Ben. "I think this is orange Kool-Aid." I peer at the plastic jug.

"Water would be great."

I grin as I pluck a bottle from the shelf inside the fridge door and lob it to him. He catches it easily and pops the top, then takes a big pull. I watch his strong throat move as he swallows.

Brooklyn is dropping bread into the toaster and still Ben isn't looking at her bare legs or braless breasts. He's looking at me. My skin heats. Where the hell are Sky and Jacob?

Finally, I hear footsteps on the stairs and they appear in the kitchen, Skylar dressed in her pink diner uniform.

"We better get going, dude," Ben says. "Game day skate starts in half an hour."

"Yeah, I know." Jacob looks at Skylar. "See you at the game."

"Okay." She smiles at him. "Good luck."

"Thanks, babe." He kisses her, and then he and Ben disappear with waves.

So Skylar *is* going to the game. I wait for her to invite me, but she rushes out to the door too, off to work.

I chat with Brooklyn while she eats her toast, and I put things back in the fridge and clean up after making the sandwiches. "What are you up to today?" I ask her.

"Shopping. We're going to get some things for the party tonight. Booze and food. You want to come?"

"Um . . ." I debate this. I should do homework, but I have all day . . . since Skylar didn't invite me to go to the game with her. I try to ignore the rock in the pit of my stomach at the fact that she's going without me. Just because we're friends doesn't mean we have to do *everything* together. "I can't go until Elvis's owner picks him up."

As if on cue, my phone rings. I answer it and find myself talking to a breathlessly relieved woman. "I can't believe you found him! Thank you so much! We've been worried sick."

"He's fine." I give her my address.

"We'll be right over."

They do arrive quickly, obviously super happy that their dog was found. "Thank you again," the woman says. "Let me reward you." She pulls out her wallet.

"No, no!" I wave my hands. "You don't need to do that. I'm just glad we got him back to you."

We have a little argument about her giving me some money, but in the end I convince her it's not necessary.

"You're a lovely young lady," she says.

My cheeks heat. "Thanks."

So I go with Nat and Brooklyn. Natalie drives us to a strip mall not far away, where there's a big supermarket and a liquor store. We buy soda and cups and big bags of chips. I throw in some cash to pay for the stuff. I also pick up some other things because tomorrow's my night to cook dinner for the girls. We've been taking turns on Sunday nights.

Now that my day stretches empty in front of me, I'm kind of happy there are people coming over tonight and I won't have to sit all alone in my room. This'll be fun.

But first I have to make sure I get some work done on the paper I need to write.

On the way home we make a detour to the mall because Brooklyn has to go to Sephora. Two hours later, we're leaving the mall with glossy black-and-white shopping bags. Damn, it's hard to resist new lip gloss and nail polish.

"I'm hungry," Natalie says. "We should go for dinner."

I glance at my watch. I really need to head home and get my school-work done before people start showing up. But then, parties don't get rocking until late, and if some of the hockey team are coming, they won't be there until after the game. I'll have lots of time.

So I agree to go for something to eat at Bandidos. We order margaritas, share some nachos, and I eat half of my taco dinner. It's really good, but I'm full. I ask for it to be packaged up to take with me; it'll be an easy lunch tomorrow.

By the time we get home, the last thing I feel like doing is homework.

Yeah, I might have made a couple of bad decisions this afternoon. Especially the margaritas. Sitting at my desk in my room, with my laptop open in front of me, I am completely unmotivated. I kill some time on TikTok.

Music starts on the floor below me. Natalie and Brooklyn are getting ready for the party. I open the document I've been working on for Media Communications class. I read through it. It sucks.

I click over to Google to do some research, and I get sidetracked by an ad for Victoria's Secret. I end up scrolling through pages of bras.

Oh my God! I have to stop this. For the love of bacon, I can do this.

I start thinking about Skylar going to the game tonight without me. Who is she with?

Then I snort. I sound like a jealous lover.

It's not as if I even like hockey. Much.

I sigh. I've enjoyed the games I went to with Skylar. It's a fun atmosphere and the game is fast and entertaining.

I hear people arriving downstairs and the music gets louder. I ignore it and focus on Media Communications. I slump lower in my seat and my bottom lip pushes out as I read what I've just written. Yes, I'm feeling sorry for myself.

It's my own fault. I should have told Brooklyn and Natalie I couldn't go shopping with them. I should have gotten my homework done sooner. And I should have asked Skylar if I could go to the game with her.

Fuck.

From the bursts of laughter I hear every so often, it sounds like everyone's having fun. I lean my head back and close my eyes, for a moment contemplating giving up on the homework and going down there. Tomorrow's Sunday. I'm meeting with some classmates from Research Methods at one o'clock to spend the afternoon on a group project. I could finish this in the morning.

No. I can't do that. Procrastination and poor choices are what got me into this. I'm damn well going to finish this fucking paper, and I'm not stepping foot out of my bedroom until it's done, no matter how much revelry is happening downstairs.

I set my teeth and once more focus on my work.

I actually lose track of time and I'm just reading through the document one last time when there's a knock on my door. "Come in!"

The door opens, and Skylar's head pops inside. "Hey! What are you doing up here?"

"Homework."

She steps farther into the room and closes the door. "Seriously?"

She looks super cute wearing a Bears jersey—number eight, Jacob's number, of course—over a pair of skinny jeans.

I'm a little grouchy at this point. "Yes, seriously. I had to get this paper done."

"Oh. Okay. Are you nearly finished?"

"Yeah, I finished." I run a hand through my hair. I feel gross. "Just now."

"So you're coming down?"

"I guess." I save my document once more. "How was the game?"

"Good! We won, three-nothing, Ben got two goals and Jacob got three assists!"

"Awesome."

"What's wrong?" She ambles over and plops down on the side of my bed.

My throat thickens. I could make some shit up. But not being honest hasn't been working so well for me. I don't know how to say it, though. I swallow. "I would've liked to go to the game with you."

Her eyes widen. "Really?"

"Yeah. Who'd you go with?"

"Some of the other girlfriends . . . Krystal, Liz, and Alessia."

"Oh."

"I thought you didn't really like hockey. I thought you only came because I needed someone to go with. So I decided to ask Krystal if I could sit with them."

"Hockey's kind of growing on me."

She tips her head and gives me a level look. "You should have said something."

"I know."

"Well, then, you'll come with me next time."

I feel like such a loser. "Okay."

"Okay." She nods. "I'm going to change. You're coming down?"

"Yeah."

"Great." She jumps up and disappears.

I should change too. I look down at my yoga pants and T-shirt. Ah, who cares? I brush my hair and swipe my new lip gloss over my lips, then jog downstairs.

I find the kitchen packed with bodies. The noise level of the music and voices makes my ears buzz. I grab a beer from the fridge, not really caring what I drink.

"There you are!" Brooklyn bumps my hip with hers. "We thought you ditched us."

"Nah." I force a smile. "Had to get some work done."

"You're so disciplined."

Ha. I am *so* not.

Skylar bounces in, now wearing a pretty top instead of a hockey jersey. "Hey. Where'd Jacob go?"

"He's in the living room," Brooklyn says.

"Come on." Skylar links her arm with mine and drags me along. The living room is full of people too. Jacob is standing by the window with—of course—Ben. And Grady, Hunter, and their goaltender John Alfredson, who they call Freddy.

"Congrats," I tell the guys. "I hear you won."

"Thanks." They're all smiles, their faces flushed and hair still damp—although, as always, Ben looks like he just walked out of a salon. He's wearing black jeans, a black T-shirt, and a thick gray cardigan—something that should look like an old man's sweater but doesn't. It hangs from his broad shoulders, emphasizing the fit of his T-shirt across his flat abs.

Heat curls low inside me.

Don't look at him. Don't look at him.

Of course I look at him, and dammit, he's looking at me, and I can tell he totally thinks I was just checking him out.

My face warms and I take a quick gulp of beer. The bubbles burn my nose and my eyes water. I cough.

"You okay?" Ben asks.

"Fine."

Jacob steps away, then returns bearing a big bowl of chips. The guys all shove their hands in and start munching.

"So, two goals," I say to Ben.

He frowns. "Were you at the game?"

"No. Skylar told me when she got home. And three assists for you," I say to Jacob. "That's great."

"Thanks." Jacob smiles. "You should have come."

"Next time." I meet Skylar's eyes, and she smiles. "When *is* the next game, anyway?"

"Next home game's not until February. Next weekend we're in Omaha."

"Omaha." I nod. "Pretty exciting."

"Hey, Clarkson has a good team this year," Jacob says with a grin.

They were just away last weekend. For the first time it occurs to me that traveling has to take up a lot of their time. I'm feeling all sorry for myself because I wasted time today trying on eye shadows at Sephora, when they have to deal with being away nearly every other weekend.

Skylar and Jacob move from the group a little bit, talking to each other. I look at Ben.

"How do you fit in schoolwork when you travel so much?" I ask. "Or maybe hockey players don't care about getting good grades."

He narrows his eyes at me. "We need to have a C average to stay on the team."

"Oh." Crap, his grades are probably better than mine lately.

"And it *is* hard." He shrugs. "I try to do as much homework as I can on the bus or the plane. A lot of our stuff gets submitted online, and our coach sets up Wi-Fi on the bus so we can work." He pauses. "Also, luckily, I'm exceptionally intelligent."

I snort out a laugh.

He lifts an eyebrow. "You don't believe me?"

"You're a jock." I pat his chest. Yow. He's solid. I already knew that from that night his hard body had me pressed up against the wall. My girl parts squeeze, remembering. I shouldn't have touched him.

"Judge much?" he murmurs, grabbing my hand so I can't move away. "I thought we were past this, party girl."

Chapter 10

Ben

"Obviously not, if you're still calling me party girl." She tries to pull her hand away, but I hold on.

"You started it with the jock comment."

"What are we? Five years old? 'You started it.' 'No, *you* did.' "

"You know, you really piss me off."

"Yeah? Well, the feeling is mutual."

We stand there glaring at each other. I feel sparks flicking against my skin, tingling; it's a wonder we can't see them flashing around us in the dimly lit room. My skin heats, and I feel a stirring in my lower regions. I find myself staring at her mouth.

God, I want to kiss her.

I start to bend my head, eyelids lowering, and her body sways toward me. Then I realize what the fuck I'm doing. We made this mistake once before. We don't even like each other. I close my eyes briefly, release her hand, and jerk my head back.

Her eyes fly open wide.

I swallow. It feels like ten minutes go by while I try to think of what to say and she stares at me. I watch emotions flicker across her face—confusion, disappointment, and what looks like hurt. She sucks in a long shaky breath and lifts her chin, and now there's no mistaking the anger flashing in her eyes. "Oh hey, there's someone I need to say hi to. Enjoy the evening, pretty boy."

She disappears across the room, and I watch her come to a halt next to a guy I recognize as a football player. I frown as she smiles at him, and he slides an arm around her waist.

She looks different tonight . . . she's not dressed in a short skirt or one of her flowery tops, just black yoga pants and a gray T-shirt. But Christ, the pants are snug and show off her tight little ass, and even though the T-shirt isn't skintight, it hugs her small breasts and narrow waist.

Although she's dressed differently, the guys she's talking to are all focused on her and smiling. She's the center of their attention, laughing and flirting.

My body is hot and my groin is tight. Goddamn, I wanted to haul her into my arms and kiss her into next fucking week. She makes me *crazy*. My gut twists, and I suck in air as I turn back to the guys.

"That's Charisse," Freddy says, lifting his chin at a girl on the couch. Now, *that's* a short skirt, and as she crosses her long, bare legs, I'm pretty sure I get a glimpse of red panties.

"Jesus," Freddy mutters. "I'm so horny the crack of dawn isn't safe. I did *not* need to see that."

Soupy and I choke on our laughter.

"Apparently, she sucks cock like a popsicle on a hot day in July," Rocket comments.

Freddy groans. "I'm goin' in." He pushes away from the wall and strolls over to the couch.

Charisse looks up at him. I can't hear what Freddy says, but she smiles, so it must've been good.

Soupy sighs. "Who else is here I can hook up with?"

"The place is full of chicks," I say, finding myself looking back at Ella. She and that big dude have separated from the group a bit and are standing really close together. The way his head is bent so he can listen to her looks . . . intimate. She nods and touches his arm, and then together they turn and stroll out of the living room.

Christ. My blood heats.

My feet move and I find myself following Ella and the guy. I think his name is Renshaw. Something Renshaw. They're grabbing beers. Renshaw pops the top off a bottle and hands it to Ella. I read the "thank you" on her lips and scowl at the smile she beams at him. He maneuvers them through the crowd to a corner of the kitchen, where she leans against the counter and he slants his body into her.

I turn away before she sees me watching them. I start to go for another beer, and then I remember last time this happened and I got wasted. Better not do that again. Maybe I should just go home.

But then Jacob pulls me into a game of Beer Pong at the kitchen table, against Skylar and Brooklyn.

Yeah, I'm competitive. I like to win. And my hand-eye coordination is pretty good. I focus intently on the red cups at the other end of the table as I take my shot. And pump my fist in the air. We easily win over the girls and await our next challengers. Soupy and some chick play against us next. We beat them too, then Ella and Renshaw arrive.

Fuck.

"Hey, let's play," Renshaw says.

Ella bumps her hip into his. "Okay, but I have to warn you, I suck at this."

He whispers something into her ear and she laughs softly. I can only imagine what he just said, no doubt something about how she can suck on something else.

The tops of my ears burn, and my jaw aches from clenching it.

"Bring it," Jacob invites them. We do Rock, Paper, Scissors to see who goes first, and it's Ella. Fine.

She *doesn't* suck at this. When she lands the ball into a cup perfectly, her eyes meet mine with a little glow of triumph and a smirk on her face.

When it's my turn, I narrow my eyes on my target and land another perfect shot. And another. This game goes fast, and Ella and Renshaw are laughing, while I'm tight-lipped and determined to win. Which we do.

"Good game," Ella says lightly as she slips her arm through Renshaw's and walks away.

Jacob slaps my back as we move away from the table. "Dude, it's not the Stanley Cup, for fuck's sake. Lighten up."

I laugh, but as we move into the living room I see Ella's now dancing in the dark dining room. With some other guy! My hands fist as she shakes her body against him. He's mesmerized by her. He's not the best dancer. I give a snort and walk past them into the living room.

Freddy and Charisse are making out on the couch, no matter that they're surrounded by people.

"Jesus, they've been lip-banging for an hour," Soupy complains. "I got wood here, just watching them."

"Thanks for that," I say. "What happened to the girl you were playing Beer Pong with?"

"She's getting us drinks."

"And hopefully condoms."

Soupy laughs.

I try to pay attention to the heated conversation that's happening about another college in our division, which has banned alcohol on campus and is also talking about banishing fraternities. Needless to say, Skylar is all up in this, and she's cute in her passion. "That college has a reputation for excessive partying and alcohol consumption," she states.

"And a reputation for the consequences, like sexual assault and rape charges," another girl says. "Their enrollment is even down because of that."

"Nobody knows that's the reason their enrollment is down," says a guy I don't know.

"And you need to be careful saying that sexual assault and rape are related to alcohol consumption." Skylar frowns. "You can't blame a college culture of partying and drinking for sexual assault and rape."

The girl blinks at Skylar. "Yeah. You're right."

"And they can't get rid of fraternities," the guy adds. "If they do, they have to get rid of sororities too."

"Sororities have issues as well," the other girl says. "There are a lot of mixed messages about sex in sororities. I used to belong to Phi Chi Pi. There was an incident where one of our pledge sisters was photographed having drunk sex with a brother. Instead of questioning whether she'd actually been raped, everyone criticized her, and when I wrote a newspaper article about it, the sorority shamed me for writing it and threatened to put my chapter on probation."

"You're not a member anymore?" Skylar asks, her face soft with sympathy.

"No." The girl shrugs. "It's too bad, because some sororities do a lot of good . . . things like teaching girls leadership and organizational and professional skills, and getting them involved in community service."

Skylar sighs.

My gaze keeps wandering back to the dark dining room, where I can just make out Ella grinding against some dude.

My hand clenches the beer bottle and my back teeth gnash.

Why is this fucking me up so bad? She can dance with whoever she wants. It looks like she's back to her old partying ways, flirting and drinking and dancing, and probably soon she'll be taking that guy up to her room and fucking him.

Pressure expands hot inside me, almost unbearable. My breath is coming in short, jagged pants. The music pulses against my eardrums in a dull roar, drowning out the voices around me. I watch Ella, framed by the open French doors, arms above her head, body swaying, the guy's hands on her hips.

Then another dude moves in. He elbows the first one out of the way. Ella laughs at the first, cups his face with both hands and kisses him, then gives his chest a playful shove. She turns to the new guy and slides her hips into a rhythm against his, giving him a sexy look from beneath her lashes.

I turn a way, stomach churning, and once more try to listen to the conversation. When I look back . . . they're gone.

Fuck.

I'm an idiot, but my blood is boiling. My head is saying *dumbass move*, but my feet are moving and I stalk through the main floor of the house, looking for them. They're not anywhere. I glance up the stairs, where all the bedrooms are, the bass of the music pounding around me.

My hands clench into fists, and I will them to relax. Is she up there with that douche? With *both* of them? My chest tightens. I know I shouldn't do this, I fuckin' *know* it, but I start up the stairs, taking them two at a time.

It's quieter up here. The hall light is on. I have no idea which room is Ella's, and I pause before I poke my head into one room. Empty.

I'm just drawing back when another door opens. Ella steps into the hall and pauses, gaping at me with her hand on the light switch. I see a bathroom behind her. "What are you doing?" she demands.

I'm too worked up to think fast enough to fib. "Looking for you," I growl.

She frowns. "Why?"

"Are you alone?"

"What the fuck? Yes, I'm alone. I went to the bathroom."

I move closer to her. "Where's the guy? The douchehole you were dancing with."

She smiles. "Which one?"

My muscles go rigid. "Fuck. The one you left with, for Chrissakes."

She gives a nonchalant lift of one shoulder. "I don't know where he is." She tips her head to one side. "Are you jealous?"

I crowd her to the wall, slapping my hands on either side of her head, not yet pressing my body against hers but definitely caging her in place. "You were fucking *trying* to make me jealous."

"I was not." Her eyes flash, and her lips part. "I don't care about you."

"I don't care about you either," I bite out. Heat explodes between us, nearly incinerating us. My face is burning, my heart pounding, my dick throbbing. "I don't care who you fucking dance with. Or flirt with. Or kiss."

"Bullshit. Why are you up here, then? Why did you ask me if I'm alone?"

She challenges me like nobody else, and lust punches through my gut.

Our eyes lock on each other, our chests rising and falling with our rapid breaths. A groan rumbles up my throat as the need to taste her and feel her and punish her for making me *want* her so goddamn much when she annoys the *hell* out of me explodes inside me, and then our mouths crash together. It's hard and fierce and intense. We kiss so desperately, my lips sting.

Her hands grip my shirt, yanking me to her. My hips push into her, pressing her to the wall. I'm sure she can feel my enthusiastic dick, which has swelled to painful proportions.

She makes needy little whimpering noises as our mouths open, still crushed together, our tongues tangling. I thrust my hips against her, and she moans into my mouth, one of her legs coming up to my hip.

Just like last time, up against the wall, hard and fast, only now it's even more powerful, because my blood has been running hot all night, watching her with those guys.

"Say it," I demand against her lips, my hands going to her small waist and curving around it. "Say you wanted me to be jealous."

"No." She nips my bottom lip. Sensation jolts through me.

"Ah. You . . ." I kiss her again, deep and openmouthed, pressing her to the wall. I slide one hand under her thigh, pulling that leg up higher and bending my knees so my dick is settled against her pussy. I give another thrust and a rub, and she makes another soft sound. "Say it."

"No!"

"Fuck, you're stubborn." I slide my open mouth over her jaw, and her head falls to the side, baring her neck. I close my mouth over the soft skin there and suck, brief but hard.

She gives a muted cry that makes my dick jump.

I soothe the spot with my tongue and take her mouth again, tasting her deeply. "I could fuck you right here, like this." I drive my hips into hers.

"Oh God." Her hands slide around my neck and pull me in for another hard kiss.

We hear voices at the bottom of the stairs and freeze. "Which room is yours?" I whisper harshly.

She rolls her head against the wall, toward the door next to the bathroom.

"Come on, sexy girl." I grab her and push her in front of me, propelling her toward her room. We shove inside, and I slam the door behind us.

The room is pitch-dark. Our hands are all over each other, our mouths fused, and we stumble toward her bed.

"I *was* jealous," I grind out between nipping at her lips. My hands find bare skin under her T-shirt. Christ, the softest skin. Warm. Silky. I run my hands up and down her back.

"Good," she gasps. "Because you pissed me off."

We hit the bed and tumble down, me on my back, her on top. I grip her ass and tip my hips up, grinding my aching dick against her. She moans into my mouth, her hands in my hair, tugging at it. Tingles slide down my spine and pool at the base.

"You pissed me off too." I tangle one hand in her hair and pull her head down to crush her mouth to mine again. Her pelvis is rocking into me, and I meet her movements, fast and desperate, pressure building in my balls. It's good, so good, but . . . I need more control. I roll her, neatly tucking her under me so I'm on top, and I rock my hips into hers, dry fucking her. "You make me crazy."

"Me too." She catches my bottom lip between her teeth but quickly releases it. Electricity jolts through me. Her fingernails dig into my back. "You're so . . . fucking . . . perfect. All the damn time."

"I'm not perfect. Not even close." I kiss her again. "Damn, your mouth . . . you're so hot." My body is trembling, straining for her, so fucking hungry for her.

Her fingernails scratch up my back and a groan rises in my throat. My head goes back as my dick contracts. Then she slides her hands inside the back of my jeans and grips my ass.

We're grinding and gasping. I palm one of her sweet little tits, and it's amazing, pliant and lush, her nipple stiff.

"Yes," she pants. "Oh God. Ben . . ." Her pelvis lifts into mine, pressing hard, and she shudders beneath me, a soft wail escaping her lips.

"Jesus fuck." I push her hair off her face and stare down at her. My eyes have grown accustomed to the dim room, the silvery moonlight glowing in the window giving just enough illumination to see her shadowed face. Her eyes stay closed, her swollen lips parted. "Did you just come?"

Her teeth sink into her bottom lip and she says nothing, still breathing fast.

She did. She came, just from that. My dick throbs with the need to be inside her.

"More," she begs. "Please. That wasn't enough."

"Fucking right that wasn't enough." I catch her mouth with mine again. "I'm so hard for you, I'm dying."

"Fuck me, then, dammit."

"You better mean that. Because damn, I want to sink my cock so deep inside you."

She gasps and squeezes my ass. Heat pumps through my veins, and my balls ache with lust. "I mean it."

Chapter 11

Ella

OH MY GOD, I'm burning up.

Even though I just had an orgasm, I'm still hurting, a deep, biting ache of need low inside me that only Ben can soothe. He's on top of me, big and heavy, pressing me into the bed, heat radiating off him. The way he kisses is turning me on like I've never been before.

He's hot for me too, I can feel it, in the intensity of his kisses, the way his body is vibrating—and most of all, his cock is huge and hard. I love that so much, the way he presses into me. I couldn't stop from rubbing myself against him, right where I needed to be touched, and I was as shocked as Ben was when I came like that.

"Please," I gasp again, gripping his amazing ass and pulling him harder to me.

"I don't have a condom."

My eyes squeeze shut. "Seriously? How can that be?"

"Fuck."

"I have one." I have a bunch, a box in my top drawer because I may have liked to sleep around, but I'm not stupid enough to have unprotected sex. Even when I'm having drunk sex, I'm smarter than that. "Get off me." I push at his massive shoulders.

He rolls away with a groan, and I scramble from the bed. I rush over to the dresser and yank open the drawer, fumbling in the dusky room for the box. I find it and grab a few small packets, then return to the bed. I toss them down, then reach for the hem of my T-shirt and pull it over my head.

"Christ." Ben's watching me, and damn, he's so beautiful. His face and body are shadowy, but I see his eyes glint and his tongue slide over his bottom lip. "Ella."

My thumbs hook into my yoga pants. "Get your clothes off too."

He chokes on a laugh and knifes up to sit. He shrugs out of the sweater and reaches behind to grasp his T-shirt and yank it off. I watch as I wriggle my stretchy pants down my thighs, and holy hunga chunga . . . I swallow and stare. His body is amazing, his torso a perfect V from broad, muscled shoulders down to narrow waist and hips. The pale moonlight carves his muscles into a shadowy sculpture. My jaw slackens as his hands go to the button and zipper of his jeans.

He rolls to his back, lifts his hips, and shoves jeans and boxers down his legs. Shoes, socks, and pants all drop to the floor, and he is gorgeously naked. On my bed. "You're staring," he says, his voice a low rasp.

I haven't moved, standing there in my lace bralette and panties. "Too bad you don't work out more." I shake my head sadly.

He laughs. "C'mere, sexy." He gestures. "Wanna get those pretty undies off you."

My chest expands and lust bursts inside me. I jump onto the bed and he sits up again and reaches for me. I find myself on his lap, my legs on either side of his hips. His thighs are thick and muscular beneath me, and his cock rises—powerful, masculine, and beautiful against his belly.

He looks down at my chest. My skin tingles. "I like this."

He kisses me hard and runs his hands over my bare thighs and up and down my back, then presses one hand in the small of my back to urge me closer still. Our mouths open and slide together, tongues licking, heat swelling around us. My body turns liquid. He finds the clasp at my back and flicks it open. He slides the straps down my arms and I pull them free so he can toss the bralette aside. My nipples tighten and my breasts ache with the need to be touched. He obliges, covering my breasts with his hands and squeezing. His touch is firm and sure, and I'm throbbing between my legs. My head falls back and my spine arches, pushing myself into his palms. "Oh God." I pull in a shaky breath.

"Sweet tits," he mumbles, opening his mouth on my jaw as he caresses me. "So damn sweet."

I'm not well endowed; I've been waiting for some kind of growth spurt since I was twelve. I've accepted that it's not going to happen and made the decision not to be self-conscious about my breasts but to enjoy the pleasure they give me. My nipples are sensitive, and I love having them tugged and sucked. Ben cups me, his fingers and thumbs squeezing each nipple, and longing throbs in my core.

"Ah." I can't stop the noises that climb my throat. "So good. More."

"Greedy girl." He pinches my nipples again. "Fuck, I want to taste you."

"Oh." I can barely speak. "Yessss."

He hauls me higher and I'm on my knees, my breasts right in front of his face. He bands an arm around my torso to pull me in tighter and closes his lips around one nipple. Sensation sears a hot path from my nipple to my pussy, and my inner muscles squeeze. I reach for his head, threading my fingers through the longer hair on top, holding him at my breast as spirals of heat twist down to my core. He makes appreciative noises, moves to the other breast, sucking hard, then closing his teeth over my sensitive flesh. I cry out, and my back arches even more, my hair hanging down, moisture flooding my panties.

"Damn, baby," he murmurs. "You are so fucking hot." His hot tongue slides over the nipple, then down to lick the undercurve of my breast. When his teeth nip there, I shudder.

That's so sexy. I melt even more.

"Condom," I gasp. "Now."

"Hmm." I feel his smile. "In a hurry, babe?"

"Yes." I wriggle against him. "And so are you. Don't pretend you're not." I curl my fingers around his cock and give a firm caress. He lets out a long groan as I slide my hand up and down. "You're huge."

"Yeah." He kisses the side of my neck, then leans over to grab a condom.

"And modest."

He snorts as he rips open the package. "Just honest, babe."

I can't help the smile that tugs my lips. We like to push each other's buttons, but there's no arguing that he is definitely hung. I pluck the condom from his fingers. "Let me."

"Aaah."

I shift so I can reach him better, and I roll the condom down his engorged length. He leans back on his hands. My gaze roams over ripped abs, a cluster of neat, dark hair at the base of his cock, and . . . his cock. I'd like to take more time to admire him, to study him, maybe even taste him . . . God. My eyes close briefly as my bones melt. But I want him inside me. So much.

I rise onto my knees and again adjust my position so I'm over him.

"Way too fast," he breathes. "I want to do so much to you, baby, to your sexy little body . . . but damn, I need to be inside you."

"I need it too."

He kisses me, one arm wrapped around me again. Then he grasps my ankle, pulls it back behind him, plants his foot into the mattress, and in a fast, smooth move swings me around and onto my back beneath him. I bounce as I hit the mattress, my head on a pillow, and I can't stop the delighted smile that springs to my lips. My belly does a little flip of lust.

"You like that," he says.

"No, I don't."

He grins, his teeth white in the dim light, kneeling between my spread thighs. He leans down to kiss me, pausing with his lips a breath away, and whispers, "Bullshit." His cock rubs over the front of my panties as his mouth covers mine and he groans into it. Back and forth he rocks his hips, rubbing his cock against me, and my clit is straining for more.

"Please," I gasp. "I need you."

He rises up and tugs my panties down. I pull my knees up and back so he can yank them off over my feet. He tosses them aside and lays his hands on my thighs to part them again. When he gazes down at my pussy, my entire body flashes hot.

"Pretty," he murmurs. "Jesus, Ella."

I whimper. "Do it!"

He finds my entrance with the head of his cock and presses in. I bite my lip and close my eyes as my body stretches around his girth, and it hurts so good as he fills me.

"Christ. You're tight. Hot."

I squeeze him tighter still and he growls. I love that. He fills me with luscious pressure and heat, sliding over tender nerve endings. Pleasure pours over me in hot waves.

He reaches for one breast and squeezes as he slides in and out of my body, slowly at first, then moving faster. He leans over me and rubs his big, naked chest and abs against mine. He's burning hot and damp with perspiration, and it feels so good. Heat spirals through me, need lifting my hips up to meet his harder strokes. He kisses me and then pauses, his nose barely touching mine, and I gaze into his shadowed eyes. Something passes between us, something intense and hot and connecting. My chest tightens. I touch his face, and he turns to take my thumb into his mouth and suck on it, grazing it with his teeth.

"Hot fucking girl," he whispers. "So hot."

"Yes, yes, I'm burning up—for God's sake, fuck me!"

He rises back onto his knees, and I can only stare in wonder at the beauty of his body carved in shadows, his big thighs spread. I pull one knee back, and he helps with a hand flat on my thigh, his other hand holding my ankle. My body jolts with each increasingly harder thrust as he fucks me. Heat twists and tightens inside me, and I slip a hand down to find my swollen clit. Just touching it nearly makes me come again and I moan.

Ben watches me with a heated gaze. "Beautiful," he rasps out. "Want you to come. Come on my cock, gorgeous."

Another orgasm is building, pressure coiling inside me, fierce and fast. I gaze at Ben's face as I clench my inner muscles, intensifying every sensation.

"Christ. That tight little pussy is working me . . ." He groans and I do it again, but that makes my orgasm come faster, faster than I want. I want to draw out the sweet sensation and make it last, but it shoots up high and hard, bursting inside me.

I know I'm making noises—whimpers and soft cries—but I can't stop them. My body tightens and pulses around his thick cock, warmth shimmering from my core through my entire body.

"Yeah, like that . . . fuck yeah." Ben comes too, his hands gripping me, his body going rigid other than the pulsation I feel inside me, our bodies straining together, as close as they can be, but trying to get even closer, even deeper.

Our eyes meet in the shadowy darkness, and we stare at each other for long, breathless moments.

My heart does something funny in my chest, a weird fluttery beating, and a sort of tender warmth spreads from my chest through my body. I touch his face with my fingertips, his stubble rough against them, our eyes locked together. The air in the room seems to thicken and heat. This is almost scaring me, the feelings rioting through me, unruly and uncontrollable. This isn't like me. Sex is good . . . I don't have to think, I just feel; forget all the shit I don't want to think about, just use my body. Not my emotions.

But this is different.

This is making me feel all kinds of things I can't even identify. A swelling in my chest like I'm going to burst out of my skin almost brings tears to my eyes.

I've screwed up so bad. I'm trying to be different, to make good decisions . . . *this* was a bad one. The worst. Ben already hates me because I've slept around a bunch; now he's really going to despise me. He's going to hate *himself* for having had sex with me, the girl he despises, the party girl. Agony shafts through me at that thought, the most painful of all. I don't want him to hate himself because of this.

This guy . . .

I wrench away from Ben, scrambling across the bed to get off.

"Hey." He reaches for me. He gets a firm grip on my arms and holds me in place, my back to him. My heart is pounding, and my breath is choppy. "What's wrong?"

"I need to go."

"You can't go. This is your room."

My head droops forward. *Fuck.*

"Calm down, Ella." He eases me back toward him so he can wrap his arms around me from behind. That feels so good, so secure, but it scares me too. "It's okay."

"It's not okay. This is fucked-up."

He rubs his face against my hair. "Maybe a little. Let's figure it out."

"We don't like each other."

I feel his smile. "Maybe we do."

"It was a hate fuck," I say. "They're always the hottest."

He goes very still behind me. "Hate fuck."

"Y-yes. It's all the, uh, emotion. I was pissed off. You were pissed off. Jealous. All the passion and adrenaline boiled over and . . . and we fucked. It was a mistake. Nothing can come of it."

He releases me, and the next thing I know he's off the bed. He grabs his jeans and takes two giant steps toward my desk, where he gets rid of the condom in the wastebasket. I pull the duvet around my shoulders and huddle there as he rapidly dresses.

He holds his sweater in his hands as he sets a hand on my doorknob. "Thanks for the hate fuck," he snaps. "You're right, it was hot." And then he's gone, the door closing with a thud.

Fingers curled into the duvet, I'm shaking, staring at the door. I swallow, and my throat feels like a hand is squeezing it.

I was right. I know I was right. Nothing can come of a hate fuck. It was just one more bad decision, when I've been doing so well lately. I've been studying and staying out of trouble. Skylar and I have been hanging out and talking about stuff. I've even been going for counseling, for the love of bacon! My plan has been working . . . up till now.

I fall onto the bed and curl up, my eyes squeezed shut, the corners of them burning.

I felt him watching me earlier, when I was with those other guys. I felt his eyes burning me up. I felt his smoldering anger. I *did* want him to be jealous.

And now he's walked out on me, and it fucking hurts like a dozen knives stabbing into my chest.

I am so fucked-up.

Chapter 12

Ben

SUNDAY IS OUR DAY OFF. Flash and I are taking turns throwing loads of laundry into the washer and dryer in the room just off our kitchen. He's bent over pulling stuff out of the dryer, and when I shove my clothes in the washer and slam the lid down with a violent clang, he jolts up, nearly cracking his head on a shelf. "Dude. Chill. Why are you so pissed at your laundry?"

I scowl at him as I cross my arms and lean against the washing machine. "Fuck off, I'm not pissed at my laundry."

"You're pissed at something." He pauses. "Or some*one*." He eyes me expectantly, as if I'm going to spill my guts to him.

"I'm not pissed."

That's totally a lie. I am fucking furious.

Not sure whether I'm angrier at Ella . . . or myself.

Hate fuck. Jesus Christ.

I rub my face. I can't even think up some bullshit to tell Flash to get him off my back. I might tell him what happened if Ella weren't Skylar's best friend. Because whoa, that's awkward.

Well, Ella was right about one thing—it was an epic mistake.

"How do you afford such expensive clothes?" Flash asks, letting me off the hook.

I shake my head. "There's a big outlet mall in Danby Heights." I name a suburb of Ridgedale. "I buy everything on sale. Also T.J.Maxx."

Flash narrows his eyes. "Really?"

"Really."

"So you're not secretly rich?"

"I, uh, have some investments. But I'm definitely not rich." Flash is the only person at school I've told about my messed-up family, and even he doesn't know how shitty things were.

"Investments, eh?"

I grin at his Canadianism but let it go.

"Come on," Flash says. "Let's go watch *How It's Made*. We're gonna learn about accordions."

I snort out a laugh and push away from the washing machine. "Fascinating."

"It is, man! It's like two musical instruments in one—I don't know how people play it."

"I don't know how anyone plays *any* musical instrument."

"Yeah. Same. No, wait, I played the recorder in school."

"I don't think that counts."

We're soon watching the assembly of the keyboard of an accordion.

I'm not really paying attention, though, because I'm remembering fucking Ella.

My body heats and my dick stirs, remembering how hot she was. How tight and slick and so damn eager . . . she made me feel like a fucking god, turning her on like that, making her so hot, making her come . . . twice.

Then my skin burns everywhere, remembering how it ended . . . how she said it was a hate fuck.

She hates me.

My eyes close and my chest tightens. Jesus. Why does that bug me so much? We both know the feeling is mutual.

Except . . . I don't believe in hate fucking. How could it be that good with someone you really don't like? Yeah, we were angry. Yeah, I was jealous. She had a point about our emotions being all riled up. But the truth is . . . I *don't* hate her.

I've seen sides of her lately that don't fit with what I used to think of her. Defending her friend. Being fiercely defended by her other friends. Studying in the library. Looking after a lost little dog, sitting on the floor cuddling it. Not drinking at a party. And now that I think of it, even though she was flirting with a bunch of guys, I'm pretty sure she hasn't been sleeping around like she used to.

Not that I see her that much, but with Skylar and Jacob being together, we've been forced into spending time together, and Ella's actually pretty smart and funny . . . and she makes a mean turkey sandwich.

I've already decided a turkey sandwich made by Ella has to be my new game day routine, since I played so well last night.

"Jesus," Flash says. "Six hundred reeds . . . no wonder it takes so long to tune it."

I blink at the TV, clueless. For once our favorite show isn't distracting me.

I gotta say, that was the hottest fuck I've ever had in my life, and if that was hate . . . well, maybe it's not so bad.

I can't have a girlfriend. Being in a relationship with someone means sharing shit about yourself, and that means opening yourself up to being ridiculed, plus running the risk that she'll tell other people. I have an image here on campus, and I'm not about to destroy it by confiding my loser upbringing to someone. But man, I could definitely fuck like that again.

What am I thinking? It's Ella. Skylar's best friend.

Wait, on the other hand, I already know Ella's DTF and doesn't appear interested in a boyfriend. Maybe this could work out.

But if it doesn't . . . *awkward*.

"Mama's got a squeezebox," Flash chortles.

I try again to focus on the TV, where The Who are singing an old song.

"They had to go there," Flash says with a grin. "Daddy doesn't sleep at night. Bahaha."

Fuck! Now I'm remembering Ella's tight little pussy squeezing my dick, milking me, making me come so hard I damn near blacked out.

"What's with you today?" Flash elbows me in the ribs. "That's funny."

I wince, since I took a hard hit to the boards last night, and rub the sore spot. "Jesus, keep your elbows to yourself, Gordie Howe."

"Ha."

Is Ella confiding in Skylar about what happened? What would she say? What would Skylar tell her?

"What's Skylar doing today?" I ask abruptly.

Flash frowns at me. "Why?"

"Just wondering."

"She's working the noon-to-six shift at the diner."

"Huh." I pause. "Does Skylar tell you . . . stuff?"

One of Flash's eyebrows shoots up. "Stuff? Like what?"

I pick at a loose thread on the couch. "I dunno. Like, girl stuff."

"Like, when she's on her period?"

"Jesus!" I scowl at him. "No, that's not what I meant."

He laughs, the bastard. "Just spill it, man; you're obviously all twisted up about something."

I hesitate.

"Okay, my guess is . . . Ella."

My head jerks up and I stare at him.

He meets my gaze steadily.

I slump back into the couch cushions. "I . . . we . . ."

He waits.

"We hooked up last night," I finally mumble.

He chokes. "Oh. Well. I guess I'm not surprised. Everyone can see the sparks flying when you two are together."

"Shut the fuck up."

"Seriously, man."

"You and Skylar *have* talked about us."

He sighs. "Yeah, a little. I like Ella, but I just have to warn you . . . she's got some fucked-up shit in her past."

I consider that. I don't actually like hearing it. Not that it bothers me, but Christ, I don't like knowing she's had a hard time. And what kind of fucked-up shit does she have? "Well, so do I."

"Just sayin' . . . I don't think she's girlfriend material."

"Well, that's perfect." I slap my knee and straighten. "Because I sure as hell am not boyfriend material."

Flash frowns. "Why not?"

"Too fucking busy trying to get drafted into the NHL." I lift my chin. "Which you should be too."

"Hey. Just because I have a girlfriend doesn't mean I'm not committed to hockey."

I huff out a breath. "I know, I know. I'm being an asshole."

I didn't tell him the real reason I don't want a girlfriend.

"So you slept with her. Not sure what to think of that. You, uh . . ."

"I called her a slut." My chest burns. "I know, I know. I feel like shit about that."

Flash is silent. I have no clue what he's thinking. I slide a glance his way and see him staring at the TV.

"The truth is . . . she's not a slut . . . I mean, I don't even know what a slut is anymore." I'm remembering Brooklyn and Natalie jumping to Ella's defense and the things they said.

"Ha. A slut is a woman with the morals of a man."

After that sinks in, I bark out a laugh. "Good one."

Flash shrugs. "Okay, it's a woman who's had sex with many partners. Again . . ." His hand goes up in a questioning gesture.

"Why is it pejorative for a woman and not for a man, for fuck's sake? What's wrong with having sex? Sex is fun."

"Because we live in a male-dominated society that still shames women for being sexual. I'm a slut. You're a slut."

A smile cracks my face. "When you put it that way . . . it's just a word."

"True."

"Huh." My forehead tightens as I contemplate this. "It's the judgment in it . . . right? Like, if a girl has a lot of sex, that makes her a bad person. A guy has a lot of sex and it makes him a stud."

"In fairness, there are probably some people who think that a guy who has a lot of sex is a bad person."

"Well, sure. I mean, each to his own. But I like sex."

"Me too," he agrees with heartfelt enthusiasm.

"When Tiffany called Ella a slut that night, I was furious."

"Interesting."

I frown at him. "Why?"

He shrugs, but he's kind of smirking. "I think girls are even worse slut-shamers than men sometimes." Flash shakes his head.

"Why is that?"

"Christ, this conversation is making my head hurt. I don't know! Maybe it's because they see themselves in competition with one another —so it's a way to devalue other women."

"That's fucked-up. Girls aren't a commodity. There's no fucking law of supply and demand when it comes to women that makes their value increase when supply is low. Jesus."

"Oh, right, Business major." Flash grins. "Well, I don't think we're going to figure out all the answers to this age-old problem. Maybe we should ask the girls."

"Ha."

"Anyway." His smile fades. "You can sleep with whoever you want. Ella can sleep with whoever she wants. I'm not gonna judge either of you. But just remember . . . emotions can get involved with sex, and that changes everything."

"Speaking from experience?"

Flash pauses. "Yeah. Hell yeah, I am." He sighs. "I never told you this, but when Skylar and I got together, it was supposed to be an arrangement. She'd pretend to be my girlfriend so I could get guys to sign her affirmative consent pledges."

"Shut the fuck up," I say again, staring at him. "But you two were hot for each other right from the puck drop."

He smiles. "Yeah. We were. It didn't take long for the sex to happen. And after that . . . it didn't take long for me to fall for her. And same for her. We kept trying to pretend it was just a deal, but . . ." He lifts one shoulder. "That's what I'm saying. So just be careful."

I nod. "Point taken." I push to my feet. "Better go check the laundry. I got some stuff in there that needs to hang dry."

Flash shakes his head with a laugh, and I head to the laundry room.

As I hang up my Rag & Bone checked shirt—the pink and tan one that apparently nobody else wanted so I pretty much stole it from T.J.-Maxx—and smooth out the wrinkles, I think about what we just talked about. Inside, I'm conflicted about what to do next. I'm annoyed at Ella for saying what we had was nothing but a hate fuck. But do I really want it to be more than that? Because I don't think she does.

And yet . . . I can't stop thinking about how good it was . . . How could she not want more? Am I being a conceited prick to think that?

Sex is a pretty powerful urge. Everyone knows that. Now I'm experiencing it.

As I return to the living room, Flash's phone rings and he answers. "Hey, Mom."

I grab the remote for the TV to turn down the volume and leave him alone to have a conversation with his parents. From the kitchen, I can overhear him talking to them, telling them about the agent he's now signed up with. I can tell how supportive they are, and he's eager to fill them in on the latest news, what the agent has said, what their plan is, how last night's game went.

I look down at the leftover pizza I'm about to slide into the oven to heat, and a feeling of emptiness hollows out my insides.

I made my decision last week too, and now I'm all set up with Jax Gardner as my adviser. He's a young guy, but I really liked him and his approach, and he represents a bunch of good players. But my mom's not calling to find out about that, and if I called her, she'd only pretend to be happy. My uncle Dave might give a shit, but I'm not sure if I should bother him with it. If my dad were here . . . he'd be proud, I guess. He was the one who got me started playing hockey when I was little. I was only six when he died, so I doubt if he ever even had an inkling that one day I might play in the NHL, but I'd like to think that if he saw me now, he'd be proud.

I swallow, my throat tight, and change my mind about the pizza. The emptiness inside me isn't because I'm hungry for food.

Ella's rejection last night is just one more confirmation that I'm a big fake, trying to pretend to be someone I'm not. Determination rises inside me. *I'm going to be someone.* I'm not there yet, but I will be.

I grab my keys and my jacket and push out the back door. Frigid air swirls around me, and I sit in my Mustang to let the engine warm up for a couple of minutes before I pull out. I'm restless and impatient, but not so much that I'd risk hurting my precious 'Stang. I'm a master of self-control and discipline. It's how I keep my life in order, keep things from spiraling into the chaos I grew up with.

I drive the few blocks to the house where Ella and Skylar live. I have no idea what I'm going to say, if she's even home. As I'm walking up the sidewalk to the front door, a car slows and parks on the street. I pause and see Ella inside. She jumps out, wearing a puffy black jacket, a knit cap pulled down over her long dark hair, and thick mitts on her hands. She stares at me.

"Hey," I call, turning and taking a few steps back toward her.

"Hey. What are you doing here?"

I pause. Fuck, I need to look more confident than I'm feeling, with my insides all knotted up. So I lift my chin and meet her eyes. "I want to talk to you."

Her eyes narrow. She ducks her head and reaches into the car for a bag, then straightens and shuts the door. She starts toward me. "About what?"

I jerk my head. "Wanna go inside?"

I watch expressions flit over her face. I feel vibrations coming off her that I think are nervousness.

"We could go somewhere else," I suggest, sensing her hesitance. "Taste of Heaven . . ." Then we both say no at the exact same time. And we both smile. "Okay, Carol's Café."

Still she hesitates. "Okay."

"Want to leave your stuff?"

"Nah, it's fine." She slings her bag over her shoulder, and I gesture to my car. She starts that way and I follow, my gaze dropping to that sweet little ass in tight jeans. I'm not a pig; it's normal to admire something so perfect. Right?

She throws her bag into the backseat, and we're on our way to campus. "I just came from here," she remarks, looking out the side window. "Had a meeting for a group project for my Media Communications class."

"I don't think you ever told me what your major is."

"You already know—I'm majoring in partying and drinking."

"Right." I grimace. "Okay, I may have been a bit of an ass to you."

I glance at her, and she's staring at me openmouthed. "What is going on?"

I shake my head. "Hang on. Let me find a parking spot."

I end up in a lot, and we have to walk a block, which we do in silence, although there are lots of people around. Inside Carol's Café it's nice and warm, almost steamy, with the scent of coffee and baked goods. It's not too busy, so I lead the way to a table at the back.

Ella unwraps her big scarf as she sits.

"What can I get you?" I ask.

She blinks at me almost suspiciously. "A latte, please. Skim milk."

"Got it." I go get our drinks, a regular coffee for me, and moments later return. As I walk back to the table, I study Ella sitting there staring at her phone. She looks . . . fragile. Her black turtleneck sweater emphasizes how slender and fine-boned she is. Her face is delicate, with a tiny nose and high cheekbones. Her long eyelashes flutter, and her elegant lips purse as she reads what's on the screen. That mole above the corner of her mouth is so sexy.

She looks up as I near and sets the phone aside. "Thanks." She accepts the cup I slide across the table and I take a seat too.

"So." I swallow. "About last night."

One corner of her mouth quirks, and she picks up her cup with two hands. "Uh-huh."

"Hate fuck? Really?"

She eyes me as she sips her drink. "You seemed annoyed when you left last night."

"I was pissed as hell."

Now both corners of her mouth lift. "No shit, Sherlock." She pauses. "Why was that?"

"Do you really hate me?" Oh, fuck me. I can't believe I just said that.

She doesn't answer right away, studying me. "I thought *you* hated *me*."

We sit there staring at each other across the tiny wood table, heat expanding, the air crackling around us. My heart is racing, and my mouth is dry. "I don't hate you," I finally say.

"Hey, just because we had sex doesn't mean you have to be nice to me," she says. "It was just sex."

Yeah, I can't let that go. I lean forward. "That was *so* not just sex," I say in a low voice. "That was a fucking fireball. Don't sit there and tell me you didn't feel it too."

Her eyes flash. "Okay, I felt it too. But I told you why . . . because we were wound up tighter than the girdle of a church minister's wife at an all-you-can-eat pancake breakfast."

My mouth falls open as her words sink in. Then I fall back in my chair laughing.

She smiles as she takes another sip of latte.

"Jesus Christ," I wheeze. "You fucking kill me."

"It's true." She lifts one narrow shoulder. "That's why it was so good."

"I think we should try it again."

Her eyes darken. Her little tongue comes out to swipe some foam off her upper lip, and my dick lurches to life. "That would be a very bad idea."

"Why?" I meet her eyes, challenging her.

She looks away. The hand holding her cup trembles.

Yeah, she's affected by this too.

"And don't tell me it's because you hate me," I say, feeling more confident now. "You can't fuck someone like that and hate them."

"Fuck someone like what?" she whispers.

I lean closer, even though there's nobody sitting near us. "Like you couldn't get enough of my cock."

Chapter 13

Ella

My eyes widen and my lips part. Heat spreads through me. My hands are shaking so much, Ben reaches over and takes the big round cup from me and sets it down on the table.

He's right. God.

I keep telling myself it was just sex, but I know I'm lying. I've had lots of sex, some of it even really good sex, but it has never been like that.

I don't know what the difference was. I've been thinking about it, but I almost feel afraid to do that too deeply, like there's something really scary way down deep beneath the surface that I'd rather not deal with.

But I know how well that worked for me when I was dealing with Brendan's death.

I can't have a boyfriend. I loved Brendan and he's gone. I loved Skylar and nearly lost her too. I'm not good at this. I make bad decisions, and falling for Ben would be the worst. Having sex with him wasn't exactly brilliant either.

I'm so confused. I don't understand why he's here, why he's talking about these things. He admits he was angry last night. Why isn't he avoiding me?

I bend my head and tuck my hair behind one ear. "Why are you doing this? You don't have to. We can just forget last night happened. I won't tell anyone."

"No." He grabs my hand again and this time holds tighter. "No, I don't think I can just forget last night. Because that was *good.*" He leans closer still. "And you pushed me away."

I bite my lip. I did. I did do that. I close my eyes as a burning wave of shame rushes over me. I was so hurt when he left last night . . . but it was my own fault. I was so damn terrified of everything he made me feel . . . I deliberately pushed him away. And when I open my eyes and look at his face, I can see that I hurt him.

He hasn't exactly said that yet. Maybe I'm wrong.

But maybe I'm not. Maybe he really *doesn't* hate me.

"You *should* hate me," I whisper. "You know what I'm like. You're the one who called me party girl."

"Yeah, well . . . you're the one who turns up your nose at me. Who looks at me like I'm something that dropped out of a duck's ass."

I blink. "I don't look at you like that."

"Sure you do. I just don't know why."

She swallows. "I told you last night . . . you're too damn perfect."

"That's why you hate me?"

The air pulses around us as I try to decide how to answer his question. "I don't hate you," I whisper. "But if I . . . didn't like you at first, it was because *you're* the one who looked at *me* that way." Might as well just say it. "Like I'm a drunken slut who doesn't deserve your respect."

My throat aches fiercely as I squeeze the words out. I realize how much it hurts that he thought that about me. Even though he's totally justified in thinking that of me . . . because it's true.

I've never cared much about what people think of me. My family got used to my crazy antics. I knew people were talking about my behavior last semester and I didn't care. But for some reason, I care what Ben thinks of me.

"Jesus." He reaches over and takes my hand, but I yank it away.

"It's okay," I try to say lightly. "You're entitled to your opinion, and frankly, you're not the only one who thinks that about me. So, I get it."

"I *don't* think that about you."

I stare at him.

He stares back at me. "Okay, the truth is, I was jealous. Even last semester before I knew you. I watched you with those guys, and it pissed me off. Because I was *jealous.*"

"Ben." My heart is thudding so hard in my chest, I'm having a hard time breathing. I don't even know what to say to that. "Really?"

"Really." He holds my gaze for a long moment, gripping my hand.

My chest tightens with a feeling that's almost panic. "What we had last night . . . that's all I have to give. If you're looking for more than that . . . I can't do it."

I have no idea what's going through his head. I'm almost afraid to look at his handsome face, but I sneak a peek. His mouth is set in a grim line, and his jaw is tight. Shadows flicker in his eyes. He's staring down at our clasped hands.

"Well, then, we're good," he finally says. "Because I'm not looking for anything more than that either."

I don't know what to make of that. "You should know," I manage to croak, "that I made a decision to change what I've been doing. I, uh, need to bring some grades up. I need to make sure my family doesn't . . . get some crazy idea that I need help." I pause. "That sounds really weird."

A notch appears between his eyebrows, but he nods.

"I've been trying so hard to make better decisions . . . not drinking as much, not partying as much, spending more time studying. I was doing so well up until last night."

He rubs his thumb over the back of my hand. "I've noticed that you've been different." Then he shocks the hell out of me by adding, "Not that there was anything wrong with you before."

I gape at him. I swallow. "Other than the fact that my grades were slipping, my best friend hated me, and my brothers were hearing stories about my whoring around campus?"

"Jesus." His eyes narrow and focus intently on me. "What the fuck?"

I shrug. "Yeah. So, I figured some changes were necessary."

He eyes me. "Why did Skylar hate you? What was going on?"

Do I really want to tell him this? Ah hell, why not. He's seen me at my worst, like that night when I had to be rescued from Jack Jones. "Last year, around this time actually, my other best friend, Brendan, died of suicide."

He presses his lips together and sighs. "I heard about that from Flash. It was hard on Skylar."

"Yes. It was hard on me too." I look down at my latte. "I'm actually going for some counseling now. Probably should have gone sooner. I didn't handle it very well." I tell him briefly what happened. One corner of his mouth lifts, but his eyes stay warm and steady on me as I talk. His calmness reassures and grounds me, giving me the courage to keep going.

"I'm an awful person, right? To blame my friend for our other friend dying like that?"

"Jesus." Ben swipes a hand across his face. "You're not an awful person."

"I know it wasn't her fault," I assure him. "But it was hard for a while. I . . . there's some stuff I won't share with you because it's Skylar's, but I was pretty shitty to her. Then . . . I was the one who told her about the situation Jacob was involved in back in Canada."

"Ah. Fuck."

"See? I *am* an awful person."

"Why did you tell her?"

I suck in a shaky breath. "I know Skylar thought I told her that to hurt her. But I really didn't. I was concerned about her . . . with her past, and his past . . . and I thought she should know."

"So she was angry at you for it?"

I shrug. "Actually, I don't know if she was. She was upset, for sure, because at first she believed it."

"I know," he says grimly.

"But she realized Jacob wouldn't have done what he was accused of, and they worked things out. She says she wasn't mad at me—it wasn't like I made up some bullshit story to hurt her. It was true." I sigh heavily. "I probably would handle it differently now, but I was hurting at the time and . . . well, like I said, I'm not known for always thinking things through before I act. But we're getting past that."

He nods slowly.

"I'm on academic probation," I blurt out. "And my brother who lives in Buffalo heard about how I was behaving last semester and basically threatened to tell our parents if I didn't settle down. They worried enough about me my freshman year, because I'm their baby girl. I don't need them freaking out even more. So that's why it was time for me to make some changes. And that's why last night was a mistake."

"Hmm." He sits back in his chair, a contemplative expression on his face.

"Now you really hate me, huh?" I meet his eyes defiantly. I just confessed all my worst sins to this guy, who never liked me to start with. I'm surprised he's not jumping up and running out of the café.

Then he leans forward. "My dad died when I was six years old."

I blink at him.

"My family is messed up. My mom tried her best, but she didn't have much. Most of my life I believed my dad was killed in a robbery gone wrong, or something like that, but it was never really investigated. Then a few years ago I found out he was actually murdered by my uncle."

My eyes pop open wide. "Oh my God."

"Yeah. My dad had a drug problem, and my uncle was dealing. They apparently got in an argument and Uncle Larry bashed him over the head and he died."

"How did you find that out?" My stomach is tight with sympathy.

"My grandma told me." He rubs his face. "As if I wanted to know. I spent years trying to get over losing my dad, and when I finally had, she . . . well, it was kind of upsetting. I was shocked, but there was nothing I could do about it at that point. Still, it explained why my mom had been avoiding my uncle for years."

"It was her brother who did it?" I know my eyes must be huge.

"Yeah. He tried to get her involved with his drug business too. Every time he showed up, she'd get upset. We had no money, and he kept saying he could solve all her financial problems, but she wanted nothing to do with him." He looks down. "If I didn't have hockey, I don't know what my life would be like. I was terrified I was going to be like them, maybe end up a drug addict. Or in jail. Or dead."

"Oh my God."

"So . . . I'm not going to judge you, Ella. I know how it feels to be judged. And I'm not perfect either."

My eyes widen again and I lean forward. "Ben. There's a big difference between my situation and yours . . . I've done stupid things and behaved badly . . . but you're not responsible for where you come from or what your family is like."

"People judge you for that, though." His jaw tightens. "I've experienced it."

"Yeah?"

"My mom works as a housekeeper." He drops his gaze and toys with his spoon. "When I was about fourteen, she got this fantastic job as a live-in housekeeper for this really rich family. She has a little apartment off the kitchen, and we lived in a nice neighborhood for the first time. The family had three daughters, all close to my age. They bitched at my mom for not doing their laundry perfectly, or for buying the wrong brand of yogurt. And they made my life hell too, by pretending they liked me, then laughing at me because I was the housekeeper's son. I was kind of a late bloomer, and I always felt intimidated and awkward around them, and they knew that. Their friends would come over and laugh at me, too."

"Oh Ben." My chest aches for him.

"One time they were having a party, and they invited me. I was so excited until I realized they wanted me there to be a waiter and bring people drinks."

I watch his face as he talks, the way his jaw tightens, his gaze dropping to the table.

"Another time they had friends over to hang out by the pool, and when I walked by, one of the friends asked who I was, and the oldest daughter told them I was the pool boy."

"Jesus." My mouth falls open. "I can't believe that."

"I know, right? They were such spoiled brats. But we couldn't leave, because we had nowhere else to live. Mom had worked as a live-in house-keeper before, and she lost that job when Uncle Larry showed up. For a while we stayed in a homeless shelter, and there was no goddamn way either of us wanted to go back to that. So we put up with the Winthrops' crap, but I couldn't wait to get away, to come to school here, where nobody knew me."

The way he dresses and his confident, sophisticated air made me believe he thinks he's better than everyone else . . . But, oh wow. The truth is, he created that image so he'd feel he was *as good* as everyone else.

Something unfurls in my chest, something warm and soft and vibrant. Suddenly we're holding hands again, this time with an equal firm pressure. I meet his eyes, and for the first time I see a reflection of my own insecurities and fears. "Why did you tell me that?" I whisper.

"I don't know." He makes a face. "I've never told anyone else. I guess I told you because I wanted you to know you're not the only one with shit to get over."

A trembling smile tugs my lips. Something draws out between us, something glowing and alive. Connecting us.

"The only other one who knows is Flash," he adds.

"You trust me not to tell people?" I can hardly believe that.

"Yeah."

That just about wrecks me.

"You're not an awful person, Ella," he says. "If you were, you wouldn't care about Skylar hating you. You wouldn't care about her. I know you do."

I nod slowly, tears brimming in my eyes. His faith in the good part of me makes me want to cry. Because even *I* haven't had faith in the good part of me lately.

"You care about your other friends too," he says. "I've seen it. And obviously you care about your parents, or it wouldn't matter if they freaked out worrying about you."

A breath shudders in and then out of my lungs.

"I need you to make me a turkey sandwich on my next game day," he says.

I choke and sputter. "What?"

He grins and rubs my hand. "A turkey sandwich. You made me that sandwich yesterday, and I played great. So now I have to eat one every game day. Every home game day," he clarifies. "Our next home game is February fifth."

I shake my head, smiling. "You're crazy."

"Hey, we hockey players are superstitious."

"Yeah? What other superstitions do you have?"

"I have to drink lemon-lime Gatorade before a game. I do my stretches in the same order every time. And I'm super picky about taping my stick."

"Right. I remember hearing how important your big stick is."

He laughs. "Right. So anyway, you *have* to make me that sandwich—come on, it's my career on the line here."

Tension eases out of my body as Ben and I sit and joke around. For once we're not pushing each other's buttons. There's still a buzz of attraction, but I feel relaxed and weirdly happy.

"Well, I guess I could do that," I say.

"Okay, now tell me what your major is."

"Communications. I wasn't sure what I wanted to do at first, so I took courses I was interested in, like English and Psychology, and one called Visual Communication that I really loved, and my faculty adviser suggested a major in Communications. I researched different jobs and the possibilities sounded really cool. I like writing and I'm kind of creative and also extroverted, so it seems like a good fit." I tell him about my courses and the project I was working on earlier, and he asks questions about what kind of jobs I could get after graduating. Then he tells me about this agent guy he's just made some kind of deal with, except he's not really acting as an agent, just an adviser, and how things are heating up for the guys who are entering the draft this year.

Somehow our conversation moves on, and we discover similar liberal views on most things, although we get into a little argument about global warming even though we both admit we aren't as fully informed on the topic as we should be.

Our coffees are long gone when I look at my watch. "Oh shit! It's my night to cook dinner!"

His forehead creases. "Uh-oh. Are you late?"

"Um, I think it's okay. I bought the things I need yesterday. But I better get home."

"Okay." He pushes back his chair and we both stand. He picks up my jacket and holds it for me, which makes my heart flutter. I shove my arms in and grab my scarf and hat, then my bag.

Ben drives me back to my place. The sun has just set and it's nearly dark. "What are you making for dinner?"

"Coconut chicken Thai curry." I grimace. "I hope it's good. Brooklyn's on this Thirty Something diet where she can only eat certain foods, so I had to go on Pinterest and find a recipe that would work for her."

"Maybe *she* should be the one cooking if she's on a special diet."

I laugh. "Yeah, she cooked last weekend. We take turns. None of us are very good at it, but we try."

"It sounds great. I'm not very adventurous when it comes to food. I pretty much eat pizza, burgers, or stuff at the dining hall, which thankfully is healthy. I got this nutrition plan from a dietician who advises the team about how to eat, so I kind of stick to basics."

The idea of inviting him to come in for dinner enters my head, but really, that's crazy. Sunday nights are for us girls. Maybe . . . no, I'm sure I'll never have a chance to cook Thai curry for Ben alone.

When he pulls up on the street, he puts the Mustang in park and turns to me. "I had fun this afternoon."

"Me too." Our eyes meet, and my skin heats up.

"We could do that again. Not the hate sex part, but maybe just have coffee and talk."

"Ben . . ."

"It wasn't that awful, was it?"

"No . . . but . . ." I don't know what to say. Maybe . . . maybe I *could* do that. It's not like we'd suddenly be dating or in a relationship. I know I can't do that . . . I'm a crappy friend, and I let down the guy I cared about by not realizing how much he was suffering. I can't let myself care that much about someone again. But this afternoon *was* fun. "Okay," I finally say. "We could do that again."

I don't mention that I wouldn't mind doing the hate sex part again too.

"Okay." He smiles at me, and then he leans across the console and brushes his mouth over mine. A sweet, barely there kiss, so completely at odds with the intense, violent way our mouths crashed together last night. And it totally makes my belly do a flip of lust and my girl parts quiver.

As I walk into the house, I'm not sure what just happened. Perhaps if I look up into the sky, I will see a pink pig flapping its wings . . . or perhaps the underworld is experiencing a blizzard . . . because Ben Buckingham was just nice to me.

As I wash my hands and then start preparing the chicken and vegetables for the curry, I think about what I just learned. Ben's childhood was truly traumatic, losing his father so young and in such a terrible way, then finding out when he was a teenager the truth of what happened . . . that had to be horrifying. And my heart hurts for him, thinking about him living with those rich bitches who were mean to him. It doesn't fit at all with the image I had of him, and I can't stop thinking about it. About him.

God, I can't be like this. I focus on preparing the meal, hoping to avoid a disaster like Skylar's first meal. When Brooklyn, Natalie, and Skylar all come into the kitchen, I make myself join their conversation and laughter as they snitch pieces of zucchini and red bell peppers.

Chapter 14

Ben

EVERY MUSCLE in my upper body is burning. Sweat stings my eyes, and my lungs are straining.

"The draft combine is tough," Jaegar tells Flash, Rocket, and me. "You're going to have to train hard for it. There are guys who puke when they're done with the VO2 Max bike test."

I've heard this.

The top one hundred prospects get invited to the combine, and apparently all three of us are on that list. Fuck me.

Not only are there a bunch of fitness tests and medical testing, we have to do psychological testing and interviews with the teams who are interested in us. Like freaking job interviews. Fuck me harder.

This only fuels my determination to succeed. I can see Flash feels the same. Rocket is so laid back, I don't know why he's not shitting pucks about it, but he still seems surprised he's even in this position. I almost envy him. What would it be like to go into this with no expectations?

Because, fuck, I'm going to be devastated if it doesn't work out.

Jaegar has met with us three guys individually to help us prepare physically for the combine. Right now he's fucking torturing us with pull-ups. "One day you'll thank me for this," he says with an evil grin. "One more."

Jesus. I've heard about the Hell Week that Navy SEALs go through, and it can't be any worse than this. Okay, we're not rolling around in sand, or swimming with our hands tied behind our back, but *fuck!* My muscles are screaming and trembling as I strain to pull myself up one more time, working on keeping my form perfect.

I've also been working on strengthening my grip, as that was causing me problems earlier in the year.

I lower myself and fall to the mat, stretching out flat on my back, staring up at the high gym ceiling, barely aware of the pumping rhythm of a Drake song. "I don't think I can move."

"Me either," Flash says.

I lift my head to peer at Rocket, his dreads spread out on the mat. His eyes are closed. Apparently he can't even speak.

As I lay there, my heaving chest slowly returning to normal, my mind drifts to Ella.

I haven't seen her since Sunday afternoon, but we follow each other on Insta, and I have to admit I've been stalking her there. She hasn't posted a lot—a video of a ridiculously adorable puppy that looks like a teddy bear, a face swap picture of her and Skylar that bordered on creepy.

I didn't want to call her the very next day. I waited out Tuesday too. Now it's Wednesday, and I messaged her before I got to the DeWitt Center to see if she wants to go out for coffee tonight. My phone is in my locker, unavailable to me, and it's making me antsy.

"Okay, you guys, get off your butts," Jaegar says.

With a sigh, I use my quivering abs to sit and roll to my feet. I swipe a hand across my forehead and back into my sweaty hair. Christ. Now we have to get on the ice and practice. My body feels like pudding.

In the dressing room, I sneak a peek at my phone and see that Ella has replied. I scroll through it and frown. But what can I say? *Today is the anniversary of Brendan's death. Skylar and I are spending it together.*

Hearing about her friend was brutal. Ella comes across as cool and tough, but her voice shook and her bottom lip quivered when she talked about him, and about what happened with her and Skylar after. Ella's a big softie on the inside. As evidenced by the way she looked after that lost dog, and the ridiculous puppy pic on her timeline.

"What are you doing tonight?" I ask Flash. If Ella and Skylar are together, he's got a free night too.

"Studying," he says.

I nod. Yeah, that would be the smart thing to do.

Luckily, Coach doesn't work us too hard in practice. I'm not sure I'm going to survive the next few months.

When we're done, Soupy and I are the last ones on the ice. I take my helmet off just as he flips a puck up and it comes at me. I see it, but the blinding flash of pain as it hits my nose has me dropping to the ice. "Fuck!"

My helmet slides across the ice. I'm on my knees, hands to my face.

"Jesus Christ." Soupy's at my side in an instant. "Fuck! Sorry, man. You okay?"

I can't speak. I'm not actually sure. The fiery pain is nearly making me puke. I pull my hands away, and they're covered in blood. It starts dripping on the ice. I'm weirdly fascinated by the bright red shapes on the white surface.

"Chuck!" Soupy yells to one of the trainers. "Get over here, quick!"

"What the fuck happened?" Chuck kneels beside me on the ice. He's got a towel and he lifts my head to peer at me. I close my eyes at the wave of pain.

"It was a freak thing," Soupy says. "I flipped the puck up, not even toward him, and he'd just taken his bucket off and . . . *fuck*."

I can hear the anguish in his voice. "S'okay, man."

"Your fucking nose is broken!"

"No, it's not." Chuck is poking at me, pressing the towel to my nose. I want to shout, but I grit my teeth. "Okay, pinch your nose here. Bend forward a bit." He helps me sit, my legs straight out in front of me. I do what he says. The towel is soaked with blood.

"I'm dying," I say. "I'm losing a lot of blood."

"You're not dying. Did you lose consciousness?"

"No."

"We'll have to check you for concussion, but let's get the bleeding stopped first."

"I don't have a concussion." Just the word makes my blood run cold. Fuck no. I can't be injured now. Not when the scouts are coming to games and my adviser is marketing me to the world, for Chrissakes.

"You have a cut on your nose too; not sure if you'll need stitches."

"Well, shit."

Chuck checks my nose again. "It's slowing. Let's get you off the ice."

They help me up, even though I could totally do it myself, it's not like my legs are broken. They do feel a little shaky, but hockey players are tough, so I have to skate off by myself. I heave a sigh as we leave the ice and I tramp into the dressing room and then to the first-aid room.

Flash is standing in front of his cubby with a towel around his hips, and his eyes widen as he watches us parade through. "What happened?"

"Soupy nailed me with a slap shot to the face." I attempt a grin beneath the towel still pressed to my nose.

"Bullshit," Soupy says, clearly not ready to joke about this. "It wasn't a slap shot."

I clap him on the shoulder and let Chuck take care of me.

I don't need stitches, just a butterfly bandage across my nose. He gives me an ice pack to hold there, which is just about as fucking painful as getting hit. We clean up all the blood, and he runs through the concussion protocol, asking me a million stupid questions about how I'm feeling: Ringing in the ears? No. Vision problems? No. Fatigue? Hell yeah, after Jaegar whipped our asses in the gym earlier. Finally, I'm all checked out, loaded up with painkillers, and I can go shower.

To my surprise, Flash is in the lounge area, slouched in a chair, looking at his phone.

"What are you still doing here?" I strip my bloody practice jersey off as I walk to my locker.

"Making sure you're okay, asshole."

"Aw." I make kissy noises at him. "Your concern is touching."

He follows me and grins as he studies my face. "Man, you are going to have two sweet shiners tomorrow."

"Ah, fuck." I head to a mirror. I wince as I examine my reflection. My nose is swollen, my whole face is red, and, yep, already forming are two big shadows under my eyes. "Great."

"Don't worry, you're still prettier than me."

"Ha."

"Are you okay to drive home?"

"Hell yeah." Flash is joking around, but I can see real concern shadowing his eyes. And that makes me feel kinda . . . good.

"Okay, now that I know you're okay and you can drive, I'll head home," he says. "See you there."

I shower and dress, then check my phone again. I tap in a reply to Ella. *I'm glad you're with Skylar today.*

I don't really know what else to say. They're probably having a hard time, reliving what happened a year ago. That really sucks.

My sore nose seems like a trivial thing compared to losing a friend to suicide.

When I get home, I figure I should eat something, but I'm not super hungry. Even with the painkillers, my whole face is throbbing and I have a headache. "What are we eating?" I ask unenthusiastically.

"Lasagna's in the oven," Soupy says. "That big frozen one I bought. It'll be ready soon."

"Okay. Call me. Gonna go lie down."

I trudge up the stairs, feeling exhausted. Pain does that to you. I've been hurt lots of times, luckily nothing serious—a few stitches here and there, some strained muscles and pretty bad bruises, broken ribs, and once I broke a finger. But it drains you. Plus, that was a little scary for a few minutes, with all the blood.

I ease myself onto my back on my bed. I like to sleep on my stomach, but I have a feeling that might not be happening tonight. I close my eyes.

I'll be fine. I'm tough.

Ella

After my session with Frances, I head home, where Skylar is waiting. She drives to the Burger House, Brendan's favorite restaurant in Ridgedale, and we're shown to a table for two.

"I don't know if this is a good idea or a bad one," she confesses, looking around. "I want to remember Brendan, but it's making me sad."

"I know. Me too. My mom used to make a point of remembering the anniversary of the day my grandpa died. I don't know why, but it always seemed morbid to me."

"Right?"

"Lots of people do that. They put little 'in memoriam' things in the newspaper on the anniversary."

"They go to the cemetery to put flowers on the grave."

"Brendan doesn't have a grave."

His parents had his remains cremated, and I think they still have them.

"If he did, would you go there?"

"I don't know. I went to my grandpa's grave a few times with my mom. I think she felt like she was closer to him by going there, but I didn't. I mean, I can think about my grandpa anytime. His spirit is always with me, it's not just where his body is buried. Oh my God, I sound like Natalie."

Skylar laughs.

"It's not that I want to forget Brendan." I pick up my napkin and refold it. "I think about him a lot. It doesn't have to be just on one day."

"I think about him too." Skylar's lips droop.

I hesitate. "Don't you hate him?"

She blinks rapidly. "I'm trying not to. I think I've forgiven him. Which doesn't mean I condone or excuse what he did. It just means I don't want to be angry and bitter for the rest of my life. He hurt me a lot." She pauses. "Frances helped me understand that forgiving him would empower me to acknowledge the pain I suffered without letting it define me. It would let me heal and move on with my life. And that's what I want to do."

My throat tightens, and I nod slowly. "I'm so sorry, Sky."

She tips her head. "For what?"

"For what happened to you. I hate that he did that. I hope . . ." I sigh. "I hope I can get to the point you're at."

"Well, you know . . . sometimes I still don't feel like I'm doing so good. Once Jacob and I were making out and he did something that reminded me of . . . what happened with Brendan. I freaked out."

"Oh no." I bite my lip.

"It was weird, because sex with Jacob is awesome, and he never scares me and I'm not even sure what exactly triggered the memory . . . He felt terrible, but it wasn't his fault."

"It wasn't your fault either."

"No," she agrees. "Apparently, it's pretty normal, I learned. How are things going for you with Frances?"

"Okay, I guess. It's hard for me to talk about such personal stuff. But she's so nonjudgmental . . . and easy to talk to."

"She is."

Our server approaches, and we order. When our menus have been taken away, Skylar says, "Let's each talk about three things we remember about Brendan. Happy things."

"Okay. I have one. Remember the time he texted his girlfriend asking if she was DTF, only he sent it to his mom instead?"

Skylar laughs. "Yes! Oh my God, he was so mortified!"

"But she didn't even know what it meant, so he said was asking if she was down to fight."

"Then he tried to text Anna to tell her what he did, and he acciden-tally texted his mom *again!*" We both laugh.

We trade memories, and this was a good idea because we're both smiling and I feel a lot better.

My phone pings and I pick it up to check the screen. It's a reply from Ben.

He'd asked me to go out for coffee tonight, and I had to say no because Skylar and I had made these plans. I'm not sure how I feel about that. I'd been thinking a lot about him after leaving him on Sunday. As usual, Ben Buckingham thoroughly confused me. The fact that he made himself so vulnerable by telling me about his childhood endeared him to me. And talking about his hockey hopes and dreams and how important it was for him to succeed, and why it was important for him to succeed, made me admire him. This all made it hard to remember exactly why I hated him.

Which made me disappointed because I couldn't see him, even though I totally wanted to be with Skylar today. The old me would've considered ditching my friend for a hot guy, but I've been practicing delayed gratification and self-discipline, and I know that this one day is important and that there'll be many more when I can see Ben.

We don't stay out late since we both have classes in the morning, and when I get home and in my room, I message Ben back. *Hi again. Sorry tonight didn't work . . . tomorrow?*

His reply comes quickly. *Sure, sounds good.*

We agree he'll pick me up at seven. I'm smiling as I get ready for bed.

The next morning after my first class, I wander into the dining hall to find a coffee. The tables are about half full, sunlight streaming in the big, high windows. I get a cup of coffee and look around to see if there's anyone I know whom I can sit with. I spot the table with the five big guys immediately, my eyes locking onto the back of Ben's head. It's weird how I know it's him. He's with his housemates and Freddy.

I head that way to at least say hi. Jacob looks up and smiles at me. "Hey, Ella," he says as I near them. "How's it going?"

"Good." I pause next to the table.

"Join us?"

"Sure." I move around to an empty chair next to Freddy, across from Ben. I set my coffee down and then look at him. My eyes damn near pop out of my head. "Jesus Christ!"

He gives me a sheepish look back, but holy crap . . .

"What happened to you?" I ask, slowly lowering myself into the chair, staring at his poor face. His nose is hugely swollen, with a bandage on it, and both his eyes are black. I cover my mouth with one hand, a sick feeling in the pit of my stomach.

"Took a puck in the face yesterday."

"Are you okay?"

He nods. "Yeah. Apparently, my nose isn't broken, which is a miracle. It looks worse than it is."

My stomach tightens even more in sympathy with his pain, as if I'm feeling it myself. "Okay, well, I guess that's good it's not worse. It happened in practice?"

"Yeah, right at the end. I had my helmet off, freak thing." He shrugs nonchalantly, no big deal.

I let out a breath and remove the lid from my coffee cup. Wow, it's really freaking me out that he's hurt. It's not that he looks bad—although he does—I just don't like thinking about him in pain. "Will you be able to play this weekend?"

"Oh yeah, for sure. We're off to Clarkson University tomorrow."

"Oh. Not far this time."

"A few hours on the bus."

I nibble my bottom lip. I want to ask if he's sure he's okay to play, but that would sound overly concerned. I also want to leap out of my chair, rush over to him, and touch his bruises, and gently kiss them to make them better. For the love of bacon, I need to get a grip here. "Well." I lean back in my chair. "You definitely look like a hockey player now, pretty boy."

He grins and our eyes meet. And somehow I know that he knows how I'm feeling. I can't stop from smiling back at him, and for a moment it's just us, across the table from each other, the hum of chatter and clink of dishes muting into the background.

The guys are talking about the upcoming games and what they're going to have to do to win. I'm not really paying attention, but I try to pretend I am while covertly studying Ben, still aching inside for him. What is happening with me?

Skylar shows up then. She says hi to everyone and flashes me a big smile. Jacob pulls her down onto his lap, and she curls an arm around his neck. Then she notices Ben's face, and we go through the story again. This time I notice Hunter's expression and the way his eyes drop. Nobody has said who shot the puck that hit Ben in the face, but I gather it was him. It had to have been an accident, and Ben doesn't seem pissed at him or anything, but Hunter definitely looks unhappy.

"It must not have been a very hard shot, if your nose isn't broken," Skylar says. "It could be so much worse."

"Totally," Ben agrees.

I guess that's one way to look at it. Some of the shots they take at the net are super hard and fast. That's why I think goalies are crazy—but then, they wear a ton of padding and protection. And if Ben'd had his helmet on, it wouldn't have been as bad because of the cage they all wear.

I check my phone for the time. "Oops, I better get going. I have Oral Communications."

"I love oral," Grady says.

Everyone laughs, and I have to shake my head and smile.

Ben pushes back from the table. "I'll walk out with you. I'm on my way to class too."

I feel Skylar's gaze on us as we say goodbye to everyone and make our way out of the dining hall. Once outside in the frosty January air, I pull in a long breath and turn to him. "Are you really okay?"

"Yeah." His smile makes my insides melt. "I'll pick you up at seven, okay?"

I bite my lip and nod.

I think we have a date.

Chapter 15

Ella

This feels really weird.

I've been with a lot of guys, but usually it's a hookup at a party or a bar. It's been a while since I've been on a date.

I'm in my room, looking into my mirror as I add a couple of waves to my hair with the curling wand and smooth some gloss over my lips. I'm hyperaware that my housemates are going to know about this. They're going to know I'm with Ben, one of Jacob's teammates. Skylar is going to know, after all my protesting about how much I hate him.

I'm not even sure I know how to do this.

Going to parties and bars and clubs made me feel all grown up. A whole night stretching in front of me, free to do whatever I wanted, no family around to tell me not to. Laughter and fun and alcohol. But looking back, I get a hollow feeling in my stomach. Nobody I drank with or danced with or even slept with really cared about me. I *felt* like I was being a grown-up, in high heels and shiny lip gloss, drinking and flirting and having sex with whoever I wanted to. But that was such a childish idea of what being an adult is.

I guess I'm still figuring out what being an adult is, because I'm still confused about a lot of things. But I think I'm making progress. I'm still not sure if going out with Ben is a good idea or a bad one, but I want to be with him so much, it's like something inside me growing, pushing at my skin, a longing I don't think I've ever really felt.

It's five minutes to seven, so I grab my purse and peek out of my bedroom. I think the others are all in their rooms. If I scoot quickly, I can make it out of the house without having to say anything to anyone.

I jog lightly down to the front door. I pull my jacket from the closet and toss a big scarf around my neck. On the street, headlights of an approaching car illuminate the neighboring yards, and I see the car slow to a stop. I let myself out, without having said a word to any of my friends about where I'm going.

Ben is just stepping from his Mustang as I skip down the sidewalk, and he pauses. "Hi."

"Hi!" I open the passenger door and slide in; he does the same on the driver's side.

"Sneaking away?" He slants me an amused, knowing smile.

"No!" I pause. "Does Jacob know we're going for coffee?"

"Yeah." He eyes me steadily. "Is that a problem?"

"Um . . . yeah."

His eyebrows pull together.

"No, I mean, not that it's a problem we're together," I say hastily. "I just mean, dammit, I should have told Skylar. If she hears it from Jacob . . ." My insides twist at the thought she might be hurt. "I should have told her. I'm an idiot."

"Want to go back in?"

I think Skylar's in her room studying. I hesitate. "You think I'm crazy, don't you."

"No."

"I'll be quick."

He smiles, and I jump out of his car and run back to the house, berating myself for being so stupid. Why hadn't I just told her?

I race upstairs and pause outside her open door. I give a thump on the door, and she looks up from her computer. "Hey."

"Hi." I stand there blinking rapidly, my hands curling inside my mittens. "I'm going out."

"Okay." She tips her head to one side.

"With Ben."

Her eyes widen. "What? Really?"

"Just for coffee." I hold up my hands. I sigh. "I'm so freaking out about this. I don't know how to go for coffee with a guy. And it's Ben."

She smiles slowly. "Ben's a good guy, El."

"He's a stuck-up, pretentious, serious jerk," I say casually, so she won't make too much of this. "But I'm going to give him a chance."

Skylar grins. "Okay. Have fun."

"Thanks."

Okay. I did it. That didn't kill me. Now back to the date part.

I rejoin Ben in the car, where it's nice and warm and smells faintly like him, like the woodsy body wash he uses and his own male scent. The Lumineers play on the radio, and he's tapping his fingers on the steering wheel to the beat of the song. "Okay," I say brightly. "It's all good."

Amusement lifts his lips as he puts the car into gear and pulls out from the curb. "Guess it's a girl thing."

I let air out of my lungs. "Yeah. I'm trying to be a better friend."

He shoots me a sideways glance. "I think you're a pretty good friend to Skylar."

"Thank you." He even knows the ugly truth, so this means a lot. "Where are we going?"

"Off campus. The Roasted Bean."

"Sounds good. How's your face?"

"Hurting." He lifts a big shoulder. "I'm trying not to take too many painkillers."

"Why not?"

"I don't like taking drugs."

"Did they give you narcotics or something?" I frown.

He laughs. "No. Just ibuprofen."

"So take it if it helps."

"I did last night and this morning. Just trying to see if I can go without."

"Tough guy." But I remember what he said about being afraid of ending up a drug addict, so I get it.

"Hell yeah. We won't talk about how I thought I was dying because I was losing so much blood."

I smile even though my stomach flips. "I'm sure it had to be scary. Was it Hunter who hurt you?"

"Yeah." He grimaces. "He feels awful about it."

"I could tell."

"It was totally an accident, though. And I'm fine."

"Other than you look like you just went ten rounds in the ring with Rocky Marciano."

He laughs. "Kinda feels like that."

The Roasted Bean isn't far, and he soon pulls into the parking lot in front of it. Inside it's about half full, and we have no trouble getting a table at a window. I take off my jacket as he goes to order our coffees. Glancing around the small coffee shop, I don't see anyone I know.

Ben carries our coffees back to the table, and I notice how people are looking at him, with the tape on his nose and the dark purplish discolorations around both eyes. He's still gorgeous, moving with athletic ease, his hair as perfect as always, his black jacket expensive-looking, and with a stylish striped scarf looped around his neck. His meticulous grooming and clothes contrast with his beat-up face.

As we sip our drinks, we talk about all kinds of things. He tells me more about this draft that's coming up and the testing and interviews he'll have to go through. It sounds crazy, but it also sounds like he's getting a lot of support and advice. His determination impresses me. He also talks about the guys and some of the crazy pranks they play when they're on their road trips, like the snake in the cooler.

"There's obviously a pretty strong bond between all you guys."

"Yeah."

"I sort of know what that's like from my dancing days." I tell him about all the dance classes my parents made me take. "When we competed, we were a team and you didn't want to let your team down. But there was also some catfighting and competition between some of the girls as we got into our teens, and I don't think we experienced the same kind of bonding as you guys."

"This is my second year on the team, and we've got a really good group. Mostly." He shrugs. "There are a couple of guys I don't care for as much."

"Jack Jones."

"Yeah." He meets my eyes. "I was there that night."

My lips tighten. "I was so stupid."

That was the night I think I kind of hit bottom. I was drunk and flirting with Jack Jones and getting ready to leave with him to go have sex somewhere when I got scared. There was an edge to him that I didn't like. When I changed my mind, he turned nasty. And then I got really scared. Luckily, Jacob stepped in and basically saved me. And I started wondering what the hell I was doing with my life.

Ben looks down at his coffee. "That's what I thought at the time. But Flash kind of opened my eyes about some things. Black Jack's an asshole, especially when it comes to women."

"I never wanted Jacob to get in trouble because of me," I whisper. "When I heard about the fight between him and Jack, I felt terrible. I still do. I apologized to Jacob about that, and thanked him for stepping in like he did."

"I thought he was crazy," Ben confesses. "I figured you knew what you were doing."

"I thought I did too. But I'd had a lot to drink. And when I changed my mind . . . and Jack kept pushing . . . I got scared. I was embarrassed, but so damn grateful to Jacob. I think that night was a bit of a wake-up call for me about what I'd been doing."

"I think it was a wake-up call for a bunch of us. When Flash laid out the reality of a girl who's drunk not being able to consent . . . I think we all had to take a hard look at ourselves." He pauses. "At least I did. When you realize . . . well, there are a lot of mixed messages and blurred lines out there about sex and consent, and you start to look back and wonder if you ever misunderstood a situation. Whether you ever unintentionally crossed a line. We've all had drunken hookups, and I felt really uncomfortable thinking that maybe one of those times . . ."

I reach across the table and cover his hand. "You know what? The fact that you're even thinking like that and questioning yourself means you're a good guy, Ben."

He looks at our hands, then up at me. "Thanks." The air around us has grown heavy with this weighty topic. Then, as if to lighten things, his lips quirk. "Never thought I'd hear that from you."

I return his smile and release his hand, sitting back. "Don't get used to it."

The look we share stretches out. That swelling feeling in my chest intensifies, stealing my breath. Need and want twisted up with a strange affection pull at me.

"Tell me more about your dancing."

"My parents started me in ballet classes when I was five. When I got older, they added jazz, and when I was about twelve, I wanted to do hip-hop. It was cooler than ballet. I had a crazy schedule, but my parents were kind of helicopter-ish, and they didn't mind driving me all over the place."

"You must have liked it."

"Actually, I did. I still love dancing. Now it's just at parties and once or twice a week Zumba classes. And on Saturday mornings, I help with ballet classes for little girls."

"You teach ballet?"

"I'm an assistant, but yeah. They're really cute."

He's silent for a moment, then says, "You must be very . . . flexible."

My belly does a little flip at the smoldery look in his eyes. I smile. "Yes. Yes, I am." I pause. "And I know what you're thinking."

"Yeah." The heat that's been building around us all evening flares up hotter. "I'm thinking about you doing the splits."

I touch my tongue to my top lip, which draws his attention there. "I *can* do the splits, as a matter of fact."

"Holy shit." His voice is hoarse.

I lean closer. "You want to see it, don't you?"

"Oh baby. I really do. I'm picturing you on your back . . ."

Heat settles right between my legs as I imagine that too.

"Maybe we should talk about something else," he says.

I heave a small sigh. "Okay."

We talk about other things for a while, until we both check our phones. It's nearly ten. "I can't believe we've been sitting here for three hours!"

"Huh. Guess we better go. It's surprising they haven't kicked us out."

I reach for my jacket. "It's not that busy; otherwise, maybe they would have."

Ben drives me home. The air in the car crackles. I want to touch him. I still want to kiss those bruises and soothe him. My body aches to be touched too—my breasts full, my pussy throbbing. All the way home I think about reaching over and laying a hand on one of his muscular thighs. It's so weird that we've already had sex—hot, dirty, desperate sex— but the last couple of times I've seen him we haven't even kissed. And I want to kiss him. So much.

He pulls up in front of my house in the dark. All the downstairs lights are on, so someone is still up.

He turns to me. I shift in my seat to face him, longing expanding in my chest, my skin tingling everywhere. He reaches out a hand and slides it around the back of my neck, inside my scarf, under my hair. His fingers caress me in slow, mesmerizing strokes. My lips part and my gaze drops to his mouth. With a groan, he leans across, putting pressure on my neck to bring me closer too, until our mouths meet.

God. He tastes so good, and feels so good. His mouth is firm and warm and demanding. I make a needy noise in my throat, and his tongue licks into my mouth to find mine. I open wider for him and grip his jacket in one fist as we kiss again and again.

My belly flips with lust, liquid heat converging there in an unrelenting ache. All the need and passion we've been keeping banked blazes up red hot around us, and we devour each other's mouths like we can't get enough, can never get enough.

"I want you so bad," he mutters in my ear. He licks my jaw, and I shudder. "So goddamn bad."

"I can't take you inside . . ."

"I know."

I don't even understand myself why this is different . . . why I don't want to bring him into the house, past my friends, as I take him up to my room to fuck him and then have him leave.

"We could go to my place." He glides his open mouth over my throat. "But I'd rather be alone with you."

"I know."

"We could drive somewhere and I could fuck you in this car," he continues, now back to nipping at my lips. "But I don't want that for you either. Sex in a car can be hot, but I want better for you. I want to make it good for you."

My skin is burning up, and my heart contracts almost painfully.

He cups my face with two hands, brushing his thumb over my bottom lip. "We're going to find a way to be together."

"God. I can't stand it. Ben . . ."

"I know. Christ, my dick is so hard it hurts."

"We could . . . just . . . um . . . you know."

"Do it. In your room. Thinking about me. Okay?"

I whimper.

"I'll be thinking about you too. About that tight hot pussy. This sexy mouth. These sweet tits." He brushes a hand over the front of my jacket, and even with the thick fabric between us, my nipples strain for his touch.

I want to weep with need and frustration. I consider just doing it anyway, taking him in the house, leading him upstairs . . . but this isn't like the other guys.

Our foreheads still together, we sit like that, our bodies trembling and aching.

"You're going away this weekend," I whisper.

"Yeah. Fuck." He pauses. "Monday. We'll figure something out. I promise."

"Okay."

With one last, clinging kiss we say good night without words, and then I force myself to shove out of the car and run to the door. My eyes are stinging; my body is pulsing with need.

Brooklyn, Natalie, and Skylar are all in the living room with the television on and a bowl of popcorn on the coffee table. They all look up and smile. Skylar gives me a little wave. "How was the date?"

Has she told Brooklyn and Natalie? They both look at me expectantly too, so I guess she has, yet they don't seem freaked out by the fact that I'd gone out with Ben Buckingham. It's clearly a bigger deal to me than to anyone else. Except Skylar . . . she understands.

"It was good." I try to keep my voice casual. "We just went to the Roasted Bean."

"You were there for a while," Natalie says with a sly smile.

They think we were out screwing around somewhere.

"Yeah, we were." I smile. "We were surprised they didn't kick us out . . . we only ordered one coffee each." I grab a handful of popcorn and head toward the stairs. "G'night!"

I get ready for bed, washing my face, the usual routine, and jump in, prepared for a little self-pleasure. Someone knocks on my door.

Argh!

"Come in!"

Skylar pokes her head in. "Oh, you're in bed already! Sorry."

"That's okay." I sit up and smile.

"I just wanted to see how things went with Ben."

"It was good. I had fun. I think he did too."

"Will you see each other again?"

"I think so. But they're going out of town tomorrow."

"Ugh. Tell me about it. I hate the weekends away."

"We can talk more about it tomorrow," I offer.

"Okay. 'Night, El."

Once the door is closed I dive back under the covers. I do think of Ben when I cup my own breasts, tweak my nipples, and slide my hand down into my panties. I'm so wet. I touch my clit, and my body jolts with electricity. I circle my slicked-up fingertip over it, finding just the right place, just the right pressure . . . Tingles radiate from a spot deep inside me, spreading through my body.

I remember Ben's body, his hard muscles, his heavy cock . . . but I'm also picturing his steady eyes focused on me, the warmth in them making my heart hurt . . . and the coil of pleasure twists up high and tight and then peaks, my body tightening and shuddering. "Ben," I whisper. I cup my hand over my pulsing flesh, my breathing short and harsh.

I did it. I was thinking about him. And it doesn't help my state to imagine him doing the same, stroking his cock while he thinks of me and coming with my name on his lips.

Chapter 16

Ben

WE LOSE both games on our road trip.

It sucks. I know I've been distracted by what's happening with Ella and me, and I have to take a long look at myself in the mirror and ask if I was playing my best.

Honestly? I think I was. Yeah, I've been thinking a lot about Ella. I've been jerking off a lot thinking about Ella. But when I step on the ice, I'm pretty good at clearing my head and focusing on the game. Which is definitely what I need to be focusing on right now.

When we analyze our games, Coach points out where we could have been better, but he tells us we did a lot of good things too, and both were one-goal games that could have gone either way. Some guys don't believe in the hockey gods, but there are times the bounces go your way and you thank them, and then there are times when you feel the crushing frustration of bad luck.

I'm messaging with Ella on the bus ride home Sunday, telling her about the games, asking what she did over the weekend. She and Skylar apparently went out to a chick flick on Saturday night, so that's good. Not that Ella and I have made any kind of commitment . . . we've had only one date, or maybe two. I don't know if those even count—it seems like nobody dates anymore. So if she'd gone out to a party and left with some other guy, I wouldn't have any right to object.

I'd be fucking furious beyond belief, though.

Yeah, this is turning into something I didn't plan for. But the last couple of times we saw each other were fun, so maybe this relationship thing isn't so bad. I've even told her about my family and my upbringing, and instead of making her hate me, it actually seems as if she likes me more.

We've narrowed down a window of opportunity: Monday afternoon. Everyone will be out of her house, and neither of us has a class. I have to be at the DeWitt Center at three for my workout, but Mondays are an easier day after back-to-back road games.

So we have a sex date.

Goddamn, my balls will be blue by then. How am I going to make it that long?

In the meantime, we're sexting. Christ, I'm getting a boner on the bus. This is not acceptable.

I text her, *I want to fuck you so bad.*

Mmm. Me too.

Before that I want to bury my face in your pussy . . . throw your legs over my shoulders and lick you until you scream.

God, you're good at this. Think you can live up to it in person?

A bark of laughter escapes me. *Witch.*

Just wait, babe.

I'm waiting. Also, I'm wet.

Now a groan escapes me. Flash shoots me a frown from the seat next to me. "What are you doing?"

"Nothing." I swipe a hand over my mouth.

I think we have to stop or I'm going to embarrass myself here on the bus.

I remember the time I was on a trip with my U.S. National Team and a guy got caught busting a nut at the very back of the bus. He never lived that down. Desperate as I am, I'm not going to risk that. I'll just think about Business Analysis and Valuation Using Financial Statements.

I'm sorry.

No, you're not, you tease.

Hey, I'm bothered too.

But you're alone in your room. You can take care of yourself. Ah shit. Imagining that just makes me hornier.

Just to be fair, I won't. I'll wait for you.

I fucking love that. You'll be all ready for me tomorrow.

I'll be SO ready.

We end our chat, and I close my eyes and fantasize again, remembering that night in her room, seeing her naked, the feel of her in my hands and around my dick, the way she came . . . Yeah, this isn't helping my persistent boner.

I force my eyes open and pull out my laptop so I can focus on homework.

The guys behind me are talking about weird sleep things.

"Like that feeling that you're falling just when you're going to sleep," Matty says. "And you wake up."

"I hate that," Soupy agrees.

"Have you ever woken up in the morning paralyzed?"

"Uh . . . no."

"I have. It scared the shit outta me. Felt like I couldn't breathe."

"That's fucked-up, man." I can hear the horror in Soupy's voice.

"Apparently, my brain woke up before the deep sleep paralysis went away."

"You sure?"

"Yeah, that's happened to me," Freddy puts in.

"You sleepwalk too. Now, *that* is freaky."

"He did sleepwalk!" Matty says. "When we were in Schenectady, he got up in the middle of the night. He was standing over at the desk in the hotel room. I asked him what he was doing, and he said he was making a peanut butter and jelly sandwich." He pauses. "Only we didn't *have* any PB or jelly. Or bread."

"I was dreaming," Freddy says mildly. "So I got up and acted it out. Big deal."

"It's a big deal if you have a knife in your suitcase and you think I'm a turkey that needs carving."

We all burst out laughing.

"Yeah, you look like a turkey." Freddy smirks. "Jesus."

"Burnsy talks in his sleep," Butch pipes up.

Fuck it, I'm not getting anything done here. I push up and turn around to listen.

"He was talking to his girlfriend," Butch adds. "Asking her to suck his toes."

"Fuck off, I did not."

Butch laughs.

"Krystal talks in her sleep," Danny says of his girlfriend. "We once had a whole conversation. She was trying to get out of bed because she left her car running. First, I was trying to tell her she didn't, but she kept insisting, so I told her I turned it off for her. She goes, Really? I say, Yeah, and I put your keys back in your purse. And she says, Thank you, baby, and that was the end of it." He shakes his head. "It was hilarious."

"How about exploding head syndrome?" I ask.

Everyone gazes blankly back at me.

"Come on, I'm not the only one it's happened to."

"I think you are," Flash says with a grin.

"No! Okay, it's not my head exploding, but I think I hear a loud noise, like a bang or a gunshot, and I wake up. But there was nothing."

"Oh yeah . . . that *has* happened to me," Freddy says.

"Sleep is weird."

Well, if nothing else, this is taking my mind off my aching dick.

I pull up in front of Ella's house on Monday afternoon feeling like I'm a spy on a secret mission. I look around, but the street is deserted.

I ring the bell, and the door is flung open immediately. Ella stands there grinning at me. "Get in here."

"Hi to you too." I grin back and step inside. "Are we alone?"

"Totally."

"Fuck yeah." I slam the door behind me.

Ella reaches over to lock it.

"That's not going to keep your housemates out, you know. They have these things called keys."

She laughs. "I know. But it will buy us a few minutes if someone does come home."

"Am I going to be jumping out your bedroom window? I hope not. I have weak ankles."

Her sultry laugh reaches right down to my balls as I move closer to her. "No, silly, there's a tree you can climb."

"Of course. That's not a cliché at all." I bump her up against the wall with my hips and smile down into her eyes. "Miss me?"

"Um, maybe. You know . . . like you miss a toothache when it's gone."

My grin slips into evil. "Ah. Smart-ass." I edge closer still, pressing my straining erection into her soft belly. "You know what happens to smart-asses?"

"No, what?" Blink, blink, blink.

My blood rushes hot through my veins. "Smart-asses get spanked." I step back and pull her with me, then bend my knees to grip her around her thighs. Then she's over my shoulder and I'm striding to the stairs. I give her ass a little tap.

"Ben!"

Her excited little cry turns me on even more. She slaps at my back, but it's feeble. "Put me down!"

"I'll put you down." I climb the stairs and head straight for her room, where I toss her to the bed. She has the blinds shut against the afternoon sun, so it's dim in here.

Her hair is hanging in front of her face, her cheeks are pink, and she's breathing fast. I know she likes it physical, from the last time. But just to make sure, I meet her eyes. Her smile steals my breath.

That connection we have sizzles between us, practically lighting up the room with electricity.

"How long do we have?" she asks.

"Not long enough." I climb onto the bed and reach for her long-sleeved T-shirt. I peel it up over her chest and shoulders, and we wrestle her out of it. Then I have to pause just to look at her in her underwear. She's wearing sort of a bra, but it's black lace, with a scalloped band around her ribs, which is hot as fuck. "This is so sexy." I reach out to run my fingers between her breasts, then cup her softness through the lace, and she fills my palms perfectly. Some girls wear these mega-padded, push-up bras and you can't even feel them through all the foam or whatever the hell. This is sweet.

She moans. "Oh God."

I remember that her breasts are sensitive. That fucking makes me even harder, seeing how much she likes it when I touch her there. I rub over her nipples, then give them a little pinch through the lace. Her breath hitches in her throat.

I trail my fingers down her stomach, and her muscles quiver at my touch. Like last time, she's wearing yoga pants, which are nice and soft and stretchy, and easy to get off. Although before I do, I pick her up and flip her onto her belly.

She gives another squeal. I lay my hand flat on one cheek of her ass. "You should wear nothing but yoga pants, with this ass," I growl, and give the pliant flesh a squeeze. "Such a tight, sweet little ass."

She moans into the bedcovers.

I'm not really going to spank her. That would be fun, but I don't think we're there yet. I have a feeling she's not totally against the idea, but that'll be for later. Right now, I just want to admire her butt with my eyes and my hands, so I rub and squeeze. Then I hook my fingers into the waistband and yank down.

Now it's my turn to groan as I reveal those cheeks, round and smooth and perfect. She's wearing a thong, so there's basically nothing hiding her from me, and I rake my gaze over her as I tug the pants down her legs.

"Oh yeah," I whisper, leaning down to plant my lips against one cheek. "Perfect."

"Th-thank you."

"I could play with this ass all day." I lick and nibble and caress her until she's squirming and panting. I'm not lying, I could do this forever, but she's getting worked up, and I like that too. I slip my fingers down between her thighs. "Dripping wet. Just what I want."

"God, Ben. You're making me crazy."

"Good." Goddammit, her body is like a smorgasbord, and I don't know where to start. I'd like to hike her hips up in the air and bury my face in her pussy from behind, but I also want to see her face. So I flip her again.

"How do you do that?" she gasps, her shiny dark hair spread around her head on the blue duvet.

I grin and flex my biceps.

The corners of her mouth lift. "Oh yeah. You do have some impressive guns there, hockey boy."

"What's that? Did I just hear a compliment from those pretty lips?"

"Don't get used to it."

I laugh. She's let compliments slip before and said the same thing. I lean down and touch my lips to her. "You like my muscles. You like when I spin you like that."

"Maybe." She pouts against my mouth, and I nip at her plump bottom lip. Her eyes darken.

"Christ, you're hot."

"You have a condom this time, right?"

"Fuck yeah." I made sure of that. I pull three condoms out of my pocket.

Her eyes widen. "Whoa."

I toss them onto the table next to her bed, and reach behind my neck to pull my sweater off over my head.

Her gaze tracks back from the condoms to me, sliding over my chest and abs, and I fucking love the look on her face . . . awe and admiration. My dick likes it too, swelling even more. And when Ella reaches out and strokes that bulge through my jeans, I just about fucking lose it and come in my pants. "Jesus," I say hoarsely, grabbing her hand. "Careful, babe."

She bites her lip and looks at me through her eyelashes. So sexy. "Get your jeans off, then," she whispers, "if you're that close."

I'm so close I'm leaking. I slide off the bed to remove my jeans, pushing everything else off too, and then I stretch out beside her, propping my head on one hand, elbow in the mattress. My other hand traces the outline of her bra, then her thong. "Show me those pretty tits."

She bites her lip again. "You think they're pretty?"

The hint of uncertainty makes my chest swell. "Christ, yeah. They're goddamn perfection."

She opens the front fastening of the bra, which I didn't know was there, and I ease the cups aside to reveal the tempting round flesh. Her nipples are tight little points, just asking to be sucked. My mouth waters and I lean over to take one into my mouth.

Soft pleasure sounds spill from her lips as she arches her back. I can tell how much she likes that and I want to give her more. I tease the other nipple with my fingers, then slide my hand down her flat belly to her panties. I cup my hand over her pussy, marveling at how tiny she is compared to my big paw. I hold her there, feeling the damp, pulsing heat. She lifts into my touch with another moan.

I tug her nipple with my lips, suck harder, and release it, then study the nub. "Perfect," I breathe. I suck the other nipple too, gently rubbing her pussy.

"God . . . please . . ."

"Just call me Ben."

She chokes on a laugh and turns her face into the pillow. "That was so bad."

I grin. "I know. Sorry." I lick her nipple, slide my tongue up over her collarbone, and then kiss her mouth. We both make hungry noises as we kiss, my hand still playing between her legs.

I can't stand it anymore. "Need to be inside you," I gasp. I slap a hand over to the table and find one of the packets. As I go up on my knees to roll it on, she pushes her bra off her arms and shimmies her panties down her hips, watching me with avid eyes. That only makes my dick ache more.

She reaches for me as I move over her, spreading her legs, and as I fit myself between them it feels so right. A flawless fit. I watch her face as I stroke the head of my dick through her slickness. Her eyelids grow heavy and her lips part. Her fingers curl around my shoulders. "You want this, baby?"

"Yes. Give it to me . . . oh yeah."

Pleasure rockets through me at the sensation of her tight body clutching me. I ease into her, deeper, deeper still, until we're both gasping, pressed tight to each other.

"Oh wow." Her fingers dig into my back. "Oh God, that feels good. Ben . . ." She rocks against me, asking for it, and I slide out and back in. I stretch out over her to bury my face in the side of her neck, breathing in the light flowery scent of her. She grabs my back and squeezes me with her thighs, which are slender but strong.

My ass clenches as I fuck her, heat washing through me, my cock tunneling in and out. My balls tighten, and the base of my spine aches.

"Oh . . . oh . . ."

"Good, baby?" I lick her throat.

"Um . . . I think . . . I'm burning."

"Yeah . . . me too."

"No, I'm really burning." Her hands come to my chest and push as she tries to shove me off her. "Jesus, Ben, my vagina is burning! Something's wrong! Ow!"

Stunned and dazed, I pull out and roll off her, blinking at her in confusion. What the fuck?

Chapter 17

Ella

My lady parts are burning, and not in a good way. I clap my hands over my crotch and let out a little scream.

"What's wrong?" Ben knifes up to sit and grabs my hands. "What the hell? What's wrong, El?"

I writhe. "Burning," I whimper. "Your cock is too much for me."

He makes a strangled noise. "We did this before, and it was fine. I don't get it."

"Me either. Oh, ow . . ."

"Is it that bad? Do you need to go to the hospital? What's happening?"

"I don't know!"

My eyes are squeezed shut. I feel Ben moving on the bed. I hear the crinkle of the condom wrapper.

"Oh, for fuck's sake."

"What?" I crack open one eye.

He holds up the wrapper. "It's a warming condom."

I squint at it. "Warming?"

"It has some kind of lube on it. It's supposed to, uh, give you more pleasure."

"My vagina is on fire!"

"Uh, I don't think it can be that bad, El," he says soothingly. "Let me see . . ."

"You can't see the burning!"

"Shhh, baby, calm down. You must be sensitive or something . . . I'll go get a washcloth."

He climbs off the bed, and his cock is still hard but has a forlorn appearance. "I'm sorry," I whimper.

"Not your fault. I'm gonna kill someone, though." He stalks out the bathroom and returns with a wet cloth and a towel. "Here. Let me wash you."

"Oh my God, this is embarrassing."

"It's okay." He makes more soothing noises as I reluctantly part my thighs and let him dab at me with the cloth.

"Oh . . . oh that feels better already."

"Damn." He wipes me, then pats me dry with the towel. "Okay, baby?"

"Yes." I sigh. "I'm sorry. God. That killed the mood, didn't it?"

He falls to his back on the bed beside me. "Apparently not." He strokes his thick cock, now bare. My breath stalls in my chest. "For me, anyway."

"What the hell is a warming condom?"

He lifts his head. "Some asshole switched my condoms. I would never buy warming condoms. I'd be too afraid of something like this happening."

"Are you kidding? Who would do that?"

"Ha. I'd put money on Soupy. Maybe Rocket."

I blink at him. "Are you going to tell them about this?"

He meets my eyes and smiles slowly. "Nah. It'll torture them more wondering about it." One corner of his mouth deepens. "Maybe one day." Then his smile fades. "Seriously, are you okay?"

"Yes." I close my eyes briefly. "Maybe I overreacted a little. I'm sure they don't put enough . . . warming stuff . . . to actually burn you."

"That would be counterproductive to the goal of increasing the lady's pleasure."

I smile too. "I'm really sorry."

"I guess you don't want to try again?"

I think about it. I assess the state of my lady parts. They're still tingling, but it does feel kind of good . . . and Ben is so beautiful, his muscled body stretched out beside me, his hand fisted around his cock and slowly stroking. And his cock . . . my chest aches with want. "I want to . . . but not with one of those condoms."

"You still have some?" he asks hopefully.

"I do." I blow out a breath and hop off the bed.

I hand him one and he takes it and opens it. I watch breathlessly as he suits up. But he doesn't immediately climb on top of me. Instead he lays his hand on my stomach and leans over to kiss me.

"Might need a little more of this," he murmurs between slow tongue kisses. "To get you back in the mood."

"I think it's working." I love his tongue in my mouth, licking over my bottom lip, then his lips gliding over my jaw. He kisses his way down to my throat, licks my collarbone, and then, oh yes, he plumps up one breast with his hand and guides my nipple into his mouth.

A shudder works over my body as sensation shoots right to my pussy. That ache returns, that empty, needy throb. Ben takes his time, building me back up to a hot glow of anticipation. When his fingers dip between my thighs, I'm so wet.

"There we go," he murmurs, licking between my breasts. "All nice and wet for me."

"Please."

"Let's try this again."

He moves over me, and once more our bodies join, mine accepting the thickness of his, closing around him. I pull him deeper, my hands on his ass, and his breath teases my ear as he moves in and out, slow at first. He's taking care with me, and that makes my heart flutter. "Harder," I whisper. "I'm okay."

"Okay, good." His hips rock faster, pumping deeper, our bodies slapping together. My clit is straining, and I tilt my hips, seeking more pressure on the right spot . . . there. "Ah." It doesn't take much . . . as he bears down on me, it's exactly what I need, his thick shaft stroking nerve endings inside me and his pelvis bumping my clit. I cry out as heat spirals up inside me in an ever-tightening coil, higher, higher . . . to a sharp crest of ecstasy. I tighten my arms and legs around his body and hold on tight as I ride the swells, pleasure pouring through me.

"Fuck yeah," he mutters, pounding faster. The agonized, tortured groans in his throat make me hold him tighter. I want this to be good for him, I want him to feel as good as I do. I slide my fingers into his hair and grip it, the fingernails of my other hand digging into his ass. *"Fuck, yeah."* He roars his release, so masculine and aggressive it thrills me to my core. "Ella. *Ella.*"

"I'm here. Come inside me . . . I love that . . ." I kiss his shoulder, openmouthed and lingering as he shudders against me.

I stroke his back in soothing gestures, savoring every ridge and muscle. He's amazing . . . but not just because of his body, which is truly a work of art. He's aggressive and strong and physical, and I love that, but he's also tender. Caring. Thoughtful.

The corners of my eyes sting with unexpected tears. Oh Jesus. I can't start crying.

Eventually, he lifts his head and gazes down at me. I hope he can't see the tears. His weight bears me into the mattress, and he props himself on his elbows to take some of it off me, even though it feels so good. He smiles at me, and my heart turns over in my chest. "That was fucking crazy."

I blink. "Crazy good?"

He chuckles and smoothes some hair off my face. "I meant the little situation with the warming condom. Jesus." He shakes his head. "One day we'll laugh about it."

He makes it sound like we're a couple. Like we're going to be together long enough for "one day." And it's scary how much I like that.

I make myself smile back at him. "Yeah. I'm still not finding it super funny right now."

"You're beautiful."

"Oh." My breath whooshes out of me. "Thank you."

His gaze roams over my face. I probably have red cheeks and smudged mascara . . . but he's looking at me as if I am, in fact, beautiful.

"You cold?" He notices my shiver.

"A little."

"C'mon, then." He pulls back the covers and easily shifts me under them, then draws them back up over both of us. "We have a few minutes to catch our breath."

I sigh at the reminder that our time is limited, but snuggle into him.

He strokes my hair as we talk about this and that . . . the bus trip home, the assignment he was worried about getting done that he managed to finish late last night. I tell him about the picture my mom just posted on Facebook of Gracie sleeping with her head hanging off the couch, and how much I miss my pup. Then his phone starts ringing.

"It's just the alarm," he says. He rolls over and drops an arm off the side of the bed to feel around for his jeans. "I set it in case we were, uh, still occupied."

"You have to go."

"Yeah."

Our eyes meet. The air thickens around us, a dense blanket of regret surrounding us. I know he feels it too. He makes a face and touches my cheek. "Hey, Ella."

"Yeah?"

"Wanna be my girlfriend?"

I gaze back at him. Is that how it goes? Is that what he's supposed to say? I had a boyfriend in high school, but somehow we just kind of slid into the boyfriend/girlfriend thing.

"Do I have to convince you?" he asks, lips quirking. "Because I can. There are lots of reasons to date a hockey player."

I just stare at him.

"I have great hands," he says modestly. "I think you already know that."

I blink.

"Also I like to play rough. And you like that too."

My heart turns over in my chest.

"I can find the opening and get it in," he continues. "And I can go hard for sixty minutes and still be ready for overtime."

I can't stop the laugh that climbs from my belly. "Ben." I lean into him helplessly. "What will people think?"

He pulls back and frowns. "What do you mean?"

"Your friends . . . they all know me . . . they know . . ." The words clog up in my throat. "I know what people say about me."

His face darkens like a thunderstorm, his eyes flashing. "What. The. Fuck."

"Don't. You were the same."

His eyes squeeze shut as if he's in pain. For a long moment he's silent. "Ella."

I wait.

"I admit I judged you. You already know that, and you judged me too."

I nod, my throat aching.

"That doesn't matter. I know you now . . . I know how funny you are, how smart you are . . . I know that soft side you keep hidden. I know you've been through some rough shit and you're working on it. You were dealing with it the best you could. I told you before, I've done the same things you have . . . partied, drank, had sex. So what?"

"You know there's a double standard."

He swallows, but his steady gaze holds mine. "Okay, yeah. There is. We can't change the world, but maybe we don't have to. Though if anyone wants to say anything like that about you to my face . . . they'll regret it."

"Don't say things like that." I wrap my hands around his biceps. "I don't want you to get in trouble like Jacob did, fighting because of me."

"I'd do it." His jaw tightens.

My heart swells up so huge I can hardly breathe. "You're crazy," I whisper.

"Maybe." He relaxes a little. "Dammit, I have to go. Look." He tilts my chin up with the backs of his fingers. "Let's just go with it. Okay?"

Those doubts creep back. I have feelings for this guy . . . but the last thing I want is to fall in love with someone. Look what happened the last time I thought I loved someone—it turned into a tragedy. I thought I loved Brendan, but I was so selfish and oblivious, I didn't even know he had feelings for my best friend, and I didn't know how much he was suffering. Obviously I'm not capable of truly loving someone.

But I look at Ben with his strong jaw and warm eyes and hear the things he's saying to me, and I want to be with him. So I whisper, "Okay."

"No more sneaking around."

"Okay."

"It's Groundhog Day."

I smile at Ben the next evening when he shows up at my place with a bag of Skittles, my favorite candy. "Yes. Yes, it is. Six more weeks of winter."

"No, the movie. *Groundhog Day*. That's what we're gonna watch."

"I think that movie's older than I am." I lead the way to the living room.

"You gotta watch it on Groundhog Day."

"If you say so."

"I sense a lack of enthusiasm."

"I can't imagine what gave me away." But I grin at him, and the smile he beams back makes my toes curl.

We get the movie started and settle onto the couch together. He pulls me into his arms, and I curl my legs up and cuddle in. This is nice. And the movie's actually pretty funny.

"Is there a day in your life you'd like to live over and over again?" he asks me when the movie's over.

"I don't know." I think about it. I've had some crappy days in the last while. But I've had some pretty good days too. "No. I wouldn't want to live the same day over and over again, no matter how good it was."

"Huh. That's what I think too."

He nuzzles my face, tugs my hair to pull my head up, and I meet his eyes. Heat builds between us. It's been there, simmering on low all evening, but all I have to do lately is think about Ben to get turned on, and here he is, right next to me, big and warm and smiling at me with sexy hunger. My head goes a little light, and lust curls low in my belly.

He leans in to kiss me, and I slide my hands around his neck and hold on while he makes the world spin, his mouth on mine, his tongue licking inside, his hands touching me everywhere. My heart is racing, my body is fever hot. He pulls me closer still, slipping his hands under my loose top to find skin, and I'm supersensitized, electricity jolting through me. I could just melt right here in his arms.

I want to touch him too, so I explore the texture of his hair, the silky length on top and the short neat hair at his nape. His skin there is soft and I glide my fingertips under the collar of his shirt, tracing over the bulky muscle to the corner of his shoulder. I need one more button open, so I work at that while he kisses my cheek and the side of my neck. A shivery sensation shimmers down my spine. Then I've got his shirt open more, and I can rub my palm over his pec.

A groan rumbles in his throat. I think he likes that. I like it too, so I rub again, over his nipple. This reminds me of that conversation we had right here in this room, when we got talking about nipple play. I taunted him to confess whether he liked it or not . . . and he'd said he did. So I tweak his nipple again, fascinated with the tightness of it.

"Christ." He licks my throat, his body vibrating.

"You like that," I remind him, rubbing his chest again. "You admitted it."

"It's making my dick about to burst out of my jeans." He gives my skin a tiny suck that makes me shudder.

"Hey, don't put marks on me."

He nearly growls. "I want to. Then everyone will know you're mine."

"That's kind of . . . Neanderthal." I should be appalled. Instead, I'm excited.

"Not gonna do it," he mumbles. "Just saying . . . I want to."

Since he mentioned his junk, I reach down to check it out. Yep, hard as a hockey stick. Probably bigger. I mean, not longer but thicker . . . Now I'm the one who's moaning. Ben lifts his hips into my touch.

"Babe," he groans. "I'm dying here."

"Yeah?"

"Fuck yeah . . ."

I rub his erection again through his jeans. I love the feel of it, so huge and hard under the denim. "Do you want to put it in my mouth?"

"Christ! Ella . . ."

"I'd like that," I whisper, kissing his stubbled jaw. "I've wanted to do that since the first time we were together."

He makes a choked noise of anguish.

"Oh hey."

We leap apart at Skylar's voice, and the overhead light in the room blares on. I blink across at Skylar and Jacob, standing in the entrance to the living room, both of them smirking.

I told Skylar last night about Ben and me, so it's not like she's caught us in a secret. Apparently, either Ben or Skylar has told Jacob, because he doesn't look surprised either.

"Sorry to interrupt." Skylar advances into the room while she takes off her jacket. She tosses it over the back of a chair.

"No, you're not." Ben narrows his eyes at Jacob.

Jacob shrugs and sprawls in one of our armchairs.

Ben tugs at his jeans and I know he's in pain. I suck my bottom lip and widen my eyes at him. He shakes his head, but the corners of his mouth twitch.

This guy . . . We've been interrupted in the middle of things how many times now . . . three? That first night we were making out in that bedroom and those girls stormed in, one of them crying. Yesterday afternoon, with the warming condom incident. Just now. And even though the buttons on his jeans are in danger of flying off, he's still got a sense of humor about it.

"Where were you guys?" I ask Skylar.

"Library. Studying."

Guilt gives me a little smack on the back of the head. *I should be* studying. What happened to my big plan of getting my grades back up, making up with Skylar, and staying away from boys and booze? How quickly I've abandoned it for one hot guy.

"Hey!" Skylar says. "We got good news today!"

"What?"

"The administration has agreed to go forward with the sexual awareness program for athletes."

"Oh, that's great news!"

"Yes! So we're going to be working on a plan to roll it out to all the athletic departments starting in September."

Ben leans over to high-five Jacob.

Everyone else chatters on while I sink into my own thoughts. A few minutes later, Ben whispers in my ear, "What's wrong, gorgeous?"

I shape my lips into a smile. "Nothing."

"Yeah, bullshit. Wanna go upstairs?"

"Horndog."

"I meant to talk."

I give him a look up through my eyelashes.

He grins. "Okay, I'll own the horndog label. But seriously . . . you okay?"

"Of course."

I see the doubt in his eyes, but I smile and lay my palm on his cheek.

"Jesus," Jacob says. "Don't mind us over here."

We both look at Skylar and Jacob, Skylar now on his lap, but despite his words, neither of them looks annoyed. The happy look on Skylar's face actually scares the shit out of me. She's making this into more than it is. More than it can be. I need to warn her.

A panicky feeling flutters in my chest. I thought I could do this. Now I'm not so sure.

Chapter 18

Ben

I want that blow job.

That's not what motivates me to make sure Ella's okay. Seriously, she got so quiet suddenly and I didn't know what was going on with her. Girls are a mystery sometimes, and I'm not one to just let it brew. I'd rather know what twisted shit is happening in her brain so we can deal with it.

So when we finally get upstairs alone in her room and she starts unbuckling my belt, I set my hands on hers and stop her.

Yeah, it kills me. But I'm a hockey player. I'm tough.

And Ella has a history of using sex to avoid dealing with her feelings. So I gently remove her hands but keep hold of them. "Tell me what was going on for you down there," I say.

"What do you mean?"

"Don't play games, El. Please. I'm just a guy. I'm not smart enough to figure women out unless you come right out and tell me what's bugging you."

She gives me a lopsided smile. "You are so smart."

"Babe." I set my hands on her hips and pull her against me.

"Okay." She sighs. "I had goals for this semester . . . because I'm on probation. Stay out of trouble so my parents or my brothers don't come to take me home and lock me away."

I smile.

"Get my grades on track. And make up with Skylar."

"You're doing all those things. So what's the problem?"

She gazes at me, and I can see the wheels turning in her pretty head. Then her face relaxes. "You're right," she finally whispers. "I guess I am."

"Of course I'm right." I puff out my chest.

She drops her forehead to said chest. "God, you're so cocky."

"You love that about me. Admit it. And . . . you love my cock. Remember . . . ?"

She chokes on a laugh. "Actually, I kinda do."

"Okay now?"

"Yeah." She lifts her head. "I'm okay." She goes on her toes and kisses me. It's a sweet kiss, a brush of her mouth over mine, but that doesn't last long. I wrap an arm around her and bend her backward as I take her mouth in a long, deep kiss that reaches right down to my balls. She feels so damn good in my arms, slender but strong, soft in some places yet firm in others. She links her arms around my neck and holds on tight as I devour her mouth.

"Mmm." She makes a happy sound in her throat. Her head falls back, and I kiss her neck, then she's sliding out of my grip and going to her knees on the floor.

"Christ." I say the word on a groan. "Ella . . ."

I expect her to attack my belt again, but she pauses and rubs her cheek against my straining dick. "Nice," she murmurs. Then she undoes my belt and lowers my zipper. The head of my cock is poking up out of my boxers, and she makes an appreciative little noise at seeing that. She tugs down the elastic and my dick springs up eagerly.

Heat rushes through my body, and I drop my gaze to watch her. Veins pulse along my shaft, and the engorged crest throbs. Her fingers curl around me, soft and delicate compared to my aggressive, male flesh. My eyes flick to her face, taking in her parted lips and heavy eyelids as she studies me.

"Like what you see, baby?" My voice is sandpaper rough.

"Oh yeah. You know I do." She rubs her thumb over the wet tip.

My balls are tight at the root, aching with pressure. Damn, I need to come. She's testing my patience, stroking me. Sensation sizzles up my spine, shorting out a few brain cells. I plant my feet a little wider, more firmly into the floor, and let her play. It's fucking heaven.

Finally, her little tongue comes out to lick. She swirls it over the head, and it's like a jolt of electricity. I shudder and bury my hands in her silky hair. She keeps licking, sliding her tongue up and down and around, getting me wet all over.

"Goddamn," I grunt.

I can see her smile just before she opens her mouth to take me in. I swallow the shout that rises in my throat. Her lips tighten around me and slide up and down easily, and electricity zaps every nerve ending in my body. My hands want to tighten on her head and hold her so I can fuck her mouth, but I ease the pressure and just guide her, letting her set the pace, letting her go as deep as she can . . . and fuuuuuuck, she takes me deep.

"Holy hell, Ella." My eyes fall closed, much as I love the visual, and my head drops back as I give myself over to sensation. My thighs quake as tension builds, tightening my ass cheeks. My heart is racing as her clinging mouth strokes me to heaven. My skin tingles everywhere.

Then she pulls off, panting. I force my eyes open to look down and watch her lift my stiff cock so she can tease my balls with that agile little tongue. She makes little pleasure noises that hit me straight in the chest. I fucking *love* it that she loves this so much. "Christ," I mutter. Pleasure escalates. My blood runs hot and fast through my veins. A groan rumbles up my chest and my fingers tighten in her hair. "I'm close, El." I tug her hair gently. "Really close."

"Okay, good." And she takes me inside again.

Okay. Okay, she's really going to do this. I'm going to come in her mouth. Her tongue slides over me, and then my balls erupt, white hot ecstasy shooting out of me, fiery sensation racing up my spine. I make embarrassing noises as she sucks me, finishing me off. "Never," I groan. "Christ, never . . ."

My knees go weak and when she lets me slide from her mouth with one last tender lick, I drop to the floor in front of her, wrap my arms around her, and crush her to me. I can't stop muttering curses, nearly delirious with bliss.

"Goddamn." I squeeze her tighter. "Your mouth . . . holy shit."

I feel her smile against my neck, her fingers threading through my hair. "That was good?"

"That was fucking fantastic." I nudge at her face until our mouths meet in a kiss. "Babe. I can barely speak."

"Good." She strokes my cheek.

"Don't worry. As soon as I get the strength back in my legs, I'm gonna lick your sweet pussy so you get yours too."

"I certainly hope so."

I choke on a laugh. "And you're gonna show me how flexible you are."

I'm cursing our goddamn schedule that has us out of town again this weekend, this time to Niagara. That's not like me. I love hockey. I live for hockey. I've set myself some big goals, and I'm determined to achieve them.

But dammit, I miss Ella.

It's probably just all the sex. Because we've been having it. A lot.

We pull off two wins this time. Flash, Franco, and I have some good chemistry happening with our line, and we're hot on the power play Saturday night, with three power play goals, one by each of us. Franco and Flash are both great net guys, with good strong sticks down low, and having my right-handed shot out there gives us added strength with my one-timers. Flash and Franco both go to the net hard, and Flash especially creates a lot of turnovers. We feed off one another and it's great.

The mood on the bus on the way home is definitely upbeat. We're firmly in fourth place, with only eight more games in the season. We have a right to be optimistic, but we can't take anything for granted.

Ella and I see as much of each other as we can during the next week.

For a change, she's the sensible one, who insists we spend time studying before we spend time . . . er, studying each other.

"I've learned from you," she explains. "It feels so much better to get the work done and then relax and have fun. Then you don't have that homework at the back of your mind."

As we leave the library one evening, she reminds me, "February break next week."

"Lots of people are going away. Like, to Cancún or Miami Beach. That would be nice." I sigh as I sling my arm around her shoulders.

"It *would* be nice." She sighs wistfully too.

"I like picturing you on a beach in a bikini."

"Let's go, then."

"Can't. We have games Friday and Saturday and then next weekend too."

"Geez. Seriously? You don't get a break?"

"It's a break from classes. And next weekend is away."

"Boo."

"But we'll have all next week . . . to study." I leer at her.

She laughs. "Yeah, we'll be studying."

"Hey, you know what I read the other day?"

"What?"

"Sex can help you do better on exams."

She nudges me with her shoulder as we approach my car. "Shut up."

"No, really. They had a lot of valid points. Like, if you get out all your sexual energies, you can focus better on studying."

"Uh-huh."

"It makes sense to me. Also, sex apparently strengthens your immune system, and you wouldn't want to get sick right before midterms."

"No." She smiles at me as I open the car door for her. "I definitely wouldn't."

Pretty sure I'm convincing her. Although, honestly, she loves to fuck as much as I do, so it's not exactly a hard sell. Still . . . "Female orgasms produce some hormone that's been linked to increases in memory and brain functions."

"Win-win!" She high-fives me and then slides into the car.

"That's my girl." I shut the door and hurry around to get in my side.

"My parents want me to go home for the break," she says when I get in.

Huh. I start the car. "Will you?"

"I don't want to. But if I don't, they'll worry."

I don't know what to say. I don't want her to leave, but that's selfish. She should see her family and let them know she's fine.

As we're driving, an ad for a jewelry store comes on the radio, talking about a Valentine's Day sale. I have to say, the idea of Valentine's Day makes my nuts shrivel. Sure, Ella's my girlfriend now . . . for nearly two whole weeks. That's not exactly a lot of time to get serious. It's not enough time to go buy her a diamond necklace. What the fuck am I supposed to do?

"Valentine's Day," Ella remarks. "What a phony holiday that is."

"Yeah?"

"Oh yeah. I'll just tell you right now I don't believe in it. It's a mass-produced money venture, created by corporations. It shames individuals and celebrates couples—and why? There's nothing wrong with not being part of a couple."

"Uh-huh."

"I hate the fake attention and forced affections. It's just another day of the week. Really, if you care about someone you don't need a special holiday to show it—you should show it every day of the week." She gives a little laugh. "Okay, rant over. Sorry."

"Well, it's good to know how you feel about that." Because I probably would have screwed up by buying her a card and some roses or some sappy shit like that.

"Anyway, maybe I could go home next weekend when you have your road trip," she says, resuming our other conversation.

I nod. "Yeah."

"I'm sure if I tell them I need the week to study for midterms they'll understand."

Despite our joking around, we really do plan to study next week. I'll still have to work out and practice, but not having classes will really help.

"She doesn't believe in Valentine's Day."

The other guys stare at me in the dressing room after our practice the next day. Butch shakes his head. "No, no, no. Don't believe that."

I frown. "Why not?"

"Girls, they always say that," he says with his French accent. "But it's not true. They want to be wined and dined and pampered. They want the romance."

I slide a questioning glance at Flash to see what he thinks. He shrugs.

Now I'm even more fucking terrified. What if Ella was just feeding me that shit to take the pressure off me, and she really does want me to do something?

Tonight she's coming to our game for the first time as my girlfriend. That shouldn't really matter to me, but it does. It gives me an extra reason to want to play well. As if I don't have enough pressure.

"I think Butch is right," Danny says. "Krystal told me last year not to do anything special for Valentine's Day. Neither of us could afford a fancy dinner out. So I didn't do anything, and she ended up crying."

"Jesus." Women. What a fucking mystery. "I don't think Ella's like that."

Or is she? She does try to give off that cool-chick vibe, but she rescues lost dogs and cries over cellphone commercials and buys treats for the little ballerinas she teaches. Does she really believe all that stuff she said?

"I'm fucked," I groan. "Whatever I do. Or don't do." I look at Flash again. "What are you doing for Skylar?"

"We're going to a movie," he says. "I'll buy her some Twizzlers."

He thinks that'll do it? Huh.

"If she said she doesn't believe in it, I think you should believe her," Soupy says. "But it doesn't hurt to make some kind of small gesture."

I think about this as we head home to get some food. Ella said if you care about someone you should show them every day, not just one day. That makes sense to me; what difference does the date make? Maybe that's where guys fall down, though. Maybe we don't show enough that we care every other day, and that's why there *has* to be a special day for love.

Not that Ella and I are in love.

I mean, I like her a lot. I care about her.

My gut knots up and I have to choke down the last of the chicken breast on my plate. *Relax, dude. You can't be like this right before a game. Gotta eat healthy and rest up.*

It's not like we're talking about marriage or something. Just a fucking sappy holiday.

As I drift off to sleep that night, I start thinking about Valentine's Day again, goddammit. This is ridiculous. If having a girlfriend is going to make me lose my mind like this, maybe it's not such a good idea.

Chapter 19

Ella

"I'm ashamed that I blamed Skylar," I tell Frances. "Why do people think that way? That it's the victim's fault?"

Frances gives a sad smile. "I could talk for an hour on that topic. Let's see if I can sum up some thoughts about that. A couple of years ago there was an incident here at Bayard where a football player left the team because of mistreatment by other players. Basically, he was being hazed, or bullied."

I nod; I've heard this story.

"There were a lot of people who felt that he must have contributed to the bullying in some way. So it's not just rape victims who get blamed."

"But why is that?"

"There's been significant research about blaming victims, but in a nutshell, it's about feeling in control. If the victim did something that caused the rape, then that rape could have been prevented. It's why victims even blame themselves."

I remember Skylar saying she should have fought harder . . .

"It's not just about avoiding responsibility, it's also about avoiding *vulnerability*. Victims threaten our sense that the world is a safe place, where good things happen to good people and bad things happen to bad people. When bad things happen to *good* people, it makes us feel like *no one* is safe. It could happen to us."

I nod.

"Societal misogyny and stereotypes about male and female sexuality don't help," she continues. "In fact, they contribute to rape itself."

I think about what she's just said. And she's right. "So I blamed Skylar for what happened, because if it could happen to her, it could happen to anyone. It could happen to me." I pause. "You know, maybe we should all just stop asking what victims do to deserve it and start asking what allows someone to *do* such a thing. Addressing that would be a lot more effective than worrying about what women are wearing or whether she asked for it or whether she fought hard enough." I pause. "I'm so proud of Skylar for the things she's doing in that regard."

Even though I feel terrible about it, now that I understand that this is a common reaction and the reasons why, it lifts some of my guilt. "I know how horrible she feels about how she handled things . . . like me, she wishes she'd done things differently. We're both going to carry around that guilt for the rest of our lives."

"We've talked about that before," Frances says gently. "That ultimately it was Brendan's decision."

"I know. I do know it. I just feel horrible that he was so alone and felt so hopeless that he would do it. But . . . he'd done something awful, to someone he cared about. I know from his emails that he was upset, but I'll never know if it was because he knew he'd hurt his friend, or because he was worried about what would happen to him if she reported it to the police."

"This week your homework is to sit down and talk to Skylar."

I gaze back at Frances. "I have talked to Skylar."

"Does she know why you told her about Jacob's past?"

I wince. "I guess I haven't really talked to her about that."

"Have you told her that you blamed her for Brendan's death?"

I close my eyes. "No."

"You also were angry at her and jealous because Brendan loved her and not you."

"Yes. I think she knows that."

"Most important . . . have you told her that you don't blame her anymore?"

I suck on my bottom lip. "No," I whisper. "I haven't told her that."

"If one of your goals is to repair your friendship with her, you two need to have an honest conversation about everything that happened. I know it won't be easy, but unless you do that and really get to the heart of these issues, your friendship will be on a much more superficial level."

I might be okay with that.

No. I'm not serious. Yes, it will be hard to talk about these things. Yes, it will be hard to confess I'm a terrible person. No, no, I can't think like that. *I'm not a terrible person.*

I sigh. This is a slow process, but my goal was to make things better between us, and if this is what I have to do, I'll do it.

Skylar should be at home right now. I know she doesn't work today, and Jacob and Ben are both at practice. If I go home right now, we can probably have that talk. Maybe it's not the best time, but I have a feeling there's never going to be a time that feels good to do this—so I might as well just get it done.

I trudge up the stairs at home and poke my head into Skylar's room. She's on her bed, knees bent, with one leg crossed over the other knee, foot tapping in the air to the beat of music I can't hear. She's wearing her earbuds, listening to something and reading a magazine.

I step in and wave, catching her attention. She smiles and tugs the earbuds out. "Hey! How's it going?"

"Okay. Just came from my session with Frances."

"Oh yeah." She sits upright. "How was it?"

"She gave me homework," I explain. "Do you have time now to talk?"

Skylar's forehead creases, but she nods. "Of course."

"I guess it's part of my healing process," I say. "I'm supposed to be honest with you about how I felt after I found out what happened between you and Brendan."

She nods somberly.

I reiterate the things I told Frances this afternoon—my feelings of jealousy, betrayal, and blame. My victim blaming. Skylar listens and doesn't say anything, letting me word vomit until I run out. I finish by telling her, "I don't blame you anymore, Sky."

She nods again.

"The other thing you need to know is why I told you about Jacob's past."

Her face goes wary. "Okay."

"I really didn't want to hurt you. That wasn't my intent. I was worried that you were hanging out with a guy who might not be so nice."

"I wondered if you were jealous of me and Jacob," she says quietly.

"No." I give my head an emphatic shake. "Frances asked me that too, and I thought long and hard about it. I wasn't jealous of you and Jacob. I wish I'd handled it differently, but I wasn't in a good place then . . . *we* weren't in a good place then. I feel horrible that it hurt you. I'm sorry, Sky."

"Okay. Thank you." She pauses. "So . . . you said you don't blame me anymore for Brendan's death . . . does that mean you don't blame yourself?"

I suck in a long breath. "I'm getting there. But I'll always feel guilty. I'll always feel like I let him down."

"Yeah." She nods, her lips downturned. "Me too."

"Oh, Sky. He let *you* down. He betrayed your friendship and trust in the worst way."

Our eyes meet in shared understanding. My nose stings, and I press my fingers to it to stop the tears. This is something that will forever bind Skylar and me together . . . something that we let drive us apart in the past. Now I see Frances's wisdom, and I know that my friendship with Skylar is stronger and deeper than it ever has been.

I reach out to her, and she leans into my hug. "We're going to be okay," she whispers. "We *are* okay."

"Yes. We are."

Sunday morning, my phone starts buzzing. Ben and I are both sound asleep and struggle to rouse ourselves. I drag myself out of bed to grab my phone from the desk. I peer at it. "Oh my God."

"What?"

"My parents. They're here."

"What?"

I look over at Ben, my eyes popping wide, my thoughts scrambling. "They're here! My mom just texted that they're out front."

"Uh . . ." He glances wildly around. "There's not really a tree outside your window, is there?"

"Nope."

"Okay. Well. I'll just hide up here, then."

I give him a doubtful look. "That might work."

I quickly pull on a pair of sweatpants, add a long-sleeved tee, then hurry to the door. "Just hang here," I whisper. "I'll come back as soon as I can."

He falls back into the pillows and stares at the ceiling as I leave the room.

I run downstairs and open the front door. "Hi!"

Mom and Dad come in. "Surprise, honey!" Mom cries, hugging me. "Were you asleep?"

"Um, yeah, I was." I close the door against the chilly morning air and hug my dad too. "It's okay, though." My plans to sleep in late with Ben and have lazy Sunday morning sex and maybe even breakfast in bed can't compare to visiting with my parents . . . *not*.

"We haven't been to visit you once this semester, so we thought we'd drive up for the day. Take you out for brunch." Mom hesitates. "Maybe get to meet this boy you're seeing . . ."

Aha. That's what this is about. I swallow my sigh. I've mentioned Ben a couple of times when we've talked on the phone, and Mom's been full of questions about him. Of course they want to meet him.

For a moment, I consider telling them he's upstairs in my bed, but I have a feeling that might not go over well. I'd kind of enjoy shocking them, though.

Nah, I can't do that. "Well, I can call him and see. Come in, have a seat. I'll go change and freshen up. Um . . . would you like some coffee?"

"I'll make us some," Mom says, heading to the kitchen. She's hardly ever been here but apparently feels quite comfortable.

I run upstairs. Ben is sound asleep, his head buried in a pillow. I give his ass a swat through the covers, and he jerks awake. "Whaaaa . . ."

"They want to take me out for brunch," I whisper. "They're waiting while I get ready."

He blinks and rubs his eyes. "Okay. When you're gone, I can leave."

"They want you to come with us."

"They know I'm here?"

"No! I said I'd call you and see if you could join us."

He scrubs his hands over his face, sitting up now. He blinks rapidly. Tension lifts his shoulders. Clearly he's not happy about this. After a long pause during which I can see he's trying to figure out what to say, he mumbles, "Um, okay."

"I'll get ready and go with them," I whisper, stripping off my clothes.

Ben's not happy, but his gaze still tracks my movements, taking in my nakedness. "I guess this could work." He yawns as he watches me hustle around the room, finding a pair of leggings and a sweater to change into.

I run into the bathroom for a few minutes to brush my teeth and my hair, then return and start putting on makeup. In the mirror I catch his reflection as he watches me and he's smirking. "What?"

"You're cute. Does opening your mouth like that help?"

I snap my mouth shut and frown. "I don't know why I do that." I screw the cap back on the tube and drop it. "Okay." I hop over to the bed and kiss him. "We're going to Taste of Heaven. See you there in a bit." He gropes my ass as I turn to leave, and I pause to smile uncertainly at him. "You're sure you're okay with meeting them?"

"Yeah."

I'm not positive I believe him.

I shut the door on my bedroom and rejoin my parents. They're in the kitchen drinking coffee, and a few minutes later we leave through the front door. We climb into their car and I direct Dad to the diner.

We're seated in a booth for four. Taisha pours us coffee and we look at the menus, but we tell her that we'll wait for Ben to arrive before we order. So we chat about my classes and the kids I teach ballet to and what's new back in Syracuse.

I check my cellphone a couple of times, because it's taking Ben a while to get here. What the hell is he doing? But he hasn't texted to say he's not coming. Finally, he walks in. I wave at him and he strides toward us.

I shake my head. He must have gone home—he's dressed in his usual stylish clothes, a pair of narrow tan pants, a plaid shirt, expensive brogue shoes, and his hair is perfect. I guess he didn't want to wear the sweatpants and hoodie he came to my place in last night. I love seeing him dressed in sweats because I know it means he's comfortable enough with me that he can just be himself.

I give him a crooked smile as he sets his hand on my shoulder and squeezes. "You look good," I murmur. I meet his eyes, and he knows what I'm saying.

I introduce him to my parents, and he shakes their hands. "My mom, Jennifer, and my dad, Mike. This is Ben."

"So nice to meet you, Ben." Mom smiles at him. Dad does not, assessing Ben with stern eyes and a set jaw. When he shakes Ben's hand, I can see Ben almost wince. Eeep.

"So, Ben. You play hockey," Dad says.

"I do." He smiles at Dad over his menu.

"Dad's a Sabres fan," I tell Ben.

"Me too," he says. "I grew up in Buffalo. They've had a rough couple of years."

This opens up a conversation that continues until the waitress approaches to take our orders. Mom and I kind of make faces at each other about all the hockey talk. Oh well.

"Waffles?" I murmur to Ben. I know his mad love for them.

"Yeah."

"I'll have the ham and asparagus crepes," I tell Taisha.

She takes our menus, and I pick up the cup of coffee in front of me.

"Ella says you're pretty serious about your hockey. Plan to play in the

NHL." Dad directs the conversation back to Ben and hockey. I swallow a sigh.

"Yes. I do." Ben lifts his chin. "Right now I'm listed number nineteen on the ISS Top 30 prospects for the NHL draft."

I reach over and squeeze his thigh, and he slants a smile at me.

"That's pretty impressive."

"Thank you. I've been working hard, especially this year."

Dad's not entirely happy about this.

"Ben's a great player," I jump in. "One of the best on the team."

I can tell Ben's uncomfortable, so I change the subject and tell Mom and Dad my plans for studying next week.

"You could study at home," Mom says a bit reproachfully. Then she glances at Ben. "But I guess I understand why you want to stay here."

Mom gets it. Dad's a little overprotective. As usual.

"I'm going to come home next weekend, Mom," I say. "I told you that."

"I know, but we wanted to see you, and we haven't visited you on campus at all this semester."

"We talk a couple of times a week."

Mom presses her lips together like she's struggling.

Our meals arrive, and we all dig in. Dad interrogates Ben about his courses, with fifty gazillion questions. I can see Ben's trying to be patient and pleasant, but he isn't exactly enjoying this. Damn.

"I'm working on a business degree," Ben tells Dad. "I'm not sure what will happen next year, but I hope I can finish it, even if it takes a little longer."

"So you have a backup plan if hockey doesn't work out?" Dad snaps.

I bite my lip.

"Well, I don't have a *definite* plan. I'm pretty determined that hockey is it for me. But sh . . . er, stuff happens. I could get injured with one wrong hit or shot blocked. And I got a full ride here at Bayard, so I kind of feel it would be a waste not to finish my degree. I thought a business degree would be practical."

"Bayard's business program is excellent."'

"Yeah. My courses are tough."

"What are your grades like?" Dad demands.

"Dad! That's a little personal."

"I have to have at least a C average to play on the team," Ben says, his jaw tight. "I can assure you my average is higher than that."

Dad narrows his eyes at Ben.

This isn't going so well.

One tense hour later, we're walking out of the diner.

"Let's go back to your place," Dad says to me. "I'll fix that broken cabinet door in your kitchen."

"You don't have to do that." We don't even notice it anymore.

"It's not a problem."

I look at Ben and smile brightly. "Coming?"

"I'd love to, but I have to go work out."

I lift an eyebrow. It's Sunday. It's supposed to be their day off from working out and practicing. "Oh. Okay, then."

He shakes hands with my parents, kisses my forehead, and waves goodbye. We watch him climb into his Mustang and drive away.

Dad crosses his arms. "Funny," he says. "There was a Mustang exactly like that parked on the street in front of your house when we got there this morning."

Chapter 20

Ben

"You hated my parents, didn't you?"

That evening Ella and I are on her couch watching TV and eating popcorn and Skittles. That was her Valentine's Day present—a bag of only red Skittles, her favorite color, that I picked out for her at the bulk food store. She loved it. And I really think she was surprised I did it, so I learned something about Ella—she means what she says, and says what she means. I like that. A lot.

"Um, babe . . . they hated *me*."

"No, they didn't!"

"I got the message from your dad, loud and clear," I state. "It's okay, I get it. They want the best for you. And they know that's not me."

She bolts straight up, nearly clipping my chin with her head. "What? That's bullshit."

I shrug. "That's what they think." I narrow my eyes at her. "What about your last boyfriend? Did they like him?"

She stares at me with a little notch between her eyebrows. "My last boyfriend was in high school. And yeah, maybe they didn't like him at first, but they came around after a while. He was a nice guy."

Doubtful that I'll be around long enough for them to grow to like me. "It's okay, El. They're entitled to their opinion. I'll probably never see them again, so it's not a big deal."

I'm lying. It pissed me off that her dad was judging me. I could tell exactly what he was thinking . . . college athlete on a full ride, taking advantage of the system, probably a guy who screws around a lot, one of those cocky, entitled jocks. And I'm a hockey player, which means I'm a goon—all brawn and no brains.

Ella has gone silent. "Right," she finally says. "I guess it doesn't really matter." Then she sighs. "They're so overprotective. It's annoying."

"Actually, I thought it was cute. Your mom obviously misses you."

"I guess."

"And they haven't been interfering in your life that much . . . that I've seen, anyway."

She falls silent, then says, "Ugh."

"What?"

"All this time I've been so resentful of how much they try to control my life, and really they haven't been lately . . . maybe they *are* letting me grow up. Maybe I've been childishly resenting their control when they just want the best for me."

"That's what most parents want for their kids, I guess. They love you."

"I love them too," she says slowly. "Which is one of the reasons I've been trying so hard to do things differently this semester. I don't want to hurt them or let them down by finding out I messed up my friendship with Skylar, failed courses, and gained a reputation on campus as a drunken, skanky whore."

"Jesus Christ, Ella."

"You know what I mean."

"You are hardly a drunken, skanky whore." I've been in a kind of pissy mood since that brunch this morning, even though the waffles were really good. "Would you stop with that?"

She gives me a long look, then takes more popcorn and turns back to the TV. "I'll stop if you will."

"What?"

"You don't think you're good enough for my parents to like. That's bullshit. So I'll stop beating myself up for mistakes I made if you'll stop beating yourself up for having a past that you had no control over. Stop being so hypersensitive about people judging you lacking."

My jaw tightens. I stare at the TV. Minutes go by, and I haven't heard a word of the show. I'm still replaying her words in my head. My knee starts bouncing.

Then she reaches out and sets her hand on my knee and gently squeezes. I feel the warmth of her through my jeans. I still my nervous bounce.

This girl . . . I'm not used to having someone in my life who knows me so well . . . knows everything about me . . . and likes me anyway.

I cover her hand with mine. She turns hers so we're palm to palm, and our fingers interlace. I bring her hand up to my lips and kiss it.

"Ben," she whispers.

I roll my head on the back of the couch and she turns toward me too. Our eyes meet. That shared connection draws out between us. "Okay," I say.

Her chin dips. "Okay what?"

"Okay, I'll stop beating myself up if you will."

Her smile is luminous, if a little shaky, her eyes full of emotion. "I know it's not that easy. But maybe we can help each other."

"Yeah." I set the bag of microwave popcorn aside and pull her onto my lap.

Our mouths meet in such a natural, perfect way. I love how she tastes. The feel of her lips, her tongue . . . her hands moving on my shoulders, then slipping beneath the collar of my shirt. So much feeling inside me . . . damn, I like this girl. I don't have words for it all, but I can show her how I feel.

I kiss her over and over, long, deep kisses, my hands sweeping her body, enjoying the curve of waist and hip, the slight weight of a breast, tangling in her silky hair. Heat flares low inside me, building hotter, my heart pounding.

She kisses me back too, burrowing closer to me like she can't get close enough. My dick is hard now, desire surging through me. My muscles tighten. I lift her so she's straddling me. Her fingers slide around the back of my neck, teasing the sensitive skin there. She leans to my ear and catches my earlobe between her lips, giving a little tug. Her breath tickles me, and shivers work down my spine, stopping at the base, just above my ass, where I have a sharp, insistent ache of need.

Her tits are pressed to my chest and I groan, tugging her hair. Her head goes back and I taste her throat with my tongue. Then she reaches between us and presses her palm to my hard-on.

"Fuck," I mutter. She caresses me firmly through my jeans. "Dying for you, El."

"Me too." She kisses my chin, nips at my jaw, then slides her tongue over my stubble. "Dying for this." She gives me another rub that just about has me coming in my jeans.

I want to rip open my fly and shove up inside her. My dick is throbbing, begging for release. "We should go upstairs."

"Yes." She slides to her knees on the floor, between my thighs, and every nerve ending lights up as she rubs her face over my dick. She squeezes my thigh, then uses her hand on my leg to brace herself as she stands. She takes my hands and steps backward, pulling me up.

I smile as I rise to my feet. Our eyes connect again with a hot crackle of energy and I let her lead me upstairs to her bedroom.

I love how adventurous she is. Anything I've suggested for us to try sexually, she's right there with me, and a couple of times she's the one who's instigated something new. She showed me how she can do splits, and it fueled my spank bank for . . . well, possibly for the rest of my life. She wasn't lying when she said she's flexible. Tonight I feel a kind of wildness inside me. Maybe because I felt so vulnerable and that's not an easy thing for me, I want to be in control and I want to be dirty.

"Know what I want?" I ask in a low voice when we're inside her room and the door is closed.

She flicks on the light beside her bed. "What?" I can see the flare of interest in her eyes.

"I want to sit here on the bed while you dance for me."

She blinks and her tongue comes out to sweep over her bottom lip. "Dance?"

"Yeah." I sit, hands on my thighs, my dick throbbing like a red-hot spike. "While you take your clothes off."

"A striptease," she says slowly. She tilts her head, then walks to her computer on the desk. She bends over, and my gaze drops immediately to her sweet ass. With a few clicks of the mouse, she starts some music. She pauses, still with her back to me, hands on the desk as the song begins . . . I don't recognize it at first, but when I do, I laugh out loud—"Pony" by Ginuwine.

I'm delighted as fuck.

I watch with a huge grin and an even bigger boner as she spins to face me and starts moving to the music with slow, seductive slides of her hips. Well, her entire body.

Holy hotness.

Then she pumps her hips fast, one, two three . . . Jesus.

I catch her small smile as she spins again and dances around the room. "I wish I could rip my shirt off," she says breathlessly, and I laugh again, but she starts inching her T-shirt up inch by inch. Her yoga pants are so low on her hips now she's almost exposing her cooch. Damn, that's hot. As she reveals her taut torso, she does another body roll that tightens her abs. My jaw drops.

She cocks a hip and does a body roll to one side, then the other. Then, facing me, she swivels her hips in a slow circle one way . . . and the other.

I swallow.

The T-shirt eventually rises over her breasts, but she gives me her back as she takes it off the rest of the way. Tease. That's okay, though, because she's twitching her ass in an amazing fashion.

She tosses the T-shirt aside and hooks her fingers into the yoga pants. Moving to the music, they inch down her thighs . . . and off. Then my whole body jolts as she drops her upper body forward, hinging at the hips, hands on the floor in front of her. Wearing nothing but thong underwear, those sweet cheeks and long legs are right on display for me.

"Jesus Christ," I mutter. This is so much better than I even imagined. "You're a fucking fantastic dancer, El."

She slowly, gracefully straightens and smiles at me over her shoulder. Then she knocks me off balance yet again by goddamn popping her booty, shaking it for me.

I groan. "You gotta be *kidding* me."

She grins and dances over to me, reaching around to unfasten her bra. She undoes it, but holds it in place as she moves to the music in front of me. I reach up and pluck it away, and she's dancing in a tiny pair of panties. Rolling her hips, she turns and straddles me so her ass is right on my aching cock, grinding into me. She grabs my hands and brings them to her bare breasts, her body shifting to the music under my touch.

"Fuck me," I groan, reaching for her hips to lift her off me. "Take those panties off and bring that pretty pussy up here. Want you to sit on my face."

She swipes her tongue over her bottom lip again as she shimmies out of the panties. "Next time *you* dance for *me,*" she says.

I laugh and fall back on the bed and watch her climb onto me. My blood is pounding through my veins. I don't think I've ever been this turned on in my life. She amazes me. I grab her waist impatiently and easily lift her up. She gives a little squeal as I bring her pussy to my mouth.

The song has ended and another one starts, part of some playlist, I guess, a slower, sultry song, and Ella kneels over me and makes little gasping noises as I lick her. Her feminine taste tingles on my tongue as I stroke my tongue over the soft, plump lips, enticingly bare and delicate. Her hands go to her hair and her back arches.

"Yeah," I mutter, kissing her, sucking her flesh into my mouth in gentle pulls, then licking again. I slide my tongue through her liquid heat, up, down, around her clit but not over it yet. She whimpers. "Like that, sexy girl?"

"Oh yeah. God yeah . . ." Her thighs quiver.

I slide my hands around to her ass, holding her in place as I eat her. I bury my face in her, inhaling her sweet scent, probing deeper with my tongue, exploring secret, mysterious girl places, and then finally I slide my tongue over the swollen bundle of nerves. She cries out and starts shaking even more.

"You made me so goddamn hard," I mutter between licks. "I want to bury my cock in you so deep."

"Yes . . . yes . . . need you . . ."

"Need you too, baby. But wanna reward you for that fucking awesome show. So much better . . . I can't even . . . Wanna make you feel good."

"Ben." Her hands drop, and her entire body is quaking. "So close . . ."

"Good." I close my lips around her clit and suck on it so gently.

She cries out, probably loud enough for all her housemates to hear, but what the hell, I just want her to have the best orgasm. I draw it out, absorbing her frantic cries until she falls to the side and curls her legs up, panting.

I need to catch my breath too, my mouth gulping in oxygen as I stare at the ceiling. Then my hands go to the button and fly of my jeans. I rip them open, shove them down, and kick them off, then jackknife to sit up and pull my shirt off over my head, even though it has buttons. I roll to the side to grab a condom, glove up, and then move Ella into position, her head on a pillow.

She stares up at me with dazed eyes. I lean down to kiss her, and when she slides her tongue over my mouth, she whispers, "I taste myself on you."

"Fuuccck." I plunge my cock into her. "Not usually this fast, baby, but you got me so hot . . ."

She's wet and slippery, tight and hot. She tilts her hips and wraps her legs around me, and I can't stop myself from pounding into her sweet body.

Her fingernails bite into my back, and that just sends another hot rush of lust through my body. My balls are on fire, slapping against her, our skin smacking together. "Yes," she whispers. "Fuck me just like that . . . harder. God, Ben, you know just how I like it."

"Yeah. I know. Just how I like it too." We're perfect together. So fucking perfect. That heat in my body roars up into something huge and powerful, all-consuming. My ears are roaring, and I'm just vaguely aware of Ella's body convulsing around me as she comes again. She strains up against my body, taking me so deep, and then I explode into her, hot, reckless, helpless. It's wild and intense, almost violent, stealing my breath, robbing me of my senses. Everything goes black as pleasure pours through me in impossible, scorching waves.

I love you.

The words echo inside my head. It takes a minute before I'm lucid enough to wonder . . . did I say that out loud?

My heart is still hammering so hard I can hear it in my ears. I'm a weak, sweaty mess on top of Ella, breathing hard. Her hands have relaxed and are now stroking up and down my damp back, and she kisses my shoulder. She doesn't say anything.

I don't think I said it out loud. Maybe I should. But fuck . . . I'm terrified. I don't know if she feels the same. No, telling a girl you love her while you're a pile of hormones and still inside her is a dick move.

This wasn't supposed to happen. I don't need that kind of complication in my life right now. Ella and I have been having fun, but this is getting intense. I don't know what my future holds and I still have to prove myself before I can have that kind of relationship. I haven't done that yet, and it's what I need to focus on.

"Skylar and I want to come into your dressing room."

"What?" I lift my head.

"We think it would be hot. Seeing all you naked guys with gorgeous bodies walking around and showering together. We have hot male-on-male shower fantasies."

I choke.

"Like, you guys slapping each other's assess and hugging naked. Do you hug in the showers like you do on the ice?"

My reply comes out in a strangled voice. "Um, no. No hugging. There might be occasional ass slapping or homoerotic jokes."

"Really?" She perks up.

"What the hell?"

"Come on, lots of girls have hot guy-on-guy fantasies. When it's two athletic, alpha hockey dudes? Oh my God. I might have to jump you again."

I roll to my back. "Have at it, babe."

Chapter 21

Ella

I sit smiling at my computer, relief and satisfaction fizzing in my chest.

I passed all my midterms.

Which means all my grades are now passing ones. I just have to keep it up for the rest of the semester and do the same on my finals. I have another meeting with my academic adviser later this week, and I think I will be off probation. I've shown them I can do it.

I take a screenshot and send it to Ben.

He messages me back. *Hey! Looking good, beautiful! Knew you could do it.*

I actually feel a little proud of myself. *How'd you do?*

He sends me a screenshot too and I smile. I wasn't really worried about his grades, with his self-discipline and focus. I've actually learned a lot from him. The concept of delayed gratification . . . making myself work hard and then rewarding myself with what I really want to do, like spending time with him or going to a party. Ben says he learned that his freshman year. Because of the demands on his time, he trained himself to get his work done early in the week so he could focus on hockey on the weekends. Also structure. He likes to have a plan for his time, whereas I'm a little scattered, but I've come to see the value of structure.

It makes my life feel more in control, less chaotic. It makes me feel more secure.

I go check in with Skylar because she's been working really hard too.

"One B+." she says with a scowl. "The rest are As."

"That's fantastic!"

She wrinkles her nose. "My goal was straight As. But you're right. It's good."

"I think we deserve to celebrate."

"Let's go see what Brooklyn and Natalie are doing."

Natalie comes across as kind of flaky with her talk about chakras and auras, but she's really super smart and has scored straight As. Brooklyn got a couple of Ds but doesn't seem too upset about it. "I just have to pass," she says cheerfully. "How should we celebrate?"

We end up having an argument, er, discussion about where to go. Brooklyn is still on her diet and even though the rest of us want to go for sushi, she can't eat rice. Finally she gives in and says she'll order some stir-fry vegetables or something.

"Have you really not had any alcohol since you started this diet?" Skylar asks her.

"Not a drop."

"And what's the purpose of this again?" I ask, perusing the menu. "You don't need to lose weight."

"Some foods have a negative impact on your health," Brooklyn says. "They can affect your energy levels, give you headaches or sore joints, or skin problems. I cut out all these potentially problematic foods for a month, then gradually reintroduce them to see if they affect me."

I nod, even though I'm skeptical.

Brooklyn orders a shrimp and veggie stir-fry after interrogating the server about what kind of oil it's cooked in and if there is any MSG in it. Skylar and I exchange a look.

"Well, I hope you feel better," I say, not wanting to discourage her. Food's important, and it's good to eat healthy, but I think food should also be a source of pleasure. And I'm going to enjoy the hell out of the spicy tuna rolls I just ordered.

This reminds me I still need to make Thai food for Ben sometime.

"Jacob did okay too?" I ask Skylar

"Yeah." She makes a face. "He's so smart, it's not fair. Jocks are supposed to be big and dumb."

"That's a stereotype."

She laughs. "Yeah, I know. There are a couple of guys on the team who might fit that, though. So hey, you guys, I'm being interviewed by a reporter from the *New York Times* next week."

"Please tell me it's not because you're a hockey girlfriend," Natalie says.

Skylar frowns. "No. It's because I'm the coordinator of the Men's Outreach program at SAPAP. They're doing an article about us."

"That's awesome, Sky," I say. I really am proud of her.

"It's always good to bring attention to the issues," she says.

"How are things at SAPAP?"

"Busy." Skylar smiles. "The *Times* is interested in the program we're developing for athletes too."

"Ugh. Did you hear that story the other day?" Natalie asks. "I saw it online. I forget what school it was . . . somewhere in Texas? Anyway, there were a bunch of anonymous Tweets that apparently were about a freshman girl who was gang-raped by some football players."

"Oh no." I frown. "I didn't hear about that."

"We were talking about it at our last meeting," Skylar says.

"So, it was the guys who were talking about gang-raping her?" I ask.

"No." Natalie shakes her head. "The girl posted about it. But anonymously."

"Why would she do it anonymously?" Brooklyn asked.

"Duh." Skylar slants her a look. "Because she's probably terrified of being attacked if she identifies herself. It's so damn unfair that a woman can't even be honest about something like that without worrying about being attacked yet again."

"So she never reported it to the police? Or campus officials?"

"Apparently not. They reached out to her online, but who knows if she'll come forward. It's so hard." Skylar shakes her head. "We have to keep working to change the culture on campus. We're actually going to send out a survey next month, doing a temperature check on sexual misconduct. We're going to ask about attitudes and beliefs regarding the reporting process and see how much confidence people have in our policies."

I admire Skylar so much. Sometimes she makes me feel small because she loves to work on such important things. But she's not preachy about it. And I know this is her way of making something good out of what happened to her.

I should be making something good out of what happened to me. But then when I think about it, what happened to me is small peanuts compared to what happened to Skylar. Yes, I lost someone I loved. I felt betrayed by someone I loved and looked up to. And I felt guilty because I let down someone I loved when they needed help. But I wasn't violated the way she was.

Still, I'm not the only one who's lost someone to suicide, and there are a lot of complicated emotions that go along with that. I'm still struggling with the fact that I didn't know Brendan was suffering that much. I've been doing some research to learn more about it and I have an idea I've been tossing around in my mind.

I'm still thinking about that when I attend my next session with Frances the following week, which will probably be my last.

"I think we've unpacked a lot of stuff," Frances says. "The grieving process."

"Yes." I understand many of the feelings I had after Brendan's death and it helps knowing those are all very common. "I don't hate myself anymore."

"You've been honest with Skylar about everything . . . how you felt, why you did the things you did."

"I have. And amazingly, she's still my friend." I smile. I hesitate, then say, "Sometimes I've been so happy lately, and then I feel guilty for that."

Frances smiles. "Everyone grieves differently. And there are many difficult and complicated emotions associated with the grieving process. But it's okay to be happy too. Joy, satisfaction, and humor are perfectly fine to feel. You've made a lot of progress, Ella. After today, I don't know if I need to see you again. You've shown some great insights into the things that have been holding you back. You've taken positive steps to move forward."

I bite my lip. "Can I ask you about something? It's not really about me."

"Of course."

"I've been doing research into the signs of mental health problems. Like, how to know if someone you care about is struggling."

Frances nods.

"There's good information out there, but there's not a lot on what to do if you think that's the case . . . if you think someone is having a hard time and might need help. I found a few articles about mental health in the workplace, and quite a few articles about the mental health crisis on college campuses. So many kids are struggling with depression, substance abuse . . . eating disorders. And I know we have a suicide prevention program here at Bayard. I know there's a grant program that gives funds to the counseling center for services for students with mental health problems. But when I talk to people, lots of people don't know about it. Or . . ." I pause. "They don't want to talk about it. There's still such a stigma around mental health."

"Yes. That's very true," Frances says slowly.

"I have this idea—tell me if you think it's stupid—but I admire what Jacob and Skylar are doing to raise awareness of rape culture and things like bystander intervention. And I want to do something like that, only about mental health issues. I think the best way to end the stigma is to talk about it. What if we had some kind of campaign on campus where we talked about mental health issues, and offered people information about how to spot signs of trouble in your friends and what to do about it if you do." I swallow. "I'm a Communications major, and I thought maybe I could use what I'm learning to develop something like that here at Bayard."

A slow smile spreads across Frances's face. "That's an amazing idea, Ella. I'd be happy to help with it any way I can."

"I'm not sure where to start."

"I'd say we start with Dr. Ivanov. He's the director of CPSS," she says, referring to the counseling center. "Let me contact him and see if I can set up a meeting."

"Thank you! That would be great. I would definitely need input from professionals. I've learned a lot, but I'm not a psychology major. Still, I'd like to be involved in starting a conversation and sharing information."

I gather up my things, since we're finished.

"Good luck, Ella." Frances smiles warmly.

"Thank you." I almost want to hug her, but that feels awkward and she makes no move toward me, so I think that's not really something that's done. "I really appreciate how you've helped me."

"My pleasure."

I go home to grab something to eat before I immerse myself in Media Communications for the evening. I find I'm the only one home, but that's okay. I make myself some scrambled eggs and toast, and eat it while I check social media on my phone. Then I go up to my room to study.

It's a couple of hours later when I hear a voice at my door. "Ella."

I look up and see Skylar in my open doorway. When I take in her tear-streaked face, I jump up from my desk, my heart clenching. "What's wrong?"

Bottom lip trembling, she stumbles into my room and drops onto the side of my bed. Her face is pink and her puffy eyes are still leaking tears. "I think Jacob and I broke up."

"What? No!" I scurry over and sit beside her on the bed, staring at her. My stomach tightens as I take in her misery.

She wipes tears from her face. "We just had a huge fight."

"About what?" My forehead wrinkles. I'm imagining Jacob cheated or . . . or . . . I don't even *know* what could be that bad.

"About . . . about . . ." She sobs. "About where he might end up living if he gets drafted."

"*When* he gets drafted," I automatically respond. Because that shit is definitely happening for both Jacob and Ben. I refuse to think otherwise. Even though I've also thought about what that will mean for Ben and me

. . . for next year . . . or ever. We haven't been together very long; still, I can't help but think about it, especially after the day we had brunch with my parents and Ben was so confident that he'll be drafted and playing in the NHL. I always knew that, but—

"Right." She hiccups. "He's been looking at the standings and the bottom teams are Edmonton, Toronto, Vancouver, and New Jersey."

"Uh-huh . . ."

"You don't know which team gets the top picks until April. They do some kind of lottery." She waves a hand. "I don't really understand it. But he wants to go to Vancouver!"

"Okaaaaaay . . ."

"Vancouver! Do you know how far away that is?"

"Um, I guess. I know it's in Canada. But it's probably close to where he's from, right?"

"I don't want to go to Vancouver!"

"This is what you fought over?" I ask cautiously.

"Yes. He's all excited about playing there. I can't even . . ."

"Okay, calm down. Deep breath."

She gazes back at me with wet eyes. "I said Toronto would be nice . . . and he said if he gets drafted by Toronto he'll pull an Eric Lindros." Her eyebrows pull together.

"I don't know what that means."

"It means he doesn't want to play there, and he won't go."

"He doesn't mean that. He was probably joking."

"He was *so* serious!"

I suck in a patient breath. "Okay. I think both of you are stressed. We just had midterms. He's probably feeling pressure about playoffs and the draft. First of all, Jacob has no control over who drafts him, Sky."

She nods, her bottom lip quivering.

"So there's really no point in fighting about it. I mean, talking about it is even kind of useless. Who knows what will happen? Also, I know for a fact that if Jacob gets drafted, he'll play with whatever team picks him. That's what he wants. Ben is the same. They've wanted it their whole lives. I guess maybe some guys are cocky enough to say they wouldn't go to a team they don't like, but that's not them. Also, I have no idea what the odds are, but I don't think Jacob is going to go first overall. I mean, I know he's up there on the lists, but there's some hotshot player in Canada who everyone is saying will be the number one pick, and then some Swedish dude, and that guy from Boston University . . . Jacob could get drafted by a really good team."

"How do you know that? About the top draft picks."

"It's all over the Internet. I was checking out where Ben is on the lists and what the scouts are saying about him. So maybe a team in Florida will pick Jacob . . . you'd like Florida, right?"

She gazes back at me, then closes her bloodshot eyes. "I'm an idiot."

"No, you're not. It's an emotional subject. I kinda know how you feel."

"Aw, Ella." Her eyes flick open. "Are you worried too?"

"I'm not worried. Okay, that's a lie. I'm a little worried. It's hard not knowing what the future holds. But I know Ben's going to do well. And whatever happens, happens." I make a face.

"I don't know if Jacob even *wants* me to go with him," Skylar whispers. "Wherever he ends up." Another little sob escapes her, and her shoulders slump. "And *that's* what I'm really most afraid of."

"Oh, Sky." My heart squeezes.

"I couldn't tell him that . . . and we got in a stupid fight."

I put my arms around her and she leans into me. "You should tell him how you feel."

"I'm afraid. What if he doesn't want me with him?"

I can't speak for Jacob, but that doesn't seem likely. "It's something you're going to have to talk about at some point."

"True." She thinks about it. "But I don't want to influence his decisions."

"Then tell him that too."

She sniffles. "When did you get to be so smart?"

"I've always been smart." I smile wryly. "About *other* people's problems."

"Thank you for being my friend," she whispers. "I'm so glad I have you back."

My throat feels like a fist is squeezing it. "Me too," I manage to say. "Love you, Sky."

"Love you, too." She sighs as she slides off my bed. "Okay, I'm going to call Jacob and tell him I'm sorry." She heads to her own room.

I understand why Skylar's anxious. We know there are going to be big changes in Ben's and Jacob's lives—we just don't know exactly what's going to happen. Even if they get drafted, which they will, they have to go to training camp and make the team. Ben's talked to me about that, and realistically most guys don't play in the NHL the first season after they're drafted. So then he has to make decisions about what he wants to do, which could be playing for the farm team, or coming back to college.

I want Ben to be drafted. I want everything good for him. I want him to be drafted and end up playing for a team he loves. But that also makes me sad. Selfishly, I get a sick feeling in my stomach at the thought that he won't be here next year. I don't even know what's going to happen this summer. Last summer, I went home to Syracuse and waitressed to make some money. Ben says he worked in a body shop in Buffalo the last few summers. We'll be two and a half hours away from each other, which isn't the end of the world.

Then why does my stomach hurt so much thinking about it?

Oh my God. I flop onto my back on the bed.

I've fallen in love with him.

I close my eyes. This wasn't supposed to happen. Didn't I tell myself that I can't let myself care about someone like that again? Because there's no way in hell he'll ever feel the same way about me.

I'm *crazy* to be thinking about a future with Ben. I *can't* be thinking of a future with Ben. I let myself dream of a future with Brendan, which was naïve and foolish and ended in devastation. I need to seriously cool my jets here.

Chapter 22

Ben

THIS WEEKEND THE PLAYOFFS START. We won our games last weekend, the final two games of our regular season, and it was a nice ending for the fans. Also a nice ending for us, because we finished in fourth place in our conference, which means we got a bye to the quarter-finals this weekend *and* we get to play at home. We had last weekend off, to rest up and catch our breath and work on a few things we're going to need to do when we play against Rensselaer.

I'm feeling unsettled, though. Weird things are happening. I heard from my mom, and she's coming to watch my game tomorrow night. That's only the third time in two years of college. She says she has something she needs to talk to me about. Great.

Plus, Ella's acting weird. Not like she's mad at me, just . . . distant, I guess is the word to describe it. She's coming to the game tonight, but when I half-jokingly said we need to get her a jersey to wear, like Skylar and the other girlfriends, she laughed and said no way.

It doesn't really matter to me.

What does matter to me is there are all kinds of scouts here to watch these games, assessing Flash, Rocket, and me. Who knows how we'll do in the playoffs or if they'll get many more opportunities to watch us play.

I need to forget they're there. I need to forget Ella's there. I need to forget my mom's there tomorrow when we play.

We pull off a win Friday night, a convincing win with a score of five-two. This builds our confidence for the game tomorrow night. It's a best-of-three series, with a game scheduled for Sunday afternoon if needed, but we want to win again tomorrow night and move on to the semifinals next weekend in Lake Placid.

Ella texts me the next morning to see what time I want to come by for a turkey sandwich. This makes me smile. It's a new routine. But dammit, I can't do it today.

Sorry, can't. **sad face emoji** *Have to pick up my mom at the bus depot.*

Your mom is coming to the game? That's great!

It is. I want her to see how I play. I want her to know how well I'm doing. I want her to be proud of me. But somehow I have a feeling that's not why she's coming. I hold off on answering Ella because I'm not exactly sure what to say.

Bring her here, I'll make her a sandwich too.

Christ. I met Ella's parents, and it didn't go so well. And my mom said she needs to talk to me about something, and given my fucked-up family, that makes me nervous. I don't think that's a conversation I want to have around Ella. *That's okay, we'll grab some lunch somewhere.*

It takes a few minutes for her to answer, and I use that time to dress in a pair of dark jeans and a sweater. I'm messing with my hair, still distracted about what's going on with Mom, when my phone pings.

Okay. Good luck tonight.

Thanks.

I shove my phone in my pocket and head out.

"Want to go back to my place?" I ask Mom when I've found her at the bus depot. "Are you hungry? We can get lunch."

"I'm not really hungry."

"I need to eat. It's game day and I have to fuel up."

"Of course you do. Let's go somewhere then."

I head back toward campus and pull into Mort's.

"So what's going on, Mom?" I ask after we order.

"I have something I need to talk to you about."

"What's that?"

She twists her hands together and I notice the signs of strain around her eyes and mouth. "I heard from Julie and Sharon the other day."

She's referring to her sisters—my aunts.

"Uh-huh." That's not exactly shocking news.

"They want to reconcile with your uncle Larry."

I frown and my gut tightens. Uncle Larry is the guy who murdered my dad. "Are you fucking kidding me?" Mom doesn't even flinch at my language, but I know I shouldn't talk like that to her. "Sorry. But why?"

"I don't understand it either," she says. "I asked them why now, and they just said he's our brother, and they want him to be part of our family. But after what he did . . ." She pauses. "So I'm thinking about going to the police," she continues in a low voice. "Telling them what happened. Maybe they can do something now."

"Oh Christ." My gut cramps up even worse.

"I want you to help me."

I stare at my mom. I love her, but I don't need this right now. I'm playing a championship game tonight, trying to move on to the semifinals next weekend and then maybe the Frozen Four. I'm trying to get into the NHL. How could she lay this on me now?

I close my eyes briefly. She has no idea. And it was her sisters who laid this on her. She needs support, and I'm the only one she has to turn to. It's just bad timing.

Although there's never a good time for something like this, I guess.

"God, Mom. I don't know . . . do you think that's a good idea?"

My stomach is churning. This is crazy. When I found out the truth about my dad's death, that Uncle Larry had killed him, it ripped open old wounds and I had to grieve for my dad all over again, this time knowing that it hadn't been a tragic accident, that it had been a deliberate act of murder. By someone I knew. By someone who'd gotten away with it. I managed to deal with that, but the last thing I need right now is dredging up all that old shit again. And going to the police? Jesus Christ.

"Don't you want justice for your father?" Mom asks, her eyes pleading with me.

My chest tightens and I close my eyes at the pain that stabs through me. Justice.

Do I owe my dad that?

Uncle Dave, who helped me out . . . because of him I was able to play hockey. Do I owe it to *him* to seek justice for my dad?

"I'm sorry, Mom." I rub my face and look away, then back at her. "I have a game today, and there are scouts here watching me, from teams who might want to draft me. We need to do well. I need to focus on that right now. Could we talk more about this in a few weeks?"

"Oh God. I'm sorry." She touches my arm. "I shouldn't have dumped this on you right now. I wasn't thinking. I've just been so upset about it. I can't believe they want to reconcile with Larry after all these years."

Fuck, now I'm worried about my mom. If she does this, is she putting herself at risk? "What if Uncle Larry finds out?"

She frowns. "Who would tell him?"

"I don't know. The police? I don't know. But he might be pissed. What if he . . . "

Her eyes widen, then narrow. She purses her lips. "He won't hurt me."

"How do you know? He fucking murdered Dad!" Christ, my voice got loud there. I close my eyes. I feel like my head is going to explode.

"I'll be fine," she says quietly. "But yes, let's talk about this another time."

I have to get my shit together. Get my thoughts and emotions under control so I can focus on hockey. How the fuck am I going to do that?

Mom comes home with me. She tells me to go on up for my afternoon nap, she'll entertain herself by watching some TV or something, but sleeping is a lost cause. I'm reeling from what my mom has just told me. Pissed. Anxious. Frustrated.

A weird heaviness fills me. I don't like this feeling. Next weekend is the semifinals, then it's the NCAA tournament, depending what happens. It could be the end of my college hockey career. I should be feeling on top of the world. Instead, I feel like everything is spinning out of my control.

I like things structured and ordered. I like to have a plan, and I like to be in control of that plan. Right now I have that old feeling of chaos and uncertainty that I had growing up.

I feel a huge weight pressing down on me . . . pressure and anger and worry. The shit my mom dumped on me. All the pressure I've been feeling the last few months with finding a rep, preparing for the combine and the draft, trying to play my best for my future and for the team, staying on top of schoolwork.

So I'm a little distracted, and I have to work hard to focus on the game. As usual, my routines help with that.

When I look up into the stands, I find Skylar, wearing her jersey. She's with Liz, Krystal, and Alessia. I frown when I don't see Ella. Maybe she's in the ladies' room, or getting a drink.

But she's not here. I shouldn't be noticing that, but I do. And it's distracting as hell, because instead of watching the puck, I keep looking into the stands searching for her, and it makes me screw up. I miss a pass from Flash and turn the puck over to the Engineers, who make a break for our goal in a two-on-one that damn near costs us a goal.

Fuck!

I slam my stick against the boards as I leave the ice to plant my ass on the bench. I'm panting and cursing myself up and down in my head. I gotta get my shit together.

My heart is pounding. Adrenaline tingles in my veins. I'm pissed, but I need to channel all that energy into my game and keep it under control. Control. I'm good at staying in control. I can do this.

My next shift is better. I use that adrenaline to slam Santini of the Engineers into the boards, and then deliver a crushing hit to another Engineer. This gets the crowd going, and the noise level in the DeWitt Center climbs. I ruthlessly ignore the crowd, though, and focus on the game.

The Engineers aren't making it easy for us, but we manage to come back from a three-one deficit to win four-three.

Ella's not here to see it.

We celebrate jubilantly in a big pileup, and yeah, I'm happy, especially considering that we came back and that I managed to get my shit together.

"Christ," I say in the dressing room as I pull off my shoulder pads. "We pulled that out of our asses."

"Hell yeah." But Flash gives me a look. "You were a little off your game in the first period."

I grit my teeth but nod. "Yeah. It won't happen again."

A bunch of guys are going to a party after. I haven't heard anything from Ella. Why didn't she come to the game? Annoyance rubs at me despite my elation at our win.

"Coming, Buck?" Soupy calls.

I look at Flash. "You going?"

"For a while. Not gonna stay long, though."

"Okay, I'll come. I just gotta take my mom to the bus depot, so I'll meet you there."

I walk into the house with the music blasting and voices yelling, and the first person my gaze falls on is Ella. My heart gives a happy bump against my ribs, but then I frown. Why'd she come to a party but not to my game?

Then the guy she's talking to bends down and whispers something in her ear, sliding an arm around her waist. She looks up at him, with long eye contact, apparently in the middle of some intense conversation. The way they stand together looks pretty goddamn close.

I recognize the guy. His name is Eric. And I have a weird déjà vu feeling. I've been here before . . . at a party watching Ella flirt with this guy and then leave with him. It was last fall. I didn't really even know her. I just knew her reputation. Guys talk—she's hot and fun. That time, I didn't care who she slept with. Now, remembering, it makes my blood heat.

She didn't come to the game. But she's here at the party. With Eric.

I had a bad feeling before. Now the sour feeling in my gut intensifies.

I've been fighting my feelings for Ella. Because she's starting to be really important to me. Like, the *most* important thing.

And she does this.

I should have known better. I *did* know better. I don't know what happened to my brain. Maybe lust and sex turned me into an idiot . . . yeah, that's what it was. I've been thinking with my dick, not my brain, getting all wrapped up in a girl, when I have so much else on my plate. I knew all along it couldn't work. I can't let anything distract me from my goals . . . not my messed-up family shit. And not a girl.

A beer appears in front of me. I look at it, then up at Flash. He's wearing a wry smile of sympathy.

I take the beer and look over at Ella, and Flash follows my gaze but I know he already saw her. We watch as Eric wraps his arms around her in a hug and kisses her cheek. My heart feels like a skate blade is sawing into it.

"It goes against the Bro Code to say 'I told you so,' " I tell him.

"I didn't say a word."

"You were thinking it."

"You can't penalize me for my thoughts."

"Sure I can."

"Christ," Flash mutters. "You guys make shit up on the spur of the moment, I swear. I'm just sayin', I tried to tell you Ella isn't girlfriend material."

Fuck. He did. "And I was okay with that," I remind him, even though I'm totally not now. "Because I'm not boyfriend material."

"You don't look like you're okay with it right now. And what was that earlier? In the game . . . it was because of her you had your head up your ass, wasn't it?"

I sigh.

"Has she talked to you about what happened last year?"

"Her friend dying of suicide? Yeah. I know about that."

"He was more than a friend."

I narrow my eyes at Flash. "What? She said he was a friend."

"A friend she was in love with."

My frown intensifies. "What the fuck?"

Flash nods slowly. "Yeah. That was part of what caused problems between her and Skylar. Um . . ." He rubs his face. "This is really crap, but what happened with Brendan was fucked-up."

"He committed suicide."

"Yeah." Flash's face tightens. He swallows. "Brendan thought he was in love with Skylar. But he had mental health issues and some other stuff going on. Of course Skylar felt all kinds of guilty after, because he'd been trying to get a hold of her and talk to her about . . . stuff . . . and she kept ignoring him. Anyway." He lets out a sigh. "Ella found out that Brendan was in love with Skylar. Here she'd had this crush on him or whatever, and she was pretty devastated by that. Plus, she blamed Skylar for Brendan's suicide."

"Jesus."

"They've talked about it now," Flash adds. "And they've both gone for counseling. Things are good with them again. It's been a lot for them to deal with, though."

"No shit." I press the heel of my hand between my eyebrows where my head is throbbing. "She was in love with him?"

Flash nods slowly.

"Why didn't she tell me that?" I ask the question out loud, but it's not really for Flash to answer. I thought Ella and I talked about all kinds of stuff . . . both of us . . . I thought we've been honest with each other. Meanwhile, she never told me that. She never told me about Skylar either, but I understand that, I guess, since it's Skylar's story. I can respect that Ella wouldn't share her best friend's personal stuff like that. But why didn't she ever tell me that she'd loved that guy?

I can only guess it's because she still has feelings for him. She's still grieving for him. Still missing him. Or I'm just not important enough to share things like that with.

I could keep making assumptions and guesses, but I'll never know the truth unless I ask her. Except I'm not sure I want to do that. It kind of makes me feel like puking.

I know Ella's been with other guys. But none of them meant anything to her, and I get that, because it's the same for me. I've been with lots of girls too, but I've never let myself get close enough to someone to really care about her. And I know why that is . . . if I get close to someone they'll realize I'm not the person I try to be and they'll find me lacking, just like those snotty princesses my mom worked for, and all their friends.

Ella was different.

At least, I'd thought she was.

"You okay, man?" Flash eyes me.

Nope. Not really. I look over at Ella, and fuck it, she's gone.

Some other guys join us, congratulating us on the win and talking about the game. One of them is Eric, so at least I know Ella's not with him. But where the fuck is she? I guzzle down half my beer.

"Just saw you talking to Ella," I say to him. "She still here?"

"Yeah, I think so." He grins, and it's a loose, sloppy grin. He's hammered. "I *hope* so. She is one hot piece."

I narrow my eyes at him, while Flash makes a choking noise.

But seriously, I need to calm the fuck down about this. "Yeah," I say, trying for casual. "She is."

"That chick can suck c—"

I lunge at him.

A bunch of hands grab me.

Yeah, so much for control.

Eric takes a step away. "Whoa, buddy. What the hell?"

I strain against the grips holding me. I want to fucking punch his nose down his throat.

"Easy, Buck" Flash tugs me back. "Been there, done that."

I pull in a long breath. Yeah, I know he's right. Throwing down with this guy might feel good for about two minutes, which is probably how long it would take me to win because he's drunk as fuck, and then I'll be in shit and it's the playoffs. I can't fucking do this. It burns under my skin that he can talk like that about Ella, though, and get away with it. She deserves so much better than that.

"I'm leaving," I mutter. "Fuck this."

"Yeah, I'll come with," Flash says. "Let's go. Behave, boys."

Chapter 23

Ella

I DON'T KNOW if I've ever felt this low. Maybe last year after Brendan died, but that seems like a lifetime ago.

I went to that party last night to take my mind off the fact that I wasn't at Ben's hockey game. I pretty much convinced myself he didn't care if I was there or not. His mom was in town, and he clearly didn't want us to meet. He didn't even want his turkey sandwich.

I don't know if the four times I've made him sandwiches since that first day are enough to constitute a game day routine. Or a superstition. But I guess not, because it doesn't seem to bother him at all not to come over.

This filled me with a heavy sadness that I hate feeling.

And then Ben showed up at the party.

I saw him and the other hockey guys there. I heard they won their game. I hesitated to go up to him, but we had to talk. For a minute, I watched him, and my heart ached with need for him. He had his back to me, and when he turned to say something to Flash, he looked so serious.

I had to tell him we couldn't see each other anymore. So I started walking toward the group, behind Ben. When I got closer, Eric appeared and started talking to them. I heard Ben ask Eric about me, if I was still there.

So he'd seen me. And he hadn't come up to me.

Eric said, "I hope so. She is one hot piece."

My feet stopped moving, and my body went cold. It seemed like it took an hour, with nobody saying anything. And then Ben said, "Yeah. She is."

My insides were flash frozen, my heart a lump of ice in my chest. Then the ice splintered, shards of it slicing through my body. I whirled around and ran out of there.

I hid in my bed, shivering and sobbing pretty much all night.

Clearly I'd been right all along. This relationship thing wasn't for me. I fell in love with Ben, and what was I to him? A hot piece.

The first time Ben texts me on Sunday, I ignore it. But I know I can't do that forever. I lie on my bed and try to figure out what to say to him. Finally, I pick up my phone and call him.

"Hey," he answers in a clipped tone.

"Hi." I start trembling. "I heard you won last night. Congratulations."

"Yeah. Thanks. Good that you heard about the win, since *you weren't there.*"

I bite my lip.

"Guess the party was more interesting than the game, huh?"

I squeeze my eyes shut at the sting of tears. "Yeah. Guess so."

Dense silence fills my ear. "Fuck," he mutters.

"I was going to talk to you there," I say, trying to keep my voice steady. "This isn't working for us."

"Yeah, I've been getting that feeling."

I blink. And swallow. The pain slicing through me steals my breath. All I can think of is self-preservation. Protecting my heart. And I say, "Well, so have I."

More silence.

"So I guess that's good, then," I say. "We both feel the same." I pause, and tears slide down my face. "Good luck in the playoffs."

After a short pause, he snaps, "Thanks." And ends the call.

That pretty much trashes the rest of my day. I have homework, and my proposal to work on for Dr. Ivanov. I heard from Frances, and we have a meeting with him next week to talk about my ideas. I make a big effort to concentrate on these things, but my mind is running like a squirrel on Ritalin.

Skylar has to work, so I don't see her until she gets home just after six. She knocks on my door, still wearing her pink Taste of Heaven uniform. "Hey. What's up?"

"Not much." I smile at her despite the gnawing feeling in my stomach and my gritty, sore eyes.

Yes, she and Jacob made up after their big fight. They had a good talk and were both honest with each other. Jacob told her he wants her with him no matter what, but he also didn't want to influence her decision about school or her degree, and since he has no idea what his future looks like, it's hard for him to ask her to commit. So they both agreed that what-ever happens, they'll figure it out together.

"Why didn't you come to the game last night?"

I shrug; I'm not sure what to say.

"Are you okay?" A notch appears between her eyebrows.

This is me. This is what I do. Hide my feelings inside and pretend I'm okay. Well, that hasn't worked so well for me. A tear leaks out of my eye. "No," I finally whisper. "I'm not really okay."

She hurries over. "What's wrong?"

"Things are done between Ben and me."

"What? No!"

"Yeah." I swipe at more tears. Geez, you'd think I'd be all dried out now. Where the hell is all this salt water coming from? "I knew it wasn't a good idea to get involved with him. I told him . . . I know what people think of me. I didn't want him to get dragged down by me."

"Oh no." Skylar shakes her head, frowning. "No, Ella."

I shrug. "He said . . . if anyone said anything like that about me to his face . . . they'd regret it. Only last night, someone *did* say something . . ." *Thanks, Eric.* "And you know what Ben said? He agreed with him."

"What?"

I repeat the conversation I overheard.

Skylar stares at me, openmouthed. Then she shakes her head. "I don't know what to say. That doesn't seem like Ben."

"Whatever." I let out a shaky breath. "He was probably mad because I didn't go to the game. I was mad because his mom was here yesterday and he didn't even want us to meet. We're done. It's for the best. You were talking about your future with Jacob, and it made me realize that Ben and I don't have a future together. I got scared. I figured it'd be better just to end things now. Before . . . before my heart . . ." I stop, unable to squeeze words through my aching throat.

"Ella." Skylar puts her arms around me and hugs me. "I think it might be too late to protect your heart."

"No." I shake my head. "Not too late." I sniffle. "This is hard, but I'll be fine."

Skylar stays like that for a long moment, then draws back and rubs my shoulder. "Want to do something tonight?"

"I'm okay. I have lots of work to do." I haven't told her about my idea because I want to know if this is actually going to fly before I make a big deal about it.

"I don't want to leave you alone when you're upset."

"I'll be okay," I repeat, smiling. "I'm sure you and Jacob have plans, anyway."

I'm grateful I have something to keep my mind off Ben over the next few days. When Frances and I meet with Dr. Ivanov, he's really interested in my ideas. I feel like a bit of a fraud. I'm a sophomore and certainly no expert on communications or mental health. But I have passion going for me, because I really feel like this is important and can make a difference, and Frances is so supportive too. I'm very grateful for that.

I remember when Skylar and I were in high school and working with the Tiger Cubs. I remember how good that made me feel, doing something for someone else. Giving something back. I don't know why I lost sight of that since I started college.

Dr. Ivanov, Frances, and I have to start somewhere, and that some-where is forming a committee that will start working on trying to make some of my ideas a reality. Dr. Ivanov is going to talk to the staff there, some of whom are psychologists and social workers, and the man who will probably be most important, John Zhang, the assistant director of Outreach and Community Engagement. He also suggests that some of their psychology and social work interns might be interested in partic-ipating.

"I think it will be important to remember that it's not a simple issue," Dr. Ivanov says. "Often we interpret suicide as a symptom of depression, but there are other factors that can lead people to take their own lives—stress, traumatic events, substance abuse, chronic pain. And sometimes . . ." He pauses. "Sometimes there are no warning signs at all."

His words give me pause. Because in doing my research, I kept thinking back to Brendan, wracking my brain to remember if there'd been signs I'd missed, anything that I could have picked up on that would have made a difference . . . and I've come up empty.

Hearing Dr. Ivanov confirm that, confirm what I've read elsewhere, makes me realize I don't need to feel guilty about missing something that would have helped . . . because there just wasn't anything.

"I understand that," I manage to say, refocusing. "And my goal is partly to educate people so they know what some of the signs are. But it's also a goal just to open the discussion about this, so even if someone isn't showing any signs outwardly but inside they're struggling, they can say something to someone without fear . . . so they can get help."

Dr. Ivanov nods. "Some of the stigma around psychological treatment has begun to fade, but it's still there. People need to know there's no shame in seeking help. We don't hesitate to seek treatment when we're *physically* sick."

"That is so true." I sigh inwardly, wishing I'd had that mind-set after Brendan died. Maybe I wouldn't have made the mistakes I did if I'd sought help sooner. But maybe I can use that lesson to help other people.

"This is so important," Dr. Ivanov says. "Thank you, Ella."

I smile and nod, though my heart is full of emotion, and it's hard to speak.

I'm happy about this, I really am. But I want to tell Ben about it. I want to share it with him. I want to share my life with him.

I miss him so much. My insides ache with it, and I feel heavy and listless.

Last week was supposed to be my final session with Frances, but as we leave our meeting with Dr. Ivanov on Tuesday, I ask if she has time to see me this week. She gives me a long look but says we could meet Thursday.

"I'm still struggling with something," I tell her Thursday when we meet. "Or actually, I'm struggling with something new."

"What is that, Ella?"

"I think I've fallen in love with someone."

"Oh."

As always, she's nonjudgmental. I haven't even mentioned to her that I'm seeing someone. So I tell her about Ben. And my feelings for him. And my feelings of guilt. And I tell her that I'm . . . *heartbroken,* because we broke up.

"You said last time you've been feeling happy," she comments. "Was that because of Ben?"

"Yes." I look down at my hands. "I feel so happy when I'm with him. And then I feel guilty."

"Your life is stretching out in front of you, and our goal was to help you move forward and make the most of that life," she reminds me again.

"Right." I suck in a deep breath. "That's what I'm doing. That's my goal."

"You've taken some very positive steps. Your plan for helping others, for opening a dialogue about mental illness and suicide, is a huge step, Ella."

"Thank you."

"And falling in love with someone is also a step forward."

"It doesn't feel like it," I whisper.

"That's how you honor someone's life. By properly and fully living life *yourself.*"

I let that sink in.

"And that includes love," she says. "It doesn't mean you're betraying Brendan. It doesn't mean you're forgetting him."

I start crying again. "I feel like if I love someone, I'll let them down and they'll leave me. And I already did let Ben down."

"How?"

"He wanted me to wear his jersey to the game. And I said no. Then he wouldn't bring his mom to meet me, and that . . . hurt my feelings." I close my eyes briefly. "I didn't even go to his game. I went to a party instead. And he saw me there."

"Why did you do those things? Did you want to hurt him, or make him angry in return?"

"No!" I stare at her. "No, that wasn't it. I . . . I was afraid."

"What were you afraid of?" she asks gently.

"I'm afraid . . ." I have to stop and really think hard about this. Because I know I have to be honest. But honesty about our deepest fears is the most terrifying thing in the world. "I'm afraid he doesn't love me back."

There. I said it. My worst fear.

"I'm afraid I'm not worth loving," I sob. "I've made so many mistakes. And now . . . I fell in love with Ben and he hates me." I pluck some tissues from the ever-present box on the coffee table and wipe my eyes.

"I doubt he hates you," Frances says gently. "But you know the only way to find that out . . . right?"

"I can't do it. I can't ask him." My stomach is in knots, and I twist my fingers together.

"Here's what I think. If he wanted you to wear his jersey, and if he was hurt because you didn't go to the game and instead went to a party, I think it's likely he *does* care about you."

I ponder that.

"And I also think you could apologize to him and tell him *why* you did those things. If nothing else."

I mull over that all the way home.

When I get there, Skylar's in her room. I pause in her open doorway and take in the small suitcase on her bed. "Packing?" I ask.

She turns to look at me. Her head tilts. "Yeah. For the playoffs this weekend. There are a couple of buses going to Lake Placid for the games."

I nod. "That's great. The guys will love having fans there."

"Yeah." She eyes me. "You sure you're okay, El?"

I press my hand to my mouth and nod. "I think I'm okay."

"You know . . . I was talking to Jacob today . . . about you and Ben."

I bite my lip.

"He was telling me about that party last Friday night. Jacob said you were flirting with a guy. Eric."

My eyes widen. "I wasn't flirting with him."

Skylar says nothing.

"I wasn't!" I stare at her. "Seriously, Sky. I went to the party because I was feeling so down about Ben. But I didn't go there to flirt with guys."

"You hooked up with Eric."

"Months ago. A couple of times. It didn't mean anything. He's a good guy, but . . . Okay, so on Friday night I was talking to him at the party, and I was worried about him."

"Why?"

"I was getting a weird feeling. He was pretty drunk, which wasn't like him. His conversation was all over the place. He's dropped out of one of his classes and quit working on the school blog. He used to be so passionate about that. He was dressed in a shirt with a stain on the front, his jeans were so loose it looked like he'd lost weight, and he really needed a haircut. That was *definitely* not like him."

"What are you saying?" she asks slowly.

"I've been doing a bunch of research about this stuff, for this idea I have. That's another story." I wave my hand. "So maybe because of that, those things set off warning bells in my head. So I started asking him questions about what was going on with him. And it sounded to me like he was having a hard time."

"You think he's depressed?"

I bite my lip and nod. "I knew I had to say something to him, but man, it's kind of touchy. Anyway, I did it. I told him it sounded like he might be depressed and asked him if he'd seen anyone about it. He wasn't receptive at first, but I told him I was concerned about him, that lots of people have mental health issues and they're treatable if you get help. Then I told him about Brendan and how I don't want that to happen to anyone else I know, and I think that actually got through to him. I told him to contact CPSS and they would help, and he said he would, and then he gave me a sloppy hug and a kiss on the cheek."

"Oh." She blinks. "Oh God."

Now I frown. "I guess Ben and Jacob probably saw that. It didn't mean anything, but they thought I was flirting with him."

"Yeah."

"Shit."

"Yeah."

I suck in air. "Did *you* believe that?"

She shakes her head. "No. I wondered what was going on, though, 'cause I know how much you care about Ben."

"I'm in love with him," I whisper.

"I knew it. I told you it was too late to protect your heart."

I nod slowly. "You were right. I thought if I ended things now, it would be easier. But . . . it's not." Pain carves through my heart like a hot knife. "It really isn't."

Skylar moves her suitcase and sits on the bed. She pats the mattress beside her and I sit next to her. I tell her about seeing Frances again and what she said about Ben having feelings for me.

"I think she's right," Skylar said quietly. "And I think he's hurting."

I bury my face in my hands. "Shit."

All these thoughts roll around and around in my head. Ben thought I was flirting with Eric? On top of the fact that I went to the party instead of his game, on top of the fact that I wouldn't wear his jersey. No wonder he was pissed.

I guess I can even understand why he said what he did. Even though it still hurts.

I remember Frances's words . . . *He does* care about you. *And I also think you could apologize to him and tell him* why *you did those things. If nothing else.*

I think about him. I see his smile. I remember his touch, how he knows what I like, how he takes care of me. I think about his bringing me red Skittles and that stuffed dog that looks like Gracie. The pressure in my chest grows, and it feels like a band tightening around me. Agony slashes through me at the thought that I hurt him by being so fucking stupid.

And yes . . . yes, I should apologize to him. I owe him that at least. I could explain how scared I was feeling, and that I'm not cut out for relationships and I could tell him I'm sorry.

"Jacob also said Ben was acting weird after his mom got here," Skylar adds.

I look up and frown. "He was?"

"Yeah."

I think about that. "Did Jacob tell you about Ben's family?"

She slowly shakes her head, puzzlement creasing her forehead.

"Oh." I pull in a long breath. "Geez. I hope everything's okay with them." Now I'm worried for him. And my worry for him eclipses my own damn fears. A feeling of urgency grips me, a need to take care of him and make sure he's okay. "I need to talk to him."

"They've already left for Lake Placid."

"Fuck." I tip my head back.

"Come with me. We leave tomorrow and get there in time for the Friday night game. You can talk to him there."

I close my eyes briefly. I have a class tomorrow afternoon. I'm not supposed to be that girl anymore, the one who blows off a class for a beer bash or shopping. I'm not supposed to be reckless and chase after a guy. Also, Saturday is the ballet class I help with, and I've never missed a day, no matter how hungover I was.

But I'm worried about Ben, and I want to apologize to him and tell him I never wanted to hurt him, and I really do want to be there at his game and cheer him on, because it's so important to him.

I pull in a long breath through my nose and meet Skylar's eyes. "I have to let Jen know I won't be there Saturday for ballet class. It shouldn't be a problem. So . . . Okay, I'll come."

Chapter 24

Ben

THIS WEEK'S been a fucking disaster.

I'm going through the motions, but I'm a mess. My head is fucked-up thinking about my mom and her going to the police and what could happen. And I miss Ella.

I miss her with an ache that is physical. Working out, I push myself as hard as I can, trying to make my body hurt for reasons other than her. It doesn't work.

Our practices are intense as we prepare for the semifinals. And I have two papers due that I'm having a helluva time concentrating on.

When I was a kid, I had a lot of bitter resentment inside me. There were times I was angry at the world because of the unfair hand I'd been dealt. Why did my dad have to die? I missed him so much. When I got older and the Winthrop family made me feel like a loser, that pissed me off too. Hockey was an outlet for that anger, but even so, as a teenager, I started to get a reputation as a player with an edge, a guy you didn't want to piss off. Luckily, I had coaches who steered me in the right direction, but if not for them and hockey, I might have ended up in trouble myself.

Now I'm feeling that bitterness again, that sense of unfairness and inferiority, that "why me" feeling. I don't like it. At all.

I knew better than to believe I could have something with Ella.

We leave on Thursday for Lake Placid. We're playing first against Quinnipiac. We've beaten them before. We can do this.

There are busloads of Bayard Bears fans here, including Skylar and the other guys' girlfriends. Jacob's parents have traveled all the way here from Canada for this weekend.

Today they announced award winners and the all-league teams. Flash and I both made the first all-league team. Yale's goalie Hannu Ranta won the award for outstanding goaltending. Jacob won the scoring award, and I won the best defensive forward award. All the other award winners came from Yale and Dartmouth. I guess that shows what people think of our chances of actually winning.

It's super-fucking-tense. Everything rests on this. If we lose tonight, we're done. There's still a chance we could get picked to play in the regional final, since we're in fourth place and our stats are better than some teams in other conferences. And hey, if we make it that far, who knows? We could make it to the Frozen Four. We'll find that out Sunday, when they announce the teams that are in the NCAA tournament.

But as I step onto the ice for the warm-up, I can't help but reflect that these games might be my last college hockey games ever.

The future stretches in front of me, exciting and full of promise, but so much is unknown. All my life I've been working toward my goal of playing in the NHL, and it's now so close I can sniff it. Still, I'm not there yet. I don't know what the hell is going to happen with my mom and my dad's murder. I don't want to take it for granted that I'll be drafted, or if I am, that I'll even play in the NHL next year.

And I wish Ella were here to share this with, because the last while she's been my biggest supporter. She knows when I don't want to talk about a loss, or when I've screwed up, and she listens when I do want to talk. She believes in me and somehow makes me believe in myself. And that has me missing her even more.

It has to happen. It has to happen.

But it can't happen until I play *this* game. I have to bring myself back to the moment. I have to focus on the only thing I can control . . . my own play. This moment.

We're on our game for the most part, peppering the Bobcats' goalie with shots. But no matter what we do, we can't get the puck past him. The frustration is getting to us, and Danny takes a stupid penalty for slashing. Fuck. Now we're a man down with less than ten minutes left in the game.

We kill that penalty, thank fuck, and that gives us a little boost that results in Flash scoring a goal on a sick breakaway.

And we win, two–one. Yeah!

We find out that Yale beat Dartmouth four–three, so we're up against our archrival in the final tomorrow night.

We're under curfew, so the bus takes us back to the hotel, and none of us even thinks of breaking curfew. This is too important. Some of the guys have girlfriends here, including Flash, but they have to be content with FaceTime and Snapchat.

We have a team meeting in the morning and a light skate before going back to the hotel for lunch and a nap. I'm feeling surprisingly good.

The atmosphere in the building tonight night is electric. I need to manage the adrenaline, and I work on breathing and visualization as the national anthem plays. And then we're off.

Flash and I combine for two goals in the first period, but the Bulldogs come back in the second and tie it up. We're not playing bad, but a couple of ugly turnovers in the neutral zone are our downfall. We need to play goddamn perfect to win this. There can't be any more sloppy mistakes, even small ones. We talk about that in the dressing room between the second and the third.

I'm drenched with sweat, panting, both exhausted and exhilarated. Coach is giving Flash, Franco, and me major minutes. Thank fuck for the endurance workouts or I'd be dead right now.

I take the face-off against Wharton and win it, drawing the puck back to Danny. We try to get it out of our end. The puck goes into the corner, and Barlow for the Bulldogs skates in for it. Danny tries to take it but can't before Barlow passes to Lysenko behind the net. Freddy's at the corner of the net, and when Wharton skates in and gives a poke, Freddy goes down on one knee . . . but apparently he didn't have that short side covered, because the puck goes in the net.

Fuck!

I feel like I was standing still, watching this unfold. Freddy's pissed. He smacks his stick into the goalpost and goes for a skate over to the boards while the Bulldogs celebrate their go-ahead goal.

I'm on the bench for the face-off at center ice. "Okay, boys," I yell. "We got this."

We battle hard for the next seven minutes, and with close to two minutes left in the third period, Coach pulls Freddy. He's on the bench, mask off, sweating like the rest of us and watching anxiously as we try to keep the puck out of our end.

We're facing off to the left of Ranta. I grit my teeth. He's been playing great tonight. His weakness has always been rebound control, but fuck, he must've been working on that, because every time there's a rebound, he uses his body to direct the puck into a low-traffic area, taking away our second shot.

I want to get the puck past him. I stare down my face-off opponent, Ciceron, with my meanest glare. Then I focus on the puck. It goes to Soupy. I'm trying to get to the net, but fucking Ciceron is in my way, blocking me. I'm not going to take a dumb penalty, and I manage to shove my way past him without slashing or tripping him. "Suck my dick, Sissy," I snarl as I wrestle my way around him.

Soupy passes it to Danny, and they set up on the blue line. I go to the front of the net just as Danny takes a slap shot from the blue line, but it gets deflected over to the boards. We have to battle hard and desperate to keep possession—our net is empty.

Franco and Ciceron collide hard against the boards, and Ciceron goes down. Franco has the puck and shoots at the net again. Ranta makes the save, but goddammit, this time he doesn't control that rebound and it comes right to me. Without even consciously thinking, I bring my stick back and shoot in a split second. I watch the puck clang off the crossbar and into the net, behind Ranta.

Elation bursts through me, and I pump my fist into the air, once, twice, three times before I'm mobbed by my teammates, who are literally jumping up and down with jubilation. I don't think I could smile any wider.

"Fuck yeah!" Flash yells as he smacks my bucket. "Bar down!"

"Yeah buddy!" Franco slaps my back.

Our fans go crazy in the stands, our bench goes crazy, including Freddy, who leaps up, arms in the air. We tied it up.

I skate over to the bench to bump my gloves against everyone else's. Coach, in a new suit and tie, has a rare smile on his face. He claps my shoulder as I sit on the bench. Freddy swings his legs in their huge goalie pads over the boards to take his place in net again.

There's a minute and five seconds left. We give it everything we have, but the clock runs out and we're into goddamn overtime.

"We're in the game, guys," I say in the dressing room, where we collapse onto the benches in drenched, stinking, gasping heaps. "Stay on 'em, just like we have been. We can do this."

"That goal was sick." Flash bumps my fist, then swipes his sweaty hair off his face.

"Rebound," I remind them.

Nine minutes into the first overtime period, I'm on the bench. I'm wound so tight, jumping up, sitting down, gripping the dasher board as I watch my teammates.

"They are *on* the goddamn puck!" I say with frustration to Franco beside me on the bench, referring to our opponents.

"I know, right?"

"Be smart, boys!" I yell.

The Bulldogs carry it into our end and shoot it behind the net. Black Jack picks it up. They fight for it and the puck gets loose and bounces around in front of our net. I wince, watching keenly. Ciceron from the Bulldogs bats the puck down and settles it, circles around, and gets it to his teammate on the point. He shoots . . . and our season ends as the puck goes past Freddy, who was totally screened.

I can't believe what I just saw. My chest and gut go hollow, and my chin drops to my chest. The excitement of the Bulldogs as they celebrate only emphasizes the shock and disappointment now crushing all of us Bears. Flash pats me on the back, and I lift my head to look at him. Our eyes meet, and I see disappointment reflected in his expression.

Losing is part of the game. I've always believed that you can judge the character of an athlete better in defeat rather than in victory. Holding your head up in the face of failure says more about you than how you show the thrill of triumph.

Hockey has one of the greatest traditions in all of sports. For some, it's like rubbing salt in the wound, but for most of us it's the ultimate display of sportsmanship. The handshake line at the end of a playoff series demands humility from both winner and loser. It reminds us that hockey is a team sport. We win as a team, and we lose as a team.

My heart is heavy as I move along the line, numbly saying, "Good game" over and over. When I get to Ranta, he pauses and sets a hand on my shoulder. "You really got it, kid."

It's small consolation, but I smile and say thanks. "You too, man. Maybe we'll play for the same team someday."

He grins and moves on.

There are a few media people who want to talk to us, especially Flash, Rocket, and me, but most of the attention is on the Bulldogs. After we've showered and dressed in our suits, we head out to find our families and girlfriends.

I have nobody here.

I'm not in a good mood. I'm pissed because we lost. I'm pissed because Ella's not here. I'm pissed because of my mom's sisters stirring up old shit. And I'm pissed because it's all a huge reminder that I'm a fucking loser with a loser family that I can't shake.

I know this game doesn't impact the draft . . . or maybe it does. Winning would have gotten a whole lot more positive attention heading into the draft. And digging up my past . . . Christ, there are all kinds of reporters and bloggers here, and they're looking for background stories on all the prospects. The last thing I need is that shit coming to light right now.

When we start down the stairs into the atrium, a cheer goes up from our fans waiting for us. We all manage halfhearted smiles and lift our hands in thanks for the support. Our fans *are* really great.

Then I see Ella.

My heart lurches into an uneven, thudding rhythm.

She's here. She's fucking here.

She's standing with Skylar against a wall, her long brown hair all shiny, her eyes warm and sympathetic. She looks so pretty. She's beaming a smile at me as if she's proud of me. We just lost . . . and she's proud of me.

And she's wearing a jersey.

My heart constricts painfully.

I don't know if it's *my* jersey because I can't see the back. Lots of people wear my jersey. Guys and girls. I'm not bragging when I say I'm a popular player for the Bears. But seeing Ella in that jersey does something to me.

I keep my eyes focused on her as I jog down the short flight of stairs into the atrium of the Herb Brooks Arena. People are cheering and clapping for us, and it's hard not to smile even though we just lost.

I make my way over to Ella, following Flash, who ends up in a heated clinch with Skylar. I stop in front of Ella.

"Nice suit, pretty boy." She nods at my plaid suit.

I glance down at it, and one corner of my mouth lifts. "Thanks."

"Did the guys give you a hard time about the pink?"

"It's not pink. It's plum. Charcoal and plum."

She grins. "You played great."

"Thanks." I hold her gaze steadily. "Why are you here?"

"I need to talk to you."

My gut clenches. "Okay," I manage to say.

There's a flurry of activity as Jacob's parents come up to us; he hugs them, then Skylar hugs them. They shake hands with me, and Jacob introduces Ella to them. The pride on their faces, although mingled with disappointment, is unmistakable.

"I guess we'll meet up with you later," Jacob says to Skylar. "We have to get on the bus."

"Okay, honey," Skylar says. She gives his hand a squeeze and moves over to Ella. "See you later."

I meet Ella's eyes and nod, so she gets the same message. She smiles back at me, and that smile gives me hope. And as she turns to walk away with Skylar, I see her back, with my name and number on it.

She's wearing my jersey.

Epilogue

Ella

I'm TRYING to stay calm, but my insides are a fluttering flock of birds. I keep my hands calmly folded in my lap. Ben is sitting next to me in the Staples Center in Los Angeles on a hot Friday evening in June. His mom and his uncle Dave are on the other side of us in the stands.

Ben and his mom went to talk to a lawyer about his dad's case. They got a lot of good information and advice, and his mom decided not to go to the police about it. Ben told her that he'd support her if she wanted to, but he was worried about her safety, and he'd rather put that behind them and move on with their lives. He told her he'd support her in staying away from his uncle Larry and that he wanted to help her leave it all behind when he started making some money. And that's what they're doing.

The Bears did go on to play in the NCAA tournament but lost to Boston University.

I also convinced Ben to tell some of the media people about his past. Well, not everything. Not the fact that his uncle may have killed his father. We talked about different ways to present his story, and I felt like I was actually using some things I've learned in my classes. And it *has* been a great human interest story at the draft—the kid who grew up without a father, his single mom struggling to support them; he wants to make it to the NHL and live the dream his dad would have had for him. Overcoming those obstacles has made Ben a stronger, more resilient player . . . and a stronger man.

In the row in front of me Skylar sits next to Jacob; Jacob's parents are beside him, and next to Skylar is Jacob's younger sister, who is bouncing in her seat with excitement. Behind us are a bunch of the Bayard Bears players and staff, and some of our college friends, all here to support Ben, Jacob, and Grady.

I reach out for Ben's hand, and he smiles at me. I can feel the energy vibrating through his body. He looks so sophisticated in his suit and tie, even with the faint sheen of perspiration on his forehead. I'm glad I chose a sleeveless dress because it's warm in here with all these people.

The atmosphere in the building is still electric, although the buzz has diminished somewhat since the first draft picks were announced. The floor of the arena is packed with tables and bodies, mostly men in suits, people milling about and talking on phones. There are signs on the tables identifying which team these people are from. My mind is boggled at how huge this is. It strikes me that hockey is a big business. There are media people and cameras everywhere. At one end of the arena is a stage draped with black curtains and a huge screen. And the stands are full.

I look around, taking in all the hopeful players there with their families. Everyone is nervous.

Last month Ben went to the draft combine. He was weighed and measured—they even measured his wingspan! He jumped and ran and bench-pressed, with cameras recording his every move. He did pull-ups and rode a stationary bike while people shouted at him to go harder, harder, *harder*! He had cameras and microphones shoved in his face.

Behind the scenes, he went through even more—medical testing, body fat measuring, endurance testing, psychological testing, and interviews with so many teams.

I watched TV last night where four dudes were analyzing the prospects, including Jacob and Ben. It was surreal to think they were talking about my boyfriend.

"Every part of his game is solid," one guy said about Ben. "Being in position, taking the man out, moving the puck."

"He just goes out there and gets the job done."

They showed little clips of him playing, analyzing his moves.

"He passes with authority. He shoots with authority. His game has really grown from the beginning of this season at Bayard College."

"His on-ice awareness is perhaps the best of all the prospects."

"Yes. He knows where everybody is on the ice."

Pride swelled in my chest when I heard that.

Listening to him being interviewed has been another revelation. I know Ben is smart, but when it comes to the business of hockey, he surprises me with the depth of his knowledge. I guess being a business major has helped him understand how this industry works, not only on the ice but off it. It gives him a very balanced, practical perspective on what's happening here, not like some of the others I've met, like the guy who was the number one draft pick, who is so full of himself. Ben knows that the draft picks are based on a lot of factors, not just who is the best player.

We've heard the first eight picks so far. We know the predictions for Jacob were that he could possibly go as high as number ten. Ben's ranked somewhere around fifteen. But at this point, anything can happen. Teams have different needs. I squeeze Ben's big hand.

The tension shimmers around us as the general manager of the Chicago Aces, Ian Yarish, leans into the microphone on the stage.

"The Chicago Aces would like to select for their first pick . . . from Bayard College . . . Jacob Flass."

Yes! We all stand and Ben leans forward and slaps his friend's shoulder. Jacob hugs his parents, then Skylar, who has tears running down her face, then his sister. He hugs and shakes hands with a bunch of other people around him, then makes his way down the stairs onto the floor. We clap as we watch him jog up onto the stage, shedding his suit jacket and handing it to someone from the Aces organization. He's grinning hugely, his face projected onto the big screen as he shakes hands with all the men on the stage and is presented with his new jersey. He pulls it on, adds a ball cap, and poses for pictures, beaming out at the crowd.

I link my arm with Ben's and hug it. Now it's real. It's happening. It's going to be Ben's turn soon.

We have to sit through five more picks.

"I think I'm going to puke," Ben says in my ear.

My heart squeezes for him, and I grab his hand again.

The draft picks are halted as the commissioner of the league announces a trade. I don't really understand it, but there's a ripple of excitement through the crowd as he reads the details. The Chicago Aces have traded two picks to move up, and now have the next pick, at number sixteen.

"They want somebody," Ben mutters to me.

We exchange nervous glances.

It would be crazy if Ben and Jacob ended up with the same team. How likely is that to happen? Not likely at all.

Which is why I'm barely paying attention when they call Ben's name.

". . . from Bayard College, Ben Buckingham."

I blink in shock. Ben rises to his feet, and I scramble up too, my mouth hanging open. Oh hell, there are probably cameras recording us, me looking like a shocked fool with my jaw on the floor. I smile as Ben hugs his mom and his uncle, then turns to me and wraps his arms around me so tight. I throw my arms around his neck. "You did it," I say in his ear. "You did it, Ben. I knew you would."

He moves out into the aisle, shakes the hand of his adviser, sitting near us; Coach Klausen; some of the Bears training staff; then he does his own walk up onto the stage.

Skylar turns to me and I lean down to hug her. "It's like a dream, isn't it?" she asks.

I nod and face Ben's mom. She has to be so proud. She's literally sobbing, her hands clasped in front of her. She smiles at me and holds her arms out and we hug too. Tears sting my own eyes. I don't know her well, but we both love Ben and that's a pretty powerful bond.

My heart is so full I think I'm going to burst watching him take off his suit jacket. He looks so young compared to the men on the stage, so eager and so happy. He pulls the black, silver, and white jersey on over his shirt and tie, someone hands him a ball cap, which he adjusts on his head, and his smile radiates joy.

I've got my phone out and I'm taking pictures. My hands are shaking so bad they're probably not going to be very good, but there are enough photographers here capturing the moment.

We had no idea where he was going to end up, but we've talked and agreed that I can go to school pretty much anywhere. There are lots of universities with good Communications programs. I've even talked to my parents about it. They've gotten to know Ben better the last few months, and they're hesitant but accepting of my plan to change schools. And we've talked about the fact that even though he'll be drafted, he could end up playing for a farm team.

Yes, he did it. He's been drafted into the NHL, his lifelong dream. And yet this is only the start of an amazing journey. There are more tests to come—development camp, training camp, trying to prove himself now on the big stage. The future is still uncertain. But I love Ben and he loves me. I believe in him, he believes in himself, and we believe in us—whatever the future holds, we'll get through it together.

Ben

I check my phone for the first time since my name was announced. My head is spinning. I'm trying to take it all in, but a lot of it is a blur.

Fuck! I stare at my phone. It's flooded with messages and texts and Tweets. I grin, shaking my head. There's no way I'll ever be able to read or respond to all of them. I'll have to save them for later. But as my thumb moves over the screen and I scroll through the Tweets, one catches my eye. Marc Dupuis, captain of the Chicago Aces, has Tweeted at me, *Congratulations to @BenBuckingham, and welcome to the Aces! Looking forward to playing with such a talented guy! See you in training camp!*

Jesus. It still hasn't all sunk in. But fuck! I'm going to play with guys like Marc Dupuis! Duncan Armstrong. Jared Rupp. And I'm going to do it with Flash.

And with Ella.

I can't wait.

Thank you for reading Cross Check! Would you like more of Ben and Skylar? Sign up for my mailing list and get free bonus content!
https://view.flodesk.com/pages/6430274a61b99ea5512d9d14

And read on for an excerpt from Dancing in the Rain...

Acknowledgments

Special thanks to Charity Kuczynski for reading *Cross Check,* giving me such great story feedback, and making sure I didn't screw up any college hockey details! If I did, the mistakes are mine!

I'd also like to take the opportunity to share a few resources for suicide awareness and prevention. Ella's mission to open a conversation about mental health issues is an important one, and not just in this story but also in real life. I encourage everyone to learn more about it, open a dialogue, and end the stigma.

American Foundation for Suicide Prevention: afsp.org
    The Jed Foundation: jedfoundation.org
    Canadian Association for Suicide Prevention: suicideprevention.ca
    Bell Let's Talk: letstalk.bell.ca/en

And as always, a huge thank-you to my amazing team—Stacey Price, Dar Albert, Heather Roberts. And to you—my readers are the best readers!

Dancing in the Rain - Excerpt

by Kelly Jamieson

Drew slumped down into the couch and drank more beer, watching a re-run of *Die Hard* for about the hundredth time.

The sharp peal of his doorbell startled him. His head jerked up. Shit. Who was at his door? It better not be someone trying to save his soul, because the mood he was in, he was pretty sure he was beyond redemption. Hey, maybe he'd strip down and answer the door naked. That would scare them away.

Genius idea. He stood and whipped his T-shirt over his head, shoved down the athletic shorts he wore with no underwear, and headed to the door, leaving his clothes crumpled on the rug. Seeing the look on their faces would be the highlight of his shitty week. It actually made him grin.

He yanked open his front door, ready for their shock . . . but his own mouth dropped open at seeing Peyton Watt standing there.

His grin faded.

Her eyes went huge.

Her gaze tracked down his naked body all the way to his toes, then back up. She met his eyes. "What the hell are you doing?" Her head moved from side to side in disbelief.

"Fuck me." He closed his eyes.

"No, thank you." She strode in past him. "Clearly you were expecting someone else, if that's what you want. Sorry I'm interrupting other plans."

He stepped aside and moved behind the door, poking his head around it. Christ. "I wasn't expecting anyone," he growled. "I thought you were some Jehovah's Witnesses here to tell me about salvation."

She whirled around and stared at him. "Seriously? You answered the door naked thinking it was Jehovah's Witnesses?"

"Uh, yeah." He rubbed the back of his head. "Seemed like a good idea at the time."

She gaped at him, then burst out laughing.

Drew's jaw went slack as he watched her. She stood on his shiny bamboo floor, the sun turning her blond hair to a glowing halo. She wore skinny jeans, red Converse, a flowy red-and-navy top with short sleeves, and she held the handle of her big purse in both hands in front of her thighs. Her face lit up with mirth was so incredibly beautiful, he could only stare in awe, and her laughter was captivating.

He found his lips twitching in response.

"Oh my God." She dropped her head forward briefly. "Can you imagine?"

"Uh ..."

She bit her bottom lip and looked back at him, eyes gleaming. For some reason, she wasn't freaked out by his nudity, and he found that fascinating. He wasn't freaked out by nudity either, usually; he was used to walking around dressing rooms and showers naked, all the damn time. However, he wasn't a jerk.

"I should get dressed," he said, not moving.

"Okay. Right." She straightened her shoulders and narrowed her eyes. "I came here to ream you out. I am so pissed at you right now. You need clothes on for this." She turned her back on him. "Although I have to admit, your body is totally worth looking at."

His face heated. He still didn't move.

"Go on," she said, facing away from him. "Go get your clothes, wherever they are. I'll wait here. And I won't peek."

He rolled his eyes and moved out from behind the door, closing it. "Thanks," he said dryly. "Appreciate it."

He strode behind her, past the kitchen, and around the corner to the family room. He scooped up his shorts and stepped into them. Jesus. He was drunker than he'd realized. What the fuck had he been thinking?

He nabbed his T-shirt. She could probably handle his bare chest. "Okay," he said. "I'm decent."

"Oh yes, you are," she said appreciatively as she turned. She took in his chest as he pulled the shirt on over his head. "Very decent."

He'd heard his share of compliments from women. Yeah, he was in good shape. He hadn't been working out over the last few months, and he'd been drinking too much booze and eating too much junk food, but it wasn't like he'd been doing nothing—he'd played a lot of rounds of golf and done a lot of water-skiing and biking at Dougie's lake home in Wisconsin. So he hadn't put on weight or gone all flabby. Although if he kept up the lack of workouts and proper diet, that was no doubt where he was headed. Fat old guy with a beer belly and skinny legs.

Christ.

Anyway, he was used to admiration from women, and for some reason he really liked it from her, but her praise actually made him feel guilty for taking his body for granted. Just because he wasn't earning his living with it anymore didn't mean he shouldn't take care of it. He'd been abusing it lately.

"Come in," he said shortly. "I was just having a beer." He turned back to the kitchen.

"Or six." She eyed the empties on the counter. Her gaze lifted to his face. "Is this how you spend your time now?"

His gut burned. "Yeah," he said shortly. "It is, actually."

She sighed and set her purse onto the island, then walked into the family room and dropped into one of the armchairs. "Is that why you think you shouldn't meet Chloe?"

He resumed his seat on the couch. "Partly."

"I came here to give you shit and tell you that you can't change your mind now. But I'm kind of having second thoughts too." She glanced back at the empty beer bottles. "Drinking to excess in the afternoon and answering the door naked. Not exactly appropriate paternal behavior."

"Chloe's not here," he muttered. "Also, I'm not hurting anyone. It was just a stupid prank."

"It makes me question your judgment."

"My judgment is fine," he snapped.

"Really." She lifted an eyebrow. "You'll forgive me if I disagree."

Available at all retailers

About the Author

Kelly Jamieson is a best-selling author of over seventy romance novels and novellas. Her writing has been described as "emotionally complex," "sweet and satisfying," and "blisteringly sexy." She likes coffee (black), wine (mostly white), shoes (high heels) and hockey!

Sign up for updates about her new books and what's coming up, visit her website at www.kellyjamieson.com or contact her at info@ kellyjamieson.com

Other Books by Kelly Jamieson

Heller Brothers Hockey

Breakaway

Faceoff

One Man Advantage

Hat Trick

Offside

Power Series

Power Struggle

Taming Tara

Power Shift

Rule of Three Series

Rule of Three

Rhythm of Three

Reward of Three

San Amaro Singles

With Strings Attached

How to Love

Slammed

Windy City Kink

Sweet Obsession

All Messed Up

Playing Dirty

Brew Crew

Limited Time Offer

No Obligation Required

Aces Hockey

Major Misconduct

Off Limits

Icing

Top Shelf

Back Check

Slap Shot

Playing Hurt

Big Stick

Game On

Last Shot

Body Shot

Hot Shot

Long Shot

Bayard Hockey

Shut Out

Cross Check

Wynn Hockey

Play to Win

In It To Win It

Win Big

For the Win

Game Changer

Bears Hockey

Must Love Dogs...and Hockey

You Had Me at Hockey

Talk Hockey to Me

Bears Hockey II

The O Zone

Good Hands

Scoring Big

Stand Alone

Three of Hearts

Loving Maddie from A to Z

Dancing in the Rain

Love Me

Love Me More

Friends with Benefits

2 Hot 2 Handle

Lost and Found

One Wicked Night

Sweet Deal

Hot Ride

Crazy Ever After

All I Want for Christmas

Sexpresso Night

Irish Sex Fairy

Conference Call

Rigger

You Really Got Me

How Sweet It Is

Screwed

Firecracker

Royally Indecent